Sisters by blood, friends by choice. *Unknown*

Chapter One

One, two,
Buckle my shoe.
Beware the mums
Who'll talk about you.

As we walked into the playground I clutched the hands of my twin boys – for my comfort, more than theirs. The cacophony of sound – children laughing and shouting, adults chatting loudly – caused me to catch my breath, momentarily disoriented. I scanned the sea of faces, vainly hoping I might spot someone I recognised.

Charlie and Jack wriggled free from my tight grip and slipped into school life, running around with children they didn't know, laughing and whooping in excitement. I stood holding their assortment of bags and lunch boxes, feeling suddenly unsure of myself. What was I supposed to do now? Everyone else seemed to know what was expected.

I glanced at the nearest group of women. Their relaxed body language and easy banter told me they'd known each other for years. That was the thing about starting all over again – it took time to make new friends. I took a deep breath and smiled in the general direction of some other mums.

A slim lady with straightened light-brown hair glanced

over and waved. I recognised her from my visit to the school, back in July. I'd had coffee with her and a few other mums while the children spent time with their new teacher. I waved back.

She grabbed her toddler son's hand and walked over to me. 'Hi, Becky. It's good to see you again.'

'Yes, you too...' I smiled hopefully. 'Kate?'

She nodded, laughing. 'How are you feeling today?'

I considered her question, not wanting to admit to someone I barely knew that I'd sobbed in the shower. 'It's a strange feeling – a mix of emotions, really.'

'I've cried already this morning,' she told me, before moving closer and lowering her voice. 'Half of me is relieved I won't have to entertain Lucy every afternoon anymore.' Her voice dropped to a whisper. 'I don't think we're supposed to admit to that, though.'

I giggled, but before I could reply the bell sounded and there was a sudden surge towards the classroom doors. I looked round in panic – suddenly every boy looked alike in their white polo shirts, green jumpers and grey trousers. Not even my sons' dark curly heads could help me spot them.

Something solid crunched into my back and I spun round to find Charlie looking up at me with his huge blue eyes. His father's eyes.

'Oops. Sorry, Mum.'

Jack appeared by his side and I followed them towards the Reception classroom. We found their pegs and hung up their coats and PE bags, and as they dashed off to the classroom I looked round for their teacher, Miss Whittaker. Her tiny frame was lost behind a wall of parents, all seemingly speaking to her at the same time. Although I was keen to chat to her, it could wait until another day.

I sneaked into the classroom to give Jack and Charlie another goodbye hug, despite their protests, and then joined the other parents all peering through the classroom window, waving madly and blowing kisses.

Eventually I threaded my way through the mass of parents, heading towards the gates. A lump had lodged itself in my throat and was refusing to move. Jack and Charlie had been looking forward to this day for so long; it couldn't come soon enough for them. Why, then, did I feel bereft? Maybe it was the letting go I was finding difficult?

Something caught my attention, causing me to turn to my left. A woman with short black hair was striding in my direction, and as she came nearer I stared in disbelief. She stopped in front of me, hands on her hips. 'Well, well. Becky Dixon.' Her eyes bored into mine. 'I thought it was you.'

It must have been five or six years since I'd seen her. She hadn't changed much, but the power suits that had been her trade-mark had been replaced by a skirt, blouse and high heels. A school uniform for mothers, I'd noticed, suddenly conscious of my jeans and jumper. 'Hello, Helen.' I smiled, but it wasn't returned.

An awkward silence hung between us and I wondered if she was thinking about the last time we'd seen each other. Her expression gave nothing away. Silences made me uncomfortable and I felt compelled to fill this one by gabbling. 'You obviously have children at this school.'

She rolled her eyes, as if I was stating the obvious, then pursed her lips, taking her time to reply. 'My daughter is in the juniors and my son has started today.'

'Oh, he must be in the same class as my boys, Charlie and Jack.' I was relieved we now had something to talk about.

The tight set of her mouth told me she didn't want to continue the conversation. She glanced around, as if bored of talking to me, and raised her hand to someone behind me. 'Sue, I need a word,' she called out before walking away, leaving me open-mouthed. Helen Stevens. I hadn't expected to bump into her again.

*

At three o'clock – fifteen minutes before school ended – I was standing outside the Reception classroom, trying to peer through the window without Miss Whittaker spotting me.

'Hi.' Kate's voice made me jump.

I turned and smiled at her. 'I came early to sneak a peek at Charlie and Jack.'

'I had the same thoughts about Lucy.' She stepped forward, almost pressing her face against the glass. 'I've been thinking about her on and off all day. Oh, there she is – she looks okay.'

Miss Whittaker glanced at us and we both took a step backwards.

'How was your day?' Kate asked. 'What did you do with your free time?'

'I run my own copywriting business from home, so having the extra hours will mean less evening working, which is great.' I didn't add that my dismal social life meant I would still work in the evenings, just to stave off the boredom. I smiled brightly. 'How about you?'

'I'm not working because I've got Connor to look after...' She turned and shook her head. 'I'd better grab him from the play equipment before he falls off.'

The playground had filled rapidly, and I glanced round for someone else to chat to. Helen was standing not far from me, talking animatedly to a couple of women, and I turned my head the other way – Helen was someone I wanted to steer clear of.

Another group of mums was deep in conversation, but a couple of them nodded at me. One looked me up and down slowly. Was she assessing me? Judging my dress sense to see if I shopped at Prada or Primark? Checking for a wedding ring or guessing my age? I shook off these thoughts. Maybe I should break the ice and introduce myself.

As I plucked up courage, the doors opened and Jack and Charlie burst out, huge smiles on their faces, school bags and lunch boxes in hands. I was smothered by two big hugs before two sets of bags, boxes and coats were thrust at me.

'I played Batman with Josh and Harry at playtime,' Charlie told me excitedly as we walked home.

'And I chased them,' Jack added.

I smiled proudly at them both. 'Did you do any writing or sums?'

Charlie frowned. 'We did a little bit.' His face suddenly lit up again. 'But playtime was the best because—'

'Yes,' Jack interrupted. 'I love playtime – we get two, you know.'

We arrived home and the boys showed me their paintings, which I immediately put up on the kitchen wall.

'Aren't you clever?' I said as I looked at their reading books, which contained three words, repeated over and over. I signed their diaries to say we'd read together and drew a smiley face on each one, which made them laugh.

The phone rang as I cooked tea and my heart clenched, thinking it was probably Darren.

'It's Aunty Sam,' Charlie yelled, passing the phone to me.

'Hey, Sam.'

My sister laughed into the phone. 'So, how did it go? Did you cry?'

'A little,' I replied, 'but they've had a great day. They haven't stopped talking about it since they got home.'

'Enjoy it. Wait until they're teenagers – all I get from James and Joe is the four-letter 'f' word – FINE.'

I laughed out loud at my sister's imitation of my nephews.

'Has Darren phoned?' she asked.

'Not yet. But I'm sure he will.'

'Of course. How about Mum?'

'No!' I scoffed. 'She probably hasn't even remembered they were starting school today.' I shook my head, never quite able to come to terms with the hurt my mother caused. 'She hasn't been returning my calls again.'

'Nor mine.' Sam sighed. 'She'll get in touch when she's ready.'

'Sure.'

Five minutes later the phone rang again and Jack grabbed it. 'Hi, Dad,' he shouted. 'Yes, yes. It was great.' He hopped from foot to foot as he told Darren all about school before handing the phone to his brother, who had been standing by his side trying to take it from him.

'Hi, Dad,' Charlie shouted breathlessly. 'I had a great time. I played Batman with Josh and Harry.'

I left him to it, hoping Darren wouldn't want to speak to me afterwards. Our brief, weekly conversations were always difficult, but I was especially churned up with a mixture of emotions today – sadness, tinged with anger that he had missed their first day of school.

I sighed silently when Charlie handed the phone to me. 'Hello.'

'Hi, Becky.' His voice seemed flat. 'The boys have enjoyed school.'

'Yes, it went well.'

'Good.' He paused. 'Everything else okay?'

'Yes. Same as ever.'

He let out a long slow breath I couldn't fathom. 'I'll call next week, then.'

'Okay.'

Darren would be upset at not being there for the boys, but somehow I just couldn't bring myself to ask how he was feeling. My chest tightened with the familiar surge of anger towards him. I pictured him in sunny California, while I was trying to keep things together for the boys' sakes. Then I pushed these thoughts away, as I'd trained myself to do over the past eight months, and concentrated on finishing the boys' tea.

Once Jack and Charlie were in bed, I finished some copy I'd been working on, before tackling the ironing pile. I flopped into bed a couple of hours later, and as I drifted off to sleep I dreamed I was sitting on a tiny chair clutching my reading book. The teacher demanded I tell him how many words I knew, but when he turned round it was Darren.

Chapter Two

Three, four
Knock at the door,
Invite me in
And I'll tell what I saw.

'Have you managed to speak to Miss Whittaker yet?' Kate asked as we watched our children racing round the playground.

I shook my head. 'No, there's always the usual queue around her.' Privately I had named the mums who took up so much of the teacher's time "hogging mums", and I couldn't understand why the main perpetrator, "hogging mum one", and her friend, "hogging mum two", had so much to say. What did they find to discuss each day?

'I've noticed that too,' Kate replied, laughing. 'I'm torn between wanting to ask how Lucy's doing and not wanting to appear neurotic.'

I nodded slowly. I really needed to talk to Miss Whittaker about Jack. 'I'll try again next week,' I told Kate.

'It's only been their first week – I doubt we'll be judged for not saying hello.'

'You're right.' I pushed my concerns about Jack to the back of my mind and smiled. 'So has Lucy enjoyed school so far?'

'She's loved it. She has eleven best friends already, which is great because I'm getting to know plenty of the mums.'

I glanced up at the group of Reception class mums standing close to us, all laughing and chatting. During the week a couple of them had introduced themselves, and they seemed a friendly bunch. However, Helen didn't stand with us, even though her son was in the same class. She preferred to chat with her friends by the gate. I'd felt her watching me a few times, but happily she'd chosen not to say anything more to me.

Kate put her hand on my arm. 'Most of us met years ago at playgroup or toddler gym. You'll soon get to know everyone.'

I smiled at her. It felt good to have made a friend. Since we'd moved house, that's what I'd missed most – having a girlfriend round the corner. We'd moved to the less-expensive market town of Dorsley, which meant I was now fifteen miles away from my best friend Issi and the other friends I'd made through playgroup. The neighbours in our cul-de-sac were lovely, but no one was under sixty and some days I just needed a girly gossip.

We saw the children into school and then I drove the short distance to Maidenhead, looking forward to meeting up with Issi.

We had arranged to meet at our usual haunt, The Cake Stand, at nine thirty for a quick drink and a chat. I had lots of work to do, but I knew we wouldn't emerge into the daylight until at least lunchtime.

I was just walking across the bridge that linked the car park to the shops when my phone bleeped with a text message. It was from Issi: *where r u? sumthing happened 2 cake stand!!* I quickened my pace. Had our favourite coffee shop burned down? Or worse still, had it been turned into a Tesco? My mind was in overdrive as I almost ran the last hundred metres through the shopping precinct, just dodging a woman with a double buggy who was having trouble steering. I turned into a side street and saw what used to be our favourite run-down café. It now stood proudly amongst the other shops, boasting the addition of red and green awnings. The pristine sign over the door announced its new name – L'Olivo.

'The Olive Tree,' Issi said, smiling at me. She grabbed me for a hug before peering through the window, a huge grin on her face. Tall and willowy, she was immaculately dressed as always, wearing cream linen trousers and a pale pink t-shirt. Her blonde hair, an inheritance from her Scandinavian mother, was tied in a loose ponytail, giving her an air of effortless elegance.

'Wow, get a load of this,' she said. 'Our café seems to have been sold and re-named over the summer holidays.' She couldn't stop smiling.

I joined her in peering through the window. New wooden tables and chairs had replaced the old plastic ones, giving it a more contemporary look. I nudged my friend. 'Look at all the rows of muffins, cakes and pastries. This is going to be far too tempting.'

'And look at the blackboard – every variety of coffee or tea you can imagine.'

My mouth watered. 'What are you going to try first? Issi?'

She was already disappearing through the door, and by the time I caught up with her an Adonis-like waiter was showing her to a table. He must have been around six feet two, with jet-black hair gelled into position and perfect white teeth. Now I understood why she had been smiling.

I sat down, desperately combing my hair with my fingers. 'You're happily married, remember. I'm the single one.'

Issi blushed and fiddled with a strand of hair that had come loose. 'I know. I'm only having a bit of fun.'

I groaned. Why did Issi have a lovely husband and still attract other men, while I had no husband and got no second glances when I walked into a room? I sighed loudly. 'I'm going to take a long hard look in the mirror later – preferably with a glass of wine in my hand.'

'Becky,' Issi replied, grabbing hold of my hand, 'you're beautiful. You just need to start believing it again.'

I held her gaze without blinking. 'We both know I'm in need of a make-over.'

'No, not really.' She tilted her head to one side, looking me up and down. 'Why don't you have your hair highlighted again? It really suited you last time.'

'I'll get round to it,' I muttered, knowing I'd let myself go recently. My shoulder-length brown hair was badly in need of a cut and re-style, and Issi was right – highlighting would make it look better. Somehow though, taking care of myself had slipped down my list of priorities.

The waiter strolled over to take our order with the air of confidence that only truly good-looking men have. His large brown eyes seemed to penetrate deeply into mine as I ordered a latte and a blueberry muffin. I blushed and looked away. Issi ordered a cappuccino and a Danish pastry, and when the order was delivered we both received a beautiful smile. I fell in love.

'Do you think he's Italian?' I whispered to Issi.

'I think it would be a good guess,' my friend replied with mock sarcasm. 'Can you remember any Italian from school?'

I thought for a moment. 'I don't think we were taught how to say, "Are you single and do you find me attractive?"'

We both laughed. It always felt good to spend time with Issi.

'Is Ben still enjoying school?'

Issi beamed. 'He's loving being with his older brother and sister.' She frowned for a second. 'Three and a half seems so young to be going every morning, but he's coping well.' She glanced at her watch. 'Dad and Maureen are collecting him for me at half eleven – just in case we're running late.'

We both burst out laughing. Issi's dad would know that our "quick coffee" would turn out to be nothing of the sort. The waiter was leaning against the counter, smiling at us, and I blushed and looked away again, feeling ridiculous. He was probably like that with all the customers.

'How are Charlie and Jack settling in?' Issi continued.

'Everything seems fine. I'm still worried about Jack's hyperactivity, though.'

'He's always been the livelier of the boys – maybe that's just his nature?'

'I don't know. They've already been given small amounts of homework to do, and he can't seem to concentrate long enough to complete it.'

'What have school said?'

'I haven't had chance to mention it – the teacher always seems so busy.'

Issi threw her head back and laughed. 'I've learned that you just have to elbow your way in.'

'You're right. I will.'

'So have you made any friends yet?'

'There's a nice lady called Kate—ooh...' I spluttered into my coffee, wiping my chin quickly with a napkin. 'You'll never guess who I bumped into.'

Issi leaned forward, resting her elbows on the table, her blue eyes twinkling. 'This sounds like some juicy gossip. Who?'

'Do you remember when I worked at McAdam's and the creative director turned up to a meeting with a major client nursing such a bad hangover she could barely speak?'

Issi frowned in concentration. 'Yes,' she said slowly. 'Didn't you feel awful because you had to report her to your boss?'

I nodded. 'I had no choice. And in any event, the client complained as well.' I shrugged at my friend. 'I'd had no idea she'd done it before – and I certainly didn't intend for her to be sacked.' Thinking back now, Helen had never seemed to like me. Whenever we'd worked on a project together she had made my life as difficult as possible, often criticising me in front of clients. I'd never admitted to anyone that I was secretly glad when she'd been sacked.

Issi's eyes widened. 'Don't tell me that's who you saw at school?'

I nodded. 'And let's just say she didn't seem pleased to see me.'

'It's a small world – did she mention anything?'

'No, but I don't think I'm her favourite person.'

'Oh well – there's not much she can do to you in the playground.' Issi smiled playfully, rolling her eyes. 'And how about the sports teacher? Have you seen him this week?'

Heat burned into my cheeks. 'I wish I hadn't mentioned him.'

'And deprive me of dating material for you?'

'He's probably married.' I was regretting telling her about the teacher who had organised a gymnastics display on our first visit to the school. My flush deepened as I remembered how the definition of his muscles had clearly shown through his t-shirt, how his dark hair had been gelled into sexy spikes, and ooh, that designer stubble... I hadn't noticed any of the children's tumbling.

'You're smiling,' Issi teased.

'As I said, he's—'

'Becky.' Issi put her hand on mine. 'Your divorce will be finalised soon. You have to move on.'

'I know.' I ran my spoon round my empty cup, staring at the remains of froth, lost in thought. Moving on seemed fine when Issi said it, but I was scared.

'Another coffee?' she asked.

I nodded, relieved when a female waitress came to take our order, returning quickly with our drinks. Flirting was emotionally draining. I looked across at Issi. 'How's Jonathan's new job?'

'Okay.'

'Oh. Isn't he enjoying it?'

'Yes – but because it's a European role he's travelling for most of the week.' She paused and her smile dropped. 'And at the weekend he's too tired to notice me.'

'Have you tried telling him how you feel?'

'No, he's only been doing this job for a couple of months – it's not fair on him to start moaning. He's under a lot of pressure without me adding to it.' She distractedly folded her napkin into a square. 'Besides, I feel really guilty that I'm unhappy; look at what I have.' She sighed and took a sip of her drink. 'I guess I'm just a bit bored.'

'Perhaps you need to go back to work now Ben's at school? Something part-time?'

'Maybe. It's not as easy now Dad's sold his business.'

'You're brilliant at PR and marketing – anyone would employ you.'

'Maybe,' she repeated. She shrugged and smiled. 'I'll start looking round.'

'I'll keep an eye out for you.'

'Sorry, Becky.' She shook her head. 'Saying I'm bored must sound awful to you. How's your work going?'

This was one of the things that made Issi so endearing. She seemed to feel almost guilty at having a privileged life. I would have been off shopping with my husband's credit card every day, splashing his cash, but that just didn't appeal to her.

'Come on. Tell me about your new client,' she said bossily.

'It's a company that owns a vineyard in Kent and they want to focus their advertising campaign on launching an up-market wine.' I lowered my voice as the waiter wandered over to collect our cups. 'I'm writing a whole series of adverts for them.'

The waiter somehow managed to brush his hand against mine, but without making any eye contact. Tingles rippled in my stomach and I glanced up at him, but he had already turned his back on us, heading for the kitchen. I could almost sense him laughing to himself. He was probably used to serving lonely thirty-four-year-old single mums. Did we have a look of desperation he felt he could satisfy by flirting with us?

'...so maybe I could talk over some ideas with you about the campaign? That would stimulate my brain.'

I refocused my mind on Issi and my new client and we chatted at length about what I was trying to achieve. 'How are we doing for time?' I asked when we'd finished.

'Twelve fifteen.' Issi shook her head. 'How did that happen?'

'I know – it flies by,' I agreed in equal amazement.

We split the bill as we always did and left a generous tip. I surreptitiously glanced around the café, hoping to catch a last glimpse of the waiter, but he was nowhere to be seen.

Outside, we blinked in the daylight. Sometimes our conversation was so intense it was if I'd been in a time warp. We hugged and then went our separate ways across Maidenhead. Issi off to her father's house to collect Ben, and me back home to do some work.

*

'Hi, Kate.'

'Hi, Becky.' She was standing with a few other mums and I joined them for ten minutes of small talk. It started to drizzle and Kate held her umbrella over both of us. As I glanced round I realised there was a sort of playground uniform. Everyone seemed to be pulling on variations of the same coat – a type of hooded anorak. As one of the mums in our group was zipping hers up she looked over at me and shook her head.

'You'll have to sort yourself out with a proper coat for standing in the playground,' she told me. 'It needs to be windproof and waterproof, obviously, and with a hood because it's very difficult to hold an umbrella, book bags, lunch boxes and a toddler's hand.' She smiled proudly at having shared this knowledge, and I didn't know whether to laugh or cry. Certainly the information was very useful, although I was sure I would have worked it all out for myself. It was the serious way it was delivered to me which made me cringe. How could this woman be so anal about a coat?

I glanced at Kate, who seemed to be coping remarkably well with holding an umbrella and her toddler's hand – although, granted, she didn't have a book bag or lunch box at this point. She caught my eye and we both dissolved into fits of giggles. Fortunately, at that moment the doors burst open and the children poured out of the classrooms. I could see one of the "hogging mums" poised by the door, trying to squeeze her way in as the children were coming out. I made a mental note to be quicker on Monday morning so I could talk to Miss Whittaker.

As we wove our way out of the playground it started to rain harder. Many of the mums produced smaller versions of their own coats from their pockets, where they had been folded neatly into a little bag, ready for their children to pop on. I really had to pay more attention to the weather forecast. We ran home, the boys jumping in the puddles that were already forming, laughing as the rain soaked us.

Once we were all home and dried off, I was relieved that Jack and Charlie were both tired after a full day at school and wanted to flop in front of the television. I had done so little work during the day that I needed to spend a couple of hours on my laptop.

This was a good time of day to do research because I

didn't need to concentrate too hard and I didn't mind being interrupted by the boys fighting over the remote control or virtually anything else they could find to argue about. I constantly wondered if I had taken on too much, but although moving down-market had improved my financial situation, I still needed to work full-time. I was coping, but not for the first time I wished Darren didn't live so far away.

'Mum, is tea ready yet?'

Charlie's shout startled me and I shelved the thought of doing anymore work until the boys were in bed and the house was quiet again.

The boys were good sleepers, and later I curled up on the sofa with my laptop and a glass of Pinot Grigio, ready to start work. Instead, I found my thoughts drifting towards a certain rather handsome Italian waiter. Angelo? Cesare? Pleasant thoughts began filling my head, but then the phone rang and I jumped so hard I nearly spilled my wine.

'Hello, Becky, love.'

'Oh. Hello, Janet.' I enjoyed my weekly catch-up with Darren's mum and I smiled at her Yorkshire accent, which usually took me several minutes to tune into. I had always got on well with my in-laws, who were a quiet couple in their sixties. When Darren told them he had left me they rang immediately, offering support. They went about it quietly, without any show, suggesting they had the boys for holidays, knowing it gave me a break and enabled me to work. Twice, Darren had flown over to join them, which meant I hadn't had to face him.

In the beginning they told me how upset they were with Darren, but since then they rarely talked about him, and they were always careful to avoid any mention of Shelley, or Barbie, as I'd nicknamed her in my head. She was the Californian colleague with the long honey-blonde hair and perfect white teeth that he'd left me for.

'How is everyone?'

'We're all great, thanks. The boys have had a good day at school.'

She laughed – a deep, throaty laugh, which was infectious. 'They were certainly full of it when I spoke to them on Tuesday.'

'Are you and Derek all right?'

'Yes, thanks, love. We were just wondering if you had plans for the October half-term?'

'No, nothing. Would you like to come and stay?'

She paused, and then her words tumbled out in one long stream. 'We were wondering if we could take the boys out to California again?'

'Oh. I—'

'We've found some cheap flights – we'll pay – and they had such a wonderful time in the summer.'

She inhaled, giving me time to speak. I could almost feel the love for her grandchildren through the phone, and the initial hurt I'd felt at the thought of not spending the holiday with my sons disappeared. Janet and Derek must miss the boys, too. 'Of course they can,' I replied. 'We'll sort out the details nearer the time.'

'Thanks, Becky. We'll take good care of them.'

'I know.'

'We were a bit unsure about asking because we thought you might have wanted to take them on some day trips. I said to Derek—'

'It's fine,' I reassured her. 'It'll give me chance to do some work at home.'

'If you're sure, love.'

I put the phone down and mulled things over. I hated the thought of the boys being so far away from me, but they'd had a brilliant time in the summer and it would have been selfish of me to say no. I finished my wine and shelved the idea of any more work, climbing into bed with a book instead.

As I started to fall asleep later, I dreamed that "Angelo", the waiter, was parking his car on the yellow zigzags outside school, which was strictly forbidden. He wound down his window and grinned, passing me a latte and a muffin. Life doesn't get much better than this, I thought sleepily.

Chapter Three

Five, six,
Pick up sticks.
Time to start
My dirty tricks.

'What are you doing, Mum?'

I was standing with my back to the long mirror in my bedroom, craning my neck over my shoulder. 'I'm just checking things,' I said absentmindedly.

'Okay,' Charlie replied, seemingly happy with my answer.

I was trying to decide whether my bottom still looked pert or if it had travelled south with my breasts. 'Do you think I look all right?' I asked my son.

He seemed momentarily confused, then beamed at me. 'I think you're really pretty.'

I smiled at him, then peered into the mirror and pulled my hair into a ponytail. 'Don't forget you're going to Aunty Sam's later – while I'm at the hairdressers.'

'Are we sleeping over?'

'Yes – as a special treat.'

Charlie ran off, shouting for his brother. 'Jack, we're staying with Joe and James tonight!'

I had finally decided to have some highlights put in, and

Sam had offered to look after the boys. I really appreciated this, remembering the last time I had been to the hairdressers and they had almost wrecked the salon in their boredom. And the appointment couldn't have come at a better time, now that I had a gorgeous Italian to flirt with. I would ask the hairdresser to update my hairstyle as well and then I was going to spend some money on new clothes – without feeling guilty.

The drive to Sam's house in Reading took forty minutes, during which time I'd yelled at Jack twice for unbuckling his seat belt. I pulled up, and as I grabbed the boys' overnight bags out of the boot Jack and Charlie ran up the drive. Jack started kicking the front door.

'Jack!' I shouted. 'Stop that. Now!'

The door opened and the boys shot inside before I could reach them. I dropped the bags in the hall and kissed my brother-in-law on the cheek. 'I'm so sorry, Dave. I'll just go and get him to apologise.'

'Don't worry, Becky, our two were just the same.'

Dave was easy-going and good fun, but I still made Jack say sorry.

'Don't do it again,' Dave told him sternly. 'Now off you go and play.' He turned and grinned at me. 'Sam's in the kitchen.'

I sat down at the kitchen table with a sigh. 'Is it because his dad isn't around?' I asked Sam. 'Am I raising two out-of-control boys?'

She joined me, pushing a mug of tea across the table. 'You're doing a brilliant job.'

'Darren's not, though, is he?' I said angrily. 'He'll be sunning himself on the beach today – with *her* – while I'm trying to discipline his children.'

Sam took hold of my hand. 'You can't change what happened. You're doing the best you can – which is just great.'

As she took the lid off the biscuit tin I thought about how she had always been there for me. With a dad who'd walked out on his three young children and a mum who had never really known where we were, we had looked out for each other. Sam had always been the strong one, thumping anyone who upset her younger sister at junior school.

'Custard cream?'

'Thanks.' I smiled. 'Michael's favourites – has he been round this week?' Sam always kept a supply for our younger brother, who popped in when he was between relationships, which was frequently.

She laughed. 'No. He's got a new girl on the go – Sophie, I think – so we won't see him for a while.'

'I'll text him later,' I said, smiling as I finished my tea. 'Do you think he'll ever settle down?'

Sam shrugged. 'He's managed to avoid it for thirty-two years and seems happy enough.'

'There's no point, anyway,' I said morosely.

She thumped my arm. 'Yes there is. I've been happily married to Dave for fourteen years, thank you.' Her voice softened. 'You'll find someone again.'

'Sure,' I muttered, rubbing my arm.

'Have another biscuit.'

'No, I'd better go,' I said, checking my watch. 'Thanks for having the boys.'

'No problem.' She put her arms round me. 'Go and enjoy yourself.'

'Thanks – I'll see you tomorrow.'

I grabbed the boys for a kiss, making them promise to behave, and then headed back down the M4 to Maidenhead.

*

I emerged from the salon with a more fashionable look and blonde highlights. I was thrilled. By cutting off several inches of hair my cheekbones seemed to have reappeared, and I felt less "mumsy" and more "mum around town". I called in at one of the cheaper clothes shops and held up a pair of jeans.

'Would you like to try those on?' the assistant asked.

'No. I—' I stopped in mid-sentence as it dawned on me that I didn't have two inquisitive four-year-olds in tow. Boys who could demolish a stack of beautifully folded t-shirts in seconds. 'I'd love to,' I replied, grinning at her.

I left the shop with my "autumn collection", which consisted of a pair of jeans, a pair of smart trousers, a couple of t-shirts and a lovely thick cardigan with a fur collar. I loved the colour – a deep blue that looked great with my eyes and newly-highlighted hair. I was feeling so good about myself I considered calling in at L'Olivo for a coffee.

It was on my way back to the car park, so I decided I would see how brave I was feeling as I approached it. I stopped outside on the pretence of making a call on my mobile and dropped my shopping onto the pavement. I felt drawn to look through the window, and there he was, watching me. Our eyes met briefly and then I looked away, mortified. I had just made it so obvious that I liked him. He must have so many women like me flirting with him. He probably went back into the kitchen and put another notch on his chalkboard. 'That's six today, and we've not even had the evening trade yet.'

I grabbed my shopping and headed for the car park, feeling like a fool.

Once home I checked in with Sam, but the boys didn't want to talk to me; they were far too busy playing with their cousins.

I had treated myself to a lasagne from Marks & Spencer, and I sat down to enjoy it with my customary glass of Pinot. Afterwards I rang Issi for a chat and told her about my new look, but not about my close encounter at L'Olivo, because I was still cringing.

'It sounds absolutely stunning,' she told me. 'Listen, I'm really sorry but Jonathan and I are just off out to a business dinner in London, so could we catch up next week?'

'Yes, of course. What are you wearing tonight?'

'Just a simple cocktail dress.'

I knew it would be a designer dress, but Issi would never admit to it. 'Well, I bet you look stunning too – have a lovely time.'

'Thanks – see you in L'Olivo. How about a week on Tuesday?'

'Great, but shall we try somewhere else?' I didn't want the embarrassment of seeing the waiter again.

There was a slight pause. 'No – L'Olivo is fine.'

I took a comforting tub of chocolate ice cream into the lounge, where I flicked the television on to watch my favourite detective series.

The phone rang just as the murderer was confessing and I answered in annoyance, surprised to hear Darren's voice on the line. Why was he was calling at this time, when the boys would normally be asleep?

'Charlie and Jack are sleeping over at Sam's.' I wasn't going to admit that they were probably still up and watching a scary, inappropriately-rated movie.

'That's okay,' he replied. 'I was just ringing to talk to you.'

'Oh.'

'So?' He paused and I thought I heard him sigh. 'How are you?'

I was thrown into confusion. It was as if he wanted to *talk* to me, really talk, but didn't know what to say or where to start.

'I'm good,' I said quietly. I wished he were standing on the doorstep so I could invite him in, ask him how he really felt about me and tell him I missed him. 'How are you? Work good?'

'Yeah,' he replied slowly. 'Things are fine.'

'Great.' I paused, unsure what to say next. 'I've a lot of work on, which is good.'

'Juggling everything must be tough for you. I...' His voice suddenly became muffled, as if he were talking to someone else with his hand over the receiver. 'Becky, I have to go.'

'Oh.' Disappointment flooded through me.

'I'm sorry. I'll call soon.'

Thoughts whirled round and round in my head. Were things going badly with Barbie? Did he want to come home? I smiled as I picked up my spoon and licked it. Maybe my life was starting to look up.

*

'I'm not going to tell you again – eat your breakfast quickly or we'll be late for school.'

Jack pushed his bowl away from him. 'Don't want it,' he said.

'I don't want mine, either,' Charlie copied his brother.

I took a deep breath. 'Right. If staying with your cousins makes you this tired, you can't sleep over again.'

Charlie and Jack both scowled at me, before retrieving their bowls and eating as slowly as they could.

We made it into the playground with seconds to spare and I was pleased to see Kate was still there.

'Hey, nice haircut – it really suits you.'

I blushed. 'Thanks. Did you have a good weekend?'

'Just the usual, but yes, it was fine. How about you?'

I smiled. 'Great, thanks. I had some time to myself, saw my sister – yes, it was good.'

Kate smiled back. 'We'll have to get together for a coffee

when you're not too busy – have a proper catch-up.'

I glowed inside. It was great to see a friendly face each morning. I found it unnerving standing by myself – there was a definite stigma attached to it, as if you had no friends.

As the children filed into school I followed the boys into the small cloakroom area and pushed my way through the throng, towards Miss Whittaker. She saw me approaching and smiled, holding out her hand. 'Mrs Dixon, lovely to meet you at last.'

Was that a criticism? 'Oh, yes. I have tried to speak to you, but—' I was suddenly crushed by children moving towards the classroom and parents anxious to grab a word with the teacher. 'I wondered if I could have a word about Jack?'

'Of course.' She smiled at the children as they barged past. 'How about after school?'

'That would be great, thanks,' I said, before turning into the flow of oncoming children.

Kate was waiting for me. 'Everything okay?'

I nodded. 'I'm going to talk to Miss Whittaker later.' Although I hadn't known Kate long, I felt comfortable confiding in her. 'I'm worried about Jack's lack of concentration.'

'He's very young,' she said, 'but at least talking to Miss Whittaker will put your mind at rest.'

'Yes. You're right.'

We continued chatting as we walked out of the playground. Helen and two of her friends were still standing by the gate, deep in conversation. I nodded in Helen's direction, but she didn't respond.

'Do you know them?' Kate asked.

'I used to work with Helen, the one with dark hair, but that was years ago.'

'Well, all I know about them,' she muttered, 'is that they stand there every day, talking about everything and everyone.' She raised her eyebrows. 'I've heard they have a talent for knowing exactly what goes on in the classroom, who plays with who at playtime, and which mums arrive late for drop-off and pick-up.' She suddenly burst out laughing. 'Listen to me. I sound as bad as them.'

We said our goodbyes and I walked home, thinking about these women. Helen had enjoyed a good career in advertising, so why was she now spending her time gossiping in the cold?

*

'Oh, blow,' I said out loud. How could it possibly be half past two already? I flexed my aching fingers and stood up to stretch my back. I'd met one deadline but had achieved little else.

I ran downstairs to make a coffee and grabbed a handful of biscuits, eating them as I quickly ran the vacuum cleaner over the remnants of breakfast.

I opened the front door to find it was raining, so I ran back upstairs for the purchase I'd made at the end of Saturday's shopping spree – my very own playground coat. It was a navy zip-up with a concealed hood – not very flattering, but extremely practical. "Serious coat mum" may have been deadly boring, but she was right – you really did need a good coat to see you through all weathers. As I walked into the playground there were nods of approval and I giggled to myself.

Kate did a double-take. 'You succumbed then?' She looked me up and down. 'Very nice.'

I detected a hint of sarcasm and smiled. 'Ah, but wait until you see this,' I replied, and out of my pockets I produced two mini versions of the coat – one for each of the boys. Kate laughed so much people started staring, and as I glanced round at them I spotted the sports teacher talking to one of the parents. I thought again how attractive he was and tried to catch his eye, hoping he would notice me with my new hairstyle, but he didn't look up. I felt a pang of disappointment and hoped I'd see him in the playground another day.

I waited for the children to pour out and then took the boys back inside, telling them I just wanted to meet their teacher.

Miss Whittaker shook my hand warmly. 'It's lovely to meet you,' she said as she directed the boys to the home corner. Her fair hair was styled in a single plait down her back, and despite having spent the day teaching young children her make-up was still intact. Her unlined face was kind and welcoming. I perched on one of the tiny chairs feeling old and tired in comparison.

Miss Whittaker sat down next to me. 'The boys have settled in well and have made lots of friends.'

'Oh, good, that's a relief.' I smiled back. 'They're very happy here, but I just wanted to talk about Jack.'

She leaned back in her chair, encouraging me to talk.

'He's always been more active than Charlie, but recently he seems to be lacking concentration as well.'

'He is lively,' she said, 'but nothing I can't deal with. How was he at his nursery school?'

'Much the same, but they said it was too early to tell if there was a problem.'

'I'll ask our SENCO to give you a call – then you can pop in and talk it all through with her, as she's the expert.'

I stared at her dumbly. 'Senco?' I had no idea what she meant.

'Sorry – our Special Educational Needs Coordinator, Mrs Williams.'

I continued staring. 'You think he might have special needs?'

Miss Whittaker smiled kindly, as I imagined she would at one of her children. 'Not at all – she'll just talk things through with you.'

I thanked her and collected the boys, who ran ahead of me. I was walking through the corridor with my head down, thinking about Jack, when I bumped into someone. 'Sorry,' I said as I looked up.

Helen was glaring at me. 'Have you been called in to see the teacher already?' She was joking, but there was an edge to her voice that I didn't like.

'No. I…er…'

'My son, Josh,' she interrupted, 'is always telling me how naughty Jack is in class.'

I blinked in surprise, my cheeks burning. I couldn't think of anything to say, and then she turned on her high heels and clip-clopped down the corridor, leaving me staring after her.

I hurried the boys along because I needed to take them straight to their weekly swimming lesson at the local pool. They were always hungry after school so we all shared a bag of mini Mars Bars in the car and both the boys managed to squeeze their carton of blackcurrant juice down their sweatshirts. I didn't mind so much on a Friday, but it was only Monday. I sighed. Yet more washing.

Having got them undressed and into the pool for their lesson, I just had time to run round the supermarket next door to re-stock the fridge after the weekend. While I was loading the conveyor belt I became aware that the man in the next aisle was watching me. I did a quick appraisal – nice hair, about my age, buying a ready meal for one and a bottle of wine. My new hairstyle was working well for me. I took a deep breath and smiled. He gave me a quick smile back and looked away. If I'd had more confidence I would have chatted to him on some pretence, but this was a start, anyway.

On the way out of the supermarket one or two people glanced at me and once back in the car I admired myself in the rear-view mirror. It was then that I saw the string of toffee hanging from the corner of my mouth. My heart sank, and with Helen's words still ringing in my ears, any remaining shred of self-confidence drained out of me.

I returned to the leisure centre and lost patience with the boys after their lesson. 'Jack, hurry up and get dried,' I snapped as he flicked Charlie with his towel. 'And stop doing that.'

'I'm going as fast as I can, Mum,' he moaned.

Charlie threw his wet trunks at his brother, hitting him in the face, and Jack jumped off the bench and started chasing him round the changing room.

'That's enough!' I screamed at them, drawing discreet looks from other parents.

I needed to sort myself out. I was always tired, I hadn't given the house a good clean in weeks and I drank far too much coffee.

Back at home I put the coffee machine on and emptied the boys' school bags, lunch boxes and swimming bags. I shoved a load of washing into the machine as I put some chicken nuggets in the oven.

I smiled at Jack and Charlie as I sat down with them to eat, not really enjoying my chicken nuggets, but too tired to cook anything for myself. I poured them both a drink, trying not to shout when Jack took Charlie's beaker off him, spilling juice all over the table. Sadness overwhelmed me as I mopped it up – had my separation from Darren had anything to do with Jack's behaviour?

*

I sat on Charlie's bed reading his favourite bedtime story about a fox and his friends. Jack had already snuggled under his duvet and fallen asleep, and I pulled Charlie close to me, kissing the top of his head. 'So Mr Fox crept up on—'

'Mummy?'

I looked down at my son's puzzled expression. 'Yes?'

'Do you miss Daddy?'

Paralysis gripped me for a second. 'Yes. Of course I do,' I answered truthfully.

'So do I,' he said sleepily, slipping down the bed and closing his eyes.

I sat for a while, stroking his hair and face. I'd never talked to the boys about Darren leaving us. I'd thought they were too young, but maybe I should have done.

As I closed their door, my inadequacy made me want to cry. How could I explain things to them when I didn't really understand them myself? Sadness and anger jostled for position as my chest tightened until I could barely breathe. I grabbed the phone to tell Darren what he'd done to us, the impact he'd had on all our lives, but then I put it down again slowly. He could do nothing to heal the pain we felt.

I wandered into the kitchen and as I unloaded the dishwasher I spotted the overflowing bin. Remembering that the rubbish would be collected in the morning, I shoved my feet into my boots and braved the cold October evening, dragging the wheelie bin and then the recycling boxes down the drive.

My chest constricted again, and I forced myself to take deep breaths. I was overwhelmed by the enormity of my job as a single mum, on both on an emotional and a practical level, and I leaned over the bin and sobbed in huge gulps as I let it all out.

There was a polite cough to my left and I looked up to see my neighbour hovering uncertainly. 'Sorry, George,' I said, fishing in my pocket for a tissue.

'In future, Becky,' he said, 'it will be my job to put your bins out for you.'

His kindness made me cry again. 'Thank you,' I said weakly.

Chapter Four

Seven, eight,
Don't be late,
Or you'll be talked about
At the school gate.

'Hello, Becky.'

'Hello, Mum. How are you?' We hadn't spoken for a few weeks, because despite my leaving several messages on her answer phone, she hadn't called me back.

'I'm very well,' she replied brightly. 'I'm coming to stay for the weekend.'

'Oh. Right.' I couldn't have been more surprised.

'I'm arriving tomorrow afternoon, so can you collect me from the airport?'

I mentally re-arranged my work schedule. 'Of course I can. What time?'

'One fifteen. See you tomorrow,' she said quickly, and put the phone down.

I immediately phoned Sam and filled her in on the brief conversation.

'Crikey,' she said, laughing. 'What's going on? And why is it such short notice?'

'I don't know. I was so surprised I didn't ask.'

Sam tutted in mock exasperation. 'Ring me as soon as you've collected her – I'm intrigued.'

'Okay – will do.'

I'd had a difficult relationship with my mum for as long as I could remember. I was sure she genuinely cared about Sam, Michael and me – she just failed miserably when it came to communicating with us, which was why her visit was such a surprise.

*

I spotted Mum through the crowd at Arrivals and walked quickly towards her, kissing her on the cheek. Other people were locked in hugs that said how much they'd missed each other, and I felt embarrassed at our lukewarm greeting.

'Where's your luggage?' I asked.

'There.' She pointed to a man pulling two suitcases behind him and beaming at me.

He stopped and grabbed my face with his hands, kissing me noisily on both cheeks. 'Becky! It's so lovely to meet you.' He spoke perfect English, but with a heavy Spanish accent.

I looked blankly from him to my mother.

'This is Vicente,' she snapped. 'I *have* told you about him.'

She had mentioned a friend called Vicente several times, but I'd had no real idea who he was. I turned back to him and smiled. He seemed much younger than Mum, perhaps in his late forties, and was tall and well-built. He had a bit of a paunch around his stomach and he wasn't exactly good-looking, but he had a kind face and there was something about him that was attractive. 'Lovely to meet you, too,' I murmured.

I walked closer to my mother. 'I just didn't know he was coming with you,' I whispered. 'Is he staying with me as well?'

She frowned in annoyance. 'Where else would he be

going?'

I breathed deeply as we walked to the car, trying to calm down. I would have to sleep in the spare single bed and let them have my room, which meant I'd have to strip and re-make my bed. Or maybe Vicente would want the single bed and I'd have to share with Mum. I sighed.

Vicente and Mum sat in the back of the car and he chatted all the way home. 'I grow lots of vegetables on my farm,' he told me, 'and I sell them on the market. That's how I met your mother.'

For the last ten years Mum had been living in Spain. After my dad left she had drifted from one meaningless relationship to another, supporting us by taking in sewing. She had gained a good reputation as a seamstress, making a reasonable living from it.

She had always dreamed of a life in the sun, and had moved there with a boyfriend who had disappeared within a month. She had stuck it out though, and now had a small shop selling holiday clothing, which she said was doing well.

Through my rear-view mirror I saw her smile at Vicente. I was still unsure of the nature of their friendship, but there was clearly a deep affection between them.

'Yes,' my mother chipped in. 'After we're married we'll be living on the farm.'

I swerved, frightening the driver on the inside lane, who tooted loudly and gestured. 'Sorry, sorry,' I said, holding my hand up to him. I stared into the mirror. 'Married?'

Mum and Vicente were holding hands and smiling at each other. 'August the twenty-second,' Mum replied. 'Vicente suggested the summer so all of our families can be there.'

'Do you have children, Vicente?' I asked.

'No. I was never blessed, but I have lots of nephews and nieces. I love to… how do you say?'

'Spoil them all.' My mother shook her head.

He grinned broadly, kissing her cheek.

We arrived home and Mum wandered round my new house. 'It's…well, obviously a lot smaller than—'

'It's a lovely home,' Vicente interrupted quickly.

Mum stared at the out-dated wallpaper in the hall and grimaced.

'The whole house needs decorating,' I said, sighing heavily.

'It'll be *perfecto* once it's in your own style,' Vicente said simply.

Every time I thought about the huge task ahead of me, I panicked. I didn't know how I was going to find time to decorate, and I certainly couldn't afford to pay anyone. I kept wondering about asking Michael to help, but now he was seeing Sophie I didn't like to impose. I shelved those thoughts again.

I left Mum and Vicente poking round and went to collect the boys, explaining who Vicente was.

'Will he be our new grandad?' Jack asked.

'Yes, I suppose he will.'

'Good,' Charlie told me. 'He'll buy us presents, then. That's what Daniel's grandad does.'

We arrived home and Vicente scooped Charlie and Jack up in turn. 'What beautiful boys,' he told them.

Charlie stared at him. 'You sound funny.'

'That's because I'm Spanish,' he said, throwing his head back and laughing. 'I'll teach you some words.'

After dinner he sat them down and taught them how to count, but Jack soon lost interest. Charlie, however, was fascinated and walked round the house repeating *uno, dos, tres.*

After I'd bathed the boys and put them to bed, I joined Mum and Vicente in the lounge, flopping down in an easy chair.

'I'm going to have a long soak in the bath,' Mum announced, standing up.

'See you later, my darling,' Vicente said. 'I'll open that nice bottle of Rioja I brought. I'm sure Becky will enjoy it.' He poured us both a glass and sat down opposite me.

'Ooh, that tastes good,' I said, curling my feet under me, the alcohol starting to release the day's tensions.

'You have a busy life,' he said. 'You must make time to relax.'

I smiled wryly. 'If only.'

He shook his head. 'You work hard. Your mum has told me what a good job you do, with your business and looking after your children.'

'Has she?' I stared at him in surprise. 'Sorry – it's just that she's never said that to me.'

'Your mum is a complicated lady,' he said, draining his glass. He gestured for me to do the same and then filled them both back up. 'She was very hurt by your dad, and she understands how hard it is for you.'

'I don't know how she feels about my dad,' I replied. 'And she's never said she sympathises with me.' I was confused. What he was saying was very nice to hear, but I didn't think it was the truth. She had probably told him all this to show herself in a better light. I took a large gulp of wine. 'I have no idea why my dad left,' I said. 'And I'm worried my boys will grow up with the same feelings.'

'When they're older you'll talk to them.'

I nodded. 'But I don't know how it's affecting them now. I'm particularly worried about Jack.'

He smiled kindly. 'They seem fine to me.'

I smiled back, happy he had come into our lives. 'I'm seeing someone at school tomorrow, so I'll feel better after that.'

'Of course you will.'

Mum walked in, wrapped in my fluffy dressing gown.

'I borrowed this,' she told me. 'It's cold in England.' She sat down as Vicente poured her a glass of wine.

I smiled at her. She looked well, despite her grumpiness. She was tanned and had lost some weight, which suited her. The sun had naturally highlighted her hair and she looked like a woman who was finally content.

Vicente moved to sit next to her. 'Sheila, *mi amor*,' he said quietly, but firmly. 'You must talk to Becky about her father. It's important.'

Mum blinked several times and took a large swig of wine. 'I'll need a cigarette, then.'

I shook my head, hoping she wasn't going to be difficult.

'Oh, okay,' she moaned. She turned to her fiancé. 'Better open another bottle of wine if I'm not allowed to smoke.'

Vicente refilled our glasses and then discreetly took his into the kitchen. Mum looked at me and sighed. 'Your dad and I married young – basically because I was pregnant with Samantha. He was a plumber, money was tight, and by the time Michael was born he'd started to feel trapped in a never-ending world of babies and debt.' She stared into space for a moment, lost in her thoughts. 'That's what he told me as he left, anyway.'

'Oh.' It all sounded so clinical. 'So what was he like?'

She smiled sardonically. 'Good-looking, charming – all the ladies liked him. Too many.'

'Oh. He had an affair?'

Mum raised her eyebrows sharply. '*An* affair? No, there were many. I kicked him out in the end.'

'Where did he go?'

'Don't know, don't care. He didn't pay any maintenance – I know that much.' She drained her glass and refilled it. She was holding her body erect – this was clearly painful for her, even after thirty years.

I'd drunk enough wine to say things I wouldn't normally

have said. 'So if you'd been through it yourself, why didn't you support me more when Darren...' I couldn't bring myself to say it. I took a large gulp of wine. 'Where were you when he cleared off to America, leaving me to cope alone?'

Mum didn't flinch. 'I had to be tough to survive. My parents didn't support me, and I suppose I built a shell round myself in the early years.' She looked away. 'I guess because of that we've never been very close.'

Even though this was the truth, it hurt to hear my mother say it, and I vowed I wouldn't let that be the case with my boys. I stood up slowly. 'Thanks for telling me. Goodnight.'

*

My stomach churned as I walked round to the school's reception for my appointment with Mrs Williams the next morning. I wasn't sure what to expect from our meeting, and I hoped Jack didn't have any serious problems.

'Hello.' I smiled at the receptionist. 'Mrs Dixon. I've come to see Mrs Williams.'

As she checked her schedule, the security door to my right clicked open and I looked up to see the sports teacher walking towards me. 'Mrs Dixon?'

His white shirt, open at the neck and with the sleeves rolled back, showed off his post-summer tan and it took a hard shove to push away thoughts of him lying on a beach. A faint smell of aftershave wafted around him. Please don't let me be blushing. 'Yes.' I smiled and nodded.

'Rob Phillips. I'm the deputy head.' He thrust out his right hand and smiled. 'I'm really sorry, but Mrs Williams has had a family emergency and hasn't been able to come in this morning.'

'Oh, I'm sorry to hear that.'

'She briefed me on the phone, though,' he continued,

'and I've picked up all her notes – if you're happy to see me instead?'

He tilted his head to one side after he'd finished speaking, sending tingles up and down my spine. 'Yes, of course. That's fine.'

'We'll use her office,' he said, showing me into a small room crammed with two filing cabinets, a desk, two chairs and a half-dead plant on the window sill. He gestured for me to sit down. 'Would you like a coffee?'

'No, I'm fine, thanks.' I didn't trust myself not to spill it down my blouse. I looked across at this teacher, whose hazel eyes were filled with concern. He was around six feet, and the tone of his muscles was clearly visible through his shirt. His dark hair was well-cut and once again gelled into soft spikes.

'I understand you have some worries about Jack?'

'Yes – he doesn't seem able to concentrate for long.'

Mr Phillips smiled kindly. 'We have noticed small behavioural problems, but we were just keeping an eye on things for the time being.'

'Oh, right. Sorry. Am I panicking?'

He leaned forward. 'Not at all. It's good that we work with parents.' He glanced down at his notes. 'If it's all right with you, we're just going to give him small targets to meet.'

I nodded. 'Such as?'

'One of them is to sit still in assembly without calling out or disturbing the other children.'

My hand flew to my mouth. 'He does that?'

Mr Phillips's eyes locked onto mine and my stomach tightened. 'He's very young – please don't worry.'

'Thank you,' I replied quietly, looking away.

'Is there anything else that's concerning you?'

'No – on the whole, they both seem to have settled in well.'

'Yes,' he agreed. 'I take them for PE and they're both good

fun.'

I stood up and smiled. 'Thanks very much for all your help.'

'Not a problem.' He shook my hand again and I hoped mine wasn't clammy. 'I'll be in touch if there's any need.'

I walked home briskly and Vicente put the kettle on. 'How did it go?'

I nodded and smiled. 'Very well, thanks. Better than expected.'

*

'He's all right, isn't he?' Sam whispered to me. We were standing in her garden on Saturday afternoon watching Vicente play football with our sons.

'I like him,' I replied. 'I think he'll be good for Mum.' I then told her about my conversation with Mum, and Sam fell silent.

'I've always been curious about Dad,' she said after a few minutes. 'I wonder where he is now.'

I shrugged. 'I've got too many other problems to worry about him.' I looked up at the clock. 'What time's Michael coming?'

Right on cue the doorbell rang and he walked into the kitchen, kissing us all warmly. 'This is Sophie.'

We all shook hands with his latest girlfriend, who at five feet eleven towered over all of us. Her long red hair was coiled into a bun and she looked as if she'd come straight from a modelling assignment.

Even though Michael was shorter than her, they made a lovely and very attractive couple. With his blonde hair and brown eyes, his colouring was very different to Sam's and mine. We used to tease him mercilessly as children, telling him he'd been left on the doorstep, and I once asked Mum if he looked like our dad. She'd snapped 'yes' so violently that I'd never asked again.

Mum and Vicente came in from the garden and Michael hugged Mum. She treated him no differently to Sam and me, rarely remembering any of our birthdays, but he always said he couldn't be bothered to dwell on the past. 'I'm too lazy,' he often told us, and I wished I could adopt his attitude.

'Uncle Michael!' Charlie and Jack bellowed together, running towards him and almost knocking him over. They glanced up at Sophie, but then ignored her as they dragged their uncle outside to play football.

'Come on, Sophie,' Michael shouted over his shoulder, and Sam and I watched in amazement as she slipped off her four-inch heels and played football in her bare feet.

Sam and I prepared a buffet tea for everyone and the conversation flowed effortlessly. I chatted at length to Sophie, who actually was a model, and later on Michael slipped his arm round my waist. 'I think I really like her,' he told me. Because I was driving I hadn't had a drink, but the others had shared several bottles of wine. 'Really like her,' he slurred.

I was happy for him as I watched them later, lost in conversation together. Mum and Vicente had their arms round each other, watching the boys playing in the garden, and Sam and Dave were flopped out on the sofa. I missed Darren with a pain that caused me to go and sit outside and have a little cry.

*

I hurried through Maidenhead town centre, zipping my coat up against the biting wind, only glancing in the shop windows as I passed, conscious that I was running late for my get-together with Issi. Arriving at L'Olivo, I quickly checked my reflection in the window before calmly walking over to where Issi was sipping her cappuccino.

'Sorry I'm late.'

She kissed me on the cheek. 'You look great,' she enthused. 'Love the hair.'

'Thanks.' I let my eyes wander round the room, wondering if he had seen me come in.

A waitress appeared at our table ready to take my order, and I stared dumbly at her as I sat down. I wanted to say, 'Where's Angelo, or Cesare?' but instead I asked her for a latte, disappointed he wasn't there. I smiled at Issi. 'How was your weekend at Jonathan's parents?'

'A bit difficult because Ben went down with a bug and threw up everywhere.'

'Oh, gosh. Is he all right now?'

'Yes – he was fine by the time we got home. My in-laws weren't best pleased, but it couldn't be helped.'

I smiled sympathetically.

'Anyway,' she continued, 'your weekend sounded interesting. I laughed when I got your text.' She looked round the café. 'I half expected them to come with you today.'

I laughed. 'No, it was a flying visit – they went home yesterday.'

'So what was Vicente like?'

'Very nice, actually. After all the bad choices Mum's made over the years, I think she's finally found someone she can trust.'

'You think she'll stay with him then?'

'They're getting married.' I grinned at her incredulous expression. 'Over in Spain, in August.'

Issi threw her head back and laughed. 'I can imagine you at the wedding wearing a sombrero.' She narrowed her eyes. 'It just shows it's never too late to find love.'

I scowled back at her. 'If I have to wait until I'm nearly sixty for it, then I'm giving up now.' I sipped my latte before smiling again. 'By the way, you're invited too.'

'I'll look forward to it.'

'I meant to tell you,' I said, still smiling. 'I had a really strange conversation with Darren the other night.'

'Ooh, that sounds interesting.' Issi put her cup down and leaned forward as I recounted how he'd called to talk to me and not the boys.

'I don't think all's well in Barbie's Magic Kingdom,' I said. 'Maybe he wants to come home?'

'You wouldn't take him back though, would you?' She eyed me suspiciously. 'Not after all he put you through.'

I shrugged and looked away. 'I don't know. Sometimes I just get so lonely and tired. It would be nice to have someone to share things with.' I stirred my drink. 'Sex would be good, too.'

Issi smiled. 'You'll meet someone,' she said, putting her hand on top of mine and squeezing it.

'Maybe.' I concentrated on spooning out the remains of my frothy milk before glancing up at Issi. 'That reminds me. I saw one of the teachers at school about Jack.'

'Oh, well done. What did she say?'

'*He* said Jack had a few difficulties, but not to worry at the moment.'

'He?' Her eyes widened. 'It wasn't the sports teacher by any chance? Someone's made you smile.'

I grinned. 'He's also the deputy head – and he's gorgeous,' I whispered.

'Young? Old?'

I pretended I hadn't given the matter any consideration. 'About my age – possibly.'

Issi laughed again. 'Talking of teachers, we're going to be late.'

'Oh, why does this always happen?' I asked as I grabbed my coat and bag.

'Law of nature,' Issi replied, shrugging.

I arrived in the playground to collect the boys with only minutes to spare and couldn't help looking round for Mr Phillips as the doors opened. I was disappointed I didn't see him.

*

'Charlie, stop scratching your head,' I snapped during breakfast. 'You've been doing it for days – have you got something in your hair?'

'Liam's got head flies,' Jack told me, without looking up from his bowl of cereal. 'Jessica says he's got nits. What's nits?'

I froze. I had heard about head lice, but I wasn't sure what they looked like or what to do about them. I calmly finished my toast, then wandered over to where Charlie was sitting and parted his hair, hoping desperately to find dandruff. The sight of several black lice crawling over his scalp nearly made me bring the toast back.

Jack automatically started scratching and I gingerly checked his head as well. My heart sank, and I rang Sam. Fifteen years as a nurse had given her a wealth of medical knowledge and this must include nits.

'Okay,' my sister said in her usual calm manner. 'I don't believe in using chemicals, so you'll need a nit comb and lots of conditioner.' She paused for a moment. 'On second thoughts, you'll never get a nit comb through their curly hair – just go straight for the chemicals.'

'Right,' I replied, feeling less panicky. 'Do I need to keep them off school?'

'No – take them in after you've treated them, but let school know because they'll have to send a note home to the year group.'

'Oh, God,' I groaned. 'Everyone will know.'

Sam laughed. 'They keep it anonymous – no one will know it's Charlie and Jack. Oh, and don't forget to do your own hair!'

By the time we arrived at school, "hogging mums" and "chatting mums" were long gone. Miss Whittaker was busy teaching, so I explained the situation to her assistant, Mrs Collins, who assured me the matter would remain confidential.

*

While the boys liked to play together, they had also formed individual friendships and on the way to school one morning Charlie asked if Joshua could come round to play.

'He's my *best* friend,' he told me. 'And I've said he can come.'

I ruffled my son's hair as we walked along. I knew Helen was Josh's mum and I felt a little stirring of apprehension in my stomach. She wasn't someone I particularly wanted to develop a relationship with. However, we were both adults, and that must mean we'd leave the past behind for the sake of our children. 'Of course he can come,' I replied. 'I'll speak to his mum.'

I left the boys running around the playground and wandered over to the group Helen always stood with, waiting patiently for her to finish speaking.

'Hi, Helen.'

She glanced up. 'Yes?'

My jaw tightened at her rudeness, but I gave her a bright smile. 'Charlie has asked if Josh could come round to tea one day next week.'

She made a show of thinking about it and the mum standing next to her sniggered. 'Yes, okay,' Helen said with a shrug. 'Wednesday.'

'That's fine,' I replied. 'I'll jot down my address and phone number for you.' I reached into my bag and scribbled the details on a piece of paper. I tried to hand it to her, but she had already turned her back and resumed her conversation. 'Here you are,' I said loudly.

Without looking at me, she stuck her hand out for the details. I desperately wanted to say something clever about her rudeness, but I just couldn't find the words.

*

On Wednesday Charlie was in a state of high excitement. I'd started walking to school with some of the local mums and this particular morning I was chatting to Jenny, who lived on the next road to us. We smiled as we listened to Charlie telling her son Oliver all about Josh's impending visit.

'I've got my train set ready, and then we're going to play Power Rangers with Jack.'

'Oh,' replied Oliver. 'I wish I could come too.'

'Don't worry, you can come next week. Ask your mum.'

I collected the three boys after school and while Josh was as lively as Charlie and Jack, I was pleased by how well they played together, without too many spats.

Helen arrived for Josh promptly at six o'clock and I steeled myself for a confrontation. She stepped into the hall, glancing around at the out-dated wallpaper. I cringed in embarrassment, but I wasn't going to apologise for the décor. It would get changed in time.

'Would you like a coffee?' I offered out of politeness. I hoped she wouldn't accept as I felt awkward and on edge in her company. Before meeting again at school, the last time I'd seen her I was coming out of her boss's office as she was going in. It must have been obvious I'd been instrumental in her sacking, and a part of me wanted to explain, but it had all been such a long time ago. It was a shame, because working at the same company should have given us plenty to chat about.

'Nothing stronger?' she asked as she slipped her coat off.

'Oh.' After she'd left McAdam's, the office rumours of her drinking problems had begun circulating, but I'd never known how much was true. The gossip flooded back into my mind and I blushed, hoping she couldn't read my thoughts. 'I've a bottle of white wine opened,' I suggested, turning away as I spoke.

'Great.'

She followed me into the kitchen and I poured two glasses, passing one to her as she sat down at the table.

'The boys have played well together,' I said, sitting down opposite her.

'Good.' She seemed distracted as she picked up her glass, drinking half her wine quickly.

The conversation ground to a halt and I sipped my wine slowly. If she didn't want to talk about the children, what else were we going to discuss? I took a deep breath and wandered into enemy territory.

'Am I right in thinking you set up your own advertising company?'

She stared at me, her eyes unblinking. 'I did, but not anymore. I have a busy and fulfilling life at home.'

As she finished her wine I studied her more closely. Grey strands ran through her hair and spidery thread veins were spread across her cheeks. Her face seemed puffy, making her eyes look small and somehow lost. When I had worked with her she had always had immaculate make-up and well-cut hair, but I knew only too well how focusing on your children could often leave you neglecting your own needs.

'Josh must help to tidy up before he leaves,' she said suddenly, looking at her watch. 'I'll just pop upstairs and give him a five-minute warning.' She reappeared a few minutes later. 'It's not too bad up there. Now, would Charlie like to come round to me next week?'

'I'm sure he'd love to, thanks.'

'What about Jack?' She kept her gaze level. 'Probably best if he makes his own friends.'

I couldn't tell if that was a slight or not. 'You're right,' I replied, smiling. 'I'm trying to encourage them to have separate interests and friends.'

'Good.'

After they'd gone I picked up Helen's empty glass and wondered about her life.

*

Walking into the playground, I had the strange feeling some of the mums were looking at me. I smiled at a couple of them, who smiled back but then turned away quickly.

Jack called over to a boy in his class. 'Callum – come and play with me.'

'Okay,' Callum replied, but his mother held him back, whispering something in his ear.

My stomach lurched. What was wrong? Why had we suddenly become a family to avoid? My question was answered by two mums, speaking just a little too loudly.

'These mums who don't do a regular bug-bust really annoy me. If only they could be bothered, it would stop the spread.'

'I agree. It's just laziness.'

Mortified, I walked over to Kate. 'My boys didn't get head lice deliberately and I did the decent thing in telling school. Why are they picking on me?'

'I don't know,' she muttered.

'Kate?' My pulse rate quickened. 'Is there something I should know?'

Kate's cheeks flushed with colour. 'Emily's mum, Sue, said something about it this morning, but I just ignored it. She can be quite nasty at times.'

'But,' I spluttered, 'the boys didn't start it off – and I made sure the lice were treated properly – and I told the boys to keep their heads away from other chil—'

Kate put her hand on my arm to calm me down. 'I know all that, Becky. Helen Stevens just has it in for you for some reason.'

'Helen? What's it got to do with her?'

Kate sighed heavily. 'Best just to leave it.' She stared down at the ground

'Please, Kate. I need to know what's going on.'

'Helen told Sue you'd done nothing about it—'

'But that's not true!' I clenched my hands. 'I did everything I could.'

'Steer clear of her, Becky – she's saying other stuff as well.'

'Such as?' I couldn't take in what I was hearing.

'I don't really want to repeat gossip – and that's all it is.'

'I need to know,' I said in a low voice.

'Okay.' Kate sighed again. 'She's telling everyone you let Josh and the boys play out in the street unsupervised the other evening.' She spoke quickly and avoided looking at me. 'I know it's not true.'

'No it damn well isn't!' I exploded. 'Sorry, I didn't mean to take it out on you.'

Without thinking I marched over to Helen and her cronies. Helen looked at me without blinking. 'I'm afraid,' she said, before I could speak, 'I'll have to cancel Charlie's visit to my house.' She continued to hold my gaze. 'Under the circumstances.'

'Circumstances?' My throat tightened. 'What would they be, exactly?'

One of the posse giggled and my cheeks started to burn.

'Let's just leave it at that, shall we?' Helen smiled at me, before turning her back to talk to her posse.

'No, I'd like to know what I've been accused of.'

She spun round and glared at me. 'Let's just say I don't consider working mothers suitable to look after my children. And I'm not babysitting yours for you.'

'I don't work after three o'clock.' My heart was hammering, but I managed to keep my voice calm. 'That's when I spend time with my children.'

'That's not what you told me.' She spat the words out, turning back to her circle of friends.

I was shaking with anger as I walked back to Kate. 'I didn't leave them for a second,' I told her after we'd seen the children into school. 'I might have mentioned it was nice that Charlie and Jack were occupied so I could do some work, but it was only research, and I was sitting in the kitchen the whole time.'

'I know, I know,' Kate replied. 'She's obviously jealous because you have a job. Ignore her.'

On my walk home I reflected on the playground. It wasn't the way I had imagined it was going to be – pleasant mums making small talk and swapping recipes. It was more like a jungle, with predatory mums protecting their own offspring at all costs. How was I going to explain to my four-year-old son that he was being punished for something that was nothing to do with him?

Chapter Five

Fee-fi-fo-fum,
I smell the blood
Of a vulnerable mum.

'Yes, you get the *whole* week off school,' I told Jack for the third time. 'Granny and Grandad will be here tonight, but very late.'

'Can we wait up to see them?' Charlie asked.

I shook my head. 'You've got to go to the airport very early in the morning.'

'I'm going to see my daddy!' Jack shouted, jumping up and down.

'Me too!' Charlie yelled even louder. 'And Disneyland is the best place ever!'

He started shaking with excitement, and as I finished ironing their t-shirts I smiled at them both, despite fighting back the burning behind my eyes.

The phone rang and Charlie picked it up. 'Hi, Dad!' he yelled. 'Yes, I can't wait to see you, too.'

He told Darren everything he wanted to do at Disneyland before Jack grabbed the phone off him.

'Hi, Daddy!' he screamed.

Charlie was hopping up and down by my side, trying to

tell me something. 'Wait till Jack's finished speaking to Dad,' I told him, 'then you can both tell me.'

Jack put the phone down and turned and grinned at me, so excited he could hardly get the words out. Charlie, tired of waiting, butted in. 'Daddy's told us some exciting news.'

I smiled at them, wondering what treat Darren had lined up.

'We're going to have a baby brother or sister!' Jack yelled.

'What?' I grabbed the worktop to support myself, my legs suddenly unsteady. 'Barbie's pregnant?' I said it out loud without thinking.

'Who's Barbie?' Charlie asked before he chased his brother into the lounge.

I ran upstairs and locked myself in the bathroom, slumping onto the floor, where I cried uncontrollably. I cried for my stupidity in thinking Darren still wanted me; I cried for the absolute ending of our relationship, as there would be no reconciliation now; I cried with jealousy that he wanted to have a child with someone else; and I cried out of sheer loneliness.

After splashing my face with water I went back downstairs to start the bedtime process, putting on my smiley, everything's-okay face. The boys weren't fooled.

'Why are you crying?' Jack asked, peering at me.

'Have you fallen over?' Charlie said, his face contorted in concern.

I swallowed hard. 'I banged my knee upstairs, but I'm all right now.'

Jack led me to the sofa and made me put my leg up. Charlie fetched a small table and a box of tissues, which he put next to me. Jack brought me a plastic beaker half full of water, having spilled the other half on the way from the kitchen. They both sat by my side, one holding my hand and the other gently rubbing my knee. It took all my strength not to cry again.

The boys resisted my attempts to get them into bed, but eventually they gave in, and then I thought about ringing Issi. However, I decided I didn't have the emotional energy, so I poured myself a large glass of wine and sat down at the kitchen table, where I held an ice-pack against my swollen eyes. I didn't want Darren's mum and dad to see me upset.

My thoughts drifted to Darren, and back to the heady days when I'd first met him at university.

Sam had persuaded Dave to drive me up to Sheffield in his clapped-out van, and I was busy unpacking when there was a loud banging on my door. I opened it cautiously.

'Hi! I'm Suzy, your next-door neighbour!'

A stunning-looking girl with long shiny black hair was leaning against my door frame, grinning.

'I'm Becky.' I grinned back. 'I've just arrived.'

'I know – I've been dying to see who would have the room next to me. I got here yesterday, and I can show you straight to the Students' Union bar if you like.'

I concentrated hard to understand her Geordie accent, and then glanced momentarily at my suitcase. 'Okay.'

Over the first term we became inseparable. We were both studying English and we helped each other with the coursework. We partied hard and Suzy introduced me to endless boys, none of whom really took my fancy.

One particular night we were watching football on the screen in the students' bar. Suzy was yelling loudly, urging her team on, and I suddenly became aware of a group of lads hovering next to us. One of them told Suzy he supported Newcastle United as well, and they became lost in a conversation no one else could understand, so strong were their accents.

'Would you like another drink?' A tall guy with thick wavy hair and an incredibly sexy smile was standing next to me.

'Thanks.' I raised my half pint of lager. 'Same again, if that's all right?'

He joined me a few minutes later with two glasses and gestured for his friends to drink somewhere else.

'Darren.' He introduced himself formally.

'Becky.' I shook his hand, laughing as I did so.

'You like football, then?'

'I'm not as mad about it as Suzy,' I replied, 'but I enjoy watching it.'

'Perhaps you'd fancy watching it with me some time?'

'Perhaps,' I teased.

We chatted easily, half watching the football, until the bar closed. Darren leaned forward and kissed my cheek lazily, lingering momentarily and sending tingles down my spine. 'Do you have an early start tomorrow?'

Before I could reply, Suzy grabbed me. 'All back to mine for a party. Joey and I want to celebrate Newcastle's win.'

We followed the other people heading to our block, but when we reached Suzy's door Darren paused. 'Is that your room, next to her's?'

I nodded.

'Do you really fancy the party?'

I let us in and made two coffees. We talked into the early hours, exchanging our life stories, and we fell asleep fully clothed around four o'clock. He didn't push me to have sex with him, although he hinted, which meant I didn't have to say no. That was something I always stuck to – I never slept with anyone on a first date.

We saw each other every day during the next week and at the weekend we went shopping in Sheffield. When we returned to my room I tried on the new blouse I'd bought and he walked over to me, slowly kissing my neck and shoulders as he took it off again. We fell onto the bed, and as we made love I felt as if I was giving him my heart and soul; I thought I'd love him forever.

I remembered the phone call I'd made to Issi later that evening. 'I've had the most brilliant week.'

'What's he called?'

'Darren,' I replied dreamily.

'Ooh, you sound like you have it bad. Tell me all about him.'

'He's in the second year of a business degree, he's sharing a house with three other students, he comes from Harrogate. And he's absolutely gorgeous. Anything else you want to know?'

Issi laughed loudly. 'I'll look forward to meeting him when Jonathan and I come up in a few weeks' time.'

After their visit Issi wrote to me saying how much she liked him, and although I didn't need her approval, I was glad all the same.

At the start of my second year I moved into the house Darren rented, and I felt so happy and contented. We were very much part of the party scene, but we spent our free time walking in the Derbyshire countryside or visiting his mum and dad. When he graduated and took a sales job with an IT company in London, I was devastated.

He promised to drive up every weekend and the first time he visited we barely moved out of the bedroom, we'd missed each other so much. A few weeks later he took me to our favourite picnic spot. It was a beautiful September day, the sun still warm enough to be out in, but as he unpacked the hamper he wouldn't let me sit down. Suddenly he knelt down in front of me, a small box in his hand.

'Becky, I love you so utterly and completely. Please marry me.'

I looked down, now, at the solitaire diamond ring that I'd switched to my right hand and I felt as if my heart was being squeezed so tightly it hurt. Huge tears dripped onto the kitchen table. Why hadn't he wanted to be with me forever, as he had promised that day?

We got married in Maidenhead as soon as I graduated. It was a beautiful day – my mother had made my wedding dress, together with the bridesmaids' dresses for Sam, Issi and Suzy. Michael gave me away and I had never felt happier.

I had taken a job with a local advertising company and we soon settled into married life. Our first house was a modest one, but we had enjoyed decorating and furnishing it together. It was cosy and comfortable, and when we closed the front door each evening, shutting out the world, I was at my happiest. We would cook together, chatting about our respective days and later we would make love, often on the stairs, not making it to the bedroom.

Darren enjoyed his work and quickly moved up the career ladder. He started to travel abroad most weeks, but the huge salary he received softened the downside of my lonely nights and we soon had enough money to move to a bigger house in a better area.

Shortly after my twenty-eighth birthday I began to feel broody, particularly because Issi had just had her second baby. I broached the subject with Darren, but he was horrified.

'Becky, hun,' he had said to me, 'I know we talked about having a family one day, but let's wait a few years. I've got my heart set on a Porsche.'

I waited nearly a year, by which time the urge to have a baby was overwhelming. Darren reluctantly agreed and I fell pregnant more or less straight away.

When the boys were one I was asked to return to work, and I negotiated a part-time contract. While life was hectic, I felt fulfilled in every way even though it was hard work when Darren was abroad, which was becoming more and more often. When he came home I was often tired and always busy with the boys. Evenings fell into a regular pattern of me asleep on the sofa and Darren sitting at his computer, but I didn't feel this was a problem – I just saw it as part and parcel of having young children.

I couldn't tell when it started, but Darren and I slowly began to drift apart. We didn't talk much, and when we did it was only ever about the boys.

I sat bolt upright in the kitchen, feeling sick as I remembered the day my world had collapsed. I tried unsuccessfully to push the memories away, lost in my world of self-pity and despair.

I saw myself playing happily on the lounge floor with Jack and Charlie when the phone rang. I had smiled as I answered it. 'Hello?'

An American voice had drawled softly on the other end. 'Is that Becky?'

Instinct had made me cautious. 'Who's calling?'

'My name's Shelley. I work with Darren.'

I remembered the feeling of panic rising in me. 'Is everything all right?' I had asked naively. 'Has something happened?'

'Kind of,' she'd replied without any hint of apology. 'I've been seeing Darren for a while and I love him very much.'

'What?' I'd screamed into the phone, making Charlie cry.

'He loves me too,' she'd continued, 'and you're standing in the way of our happiness.' She'd then sighed heavily. 'Darren's too scared to tell you, so I thought I'd do it.'

I wanted to retch as I remembered her words. I swallowed the rest of my wine in one huge gulp. The pain was still as acute now as it had been that day

I had slammed the phone down in shock, shaking uncontrollably. I loaded the boys into my car and shot round to Issi's, immediately breaking down in tears.

'How has this happened?' I cried. 'We're happy. We're good together.'

Issi hadn't known what to say to me as I sobbed my heart out. 'Maybe she's exaggerating things,' she suggested. 'I'll look after the boys while you go and confront Darren.'

When I arrived back at the house he was already there, sitting quietly with his head in his hands. He looked up at me, tears pouring down his cheeks. 'I'm so sorry.'

I shuddered as I remembered how he had stood up and walked towards me. A part of me had wanted to collapse in his arms, for him to tell me it wasn't true; a part of me had wanted to slap his face.

'Please forgive me,' he had said, looking directly into my eyes. 'I'm so, so sorry.' He had started sobbing, but I had simply stood still, staring at him, unable to take in what was happening to me. 'I love you and the boys. It's you I want to be with – please don't leave me.'

Without replying I packed a bag for the three of us and fled to Sam's. I spent the first week hidden under my duvet while Sam cared for Charlie and Jack, and when I felt stronger I returned home and asked Darren to leave. He moved out that evening and left the country three months later after he had begged and begged me to forgive him. Pride had stopped me from saying yes.

Why hadn't I said yes? I had meant to, but somehow I hadn't been able to find the words.

Shelley was from California and Darren arranged a transfer through his company to join her. He was generous in his maintenance payments, but financially things were not as easy for me as they had been and the house had to be sold. I relied heavily on Issi and Sam to keep me sane in the early days because life wasn't easy bringing up two lively boys, and my self-confidence had taken a hard knock.

I refilled my glass, thinking about how Issi was constantly encouraging me to date, but how could I trust anyone again? I'd thought Darren was the love of my life. Deep down I didn't even know if I was over him. While he was out of sight it was easy, but what would it be like if I saw him again? Would all those old feelings return?

I felt completely drained by the time Janet and Derek arrived and was pleased when they passed on the offer of a drink, preferring to head straight to bed.

*

'Are you all done, love?' Darren's mum walked into the boys' bedroom and perched on the end of Jack's bed. She was small and overweight – cuddly, as the boys always described her – with curly grey hair and ruddy cheeks.

'Yes,' I replied as I zipped up the huge suitcase. 'That's everything.' I suddenly felt overwhelmed that I wouldn't be sharing this adventure with my sons, that Darren's new partner would be caring for them, comforting them if they missed me. I sat down next to Janet and put my head in my hands.

'I'm going to miss them,' I said, pushing my index fingers into the corners of my eyes to stop myself crying. 'And they're going so far away.'

Janet put her arm round my shoulders. 'Derek and I will take good care of them,' she said, the inflection in her voice telling me that she wouldn't let Shelley anywhere near them. I turned round and hugged her, silently thanking her for this show of support.

Derek poked his head round the door. 'Time to go. Is this case ready for me to take downstairs?' He glanced from Janet to me. 'We'll look after them, Becky.'

'I know.'

'And we're very proud of them,' he said, walking over and kissing my cheek. 'You've done a grand job.'

I drove them to the airport, kissing and hugging the boys when we had to say goodbye. Thankfully, in their excitement they didn't notice my distress.

'We're going on a *huge* airplane,' Charlie told me.

'And Daddy's taking us to *Disneyland*!' Jack shouted again, jumping up and down with such force his trainers made a squeaking noise on the hard floor.

As I kissed Janet and Derek goodbye I wondered how they felt about having a grandchild in America, who they would barely see. They hadn't said anything about Darren's news, for which I was grateful.

I held myself together during the drive home, but once inside my empty, quiet house I let the tears flow. I lay on the boys' beds in turn, holding their pillows to my face; smelling their scent as I missed my sons with an almost physical pain.

*

Issi rang early on Wednesday morning to invite me round for lunch. 'My friend Debs is coming as well,' she said, 'but I thought you might like to join us.'

'Thanks. I've been working flat out and could use some company.'

'Great. See you at one.'

I worked hard all morning and turned up at Issi's clutching a bottle of her favourite Australian Sauvignon wine, which she opened immediately.

'How are you feeling now about the baby news?' she whispered in the kitchen, rubbing my arm and smiling with her usual compassion.

'Well, not as distraught as I was when I texted you on Saturday, but I'm still a bit down.'

'I really feel for you,' she said. 'It can't be easy.'

'No,' I agreed. 'It hurts that he wants to start a family with someone else. I suppose...' I paused and took a deep breath. 'I suppose there's a part of me that isn't over him, and it's not going to be easy feigning excitement at the new arrival for the boys' sakes.'

'We need wine,' Issi said decisively, pouring me a glass. 'It'll numb the pain, for this afternoon at least.'

She introduced me to Debs, who was busy sorting out a dispute between her three-year-old son and Issi's son, Ben.

'Hi,' she said, looking up. 'I've heard a lot about you. I understand you and Issi go way back.'

'Yes, we were at junior school together.'

'I only met her a few years ago – at mother and toddler group, but we've become good friends. She keeps me sane.'

I nodded, knowing what she meant. I looked round at the houseful of children. 'Are yours at the same school as Issi's?'

'No – mine are all at the local primary school, but I'm thinking of moving them.'

'Why?'

'Because—'

'Lunch,' Issi shouted from the kitchen.

'I'll tell you later,' Debs said.

We joined the children, sitting down at the huge farmhouse table for pizzas and salad. After we'd eaten the children were wrapped up warmly and sent out into the garden, and we settled down in the conservatory with our coffees.

'So why are you thinking of moving your children?' I asked Debs. I guessed they went to the school Charlie and Jack would have gone to, had we not moved. It had an excellent reputation and I'd been looking forward to sending them there.

Debs rolled her eyes. 'There's a set of mums who rule the roost, and I can't bear it.'

I frowned at her, not understanding what she meant.

'There's a group that runs the Parent-Teacher Association, and they seem to have more power than the head teacher.'

'But surely that's a good thing?' I interrupted. 'I feel guilty because I can't help out with the PTA.'

'Yes, of course.' Debs smiled at us both. 'But should their duties extend to handing out slips of paper to anyone who's late for drop-off or pick-up?'

I raised my eyebrows. 'That really happens?'

Debs nodded. 'They say they're doing it to maintain the high standard of the school, but it's done in a very intimidating way.'

'It does sound a little extreme,' Issi said, standing up to refill our coffee cups.

I thought about Helen and her cronies for a moment and wondered if every playground had someone who liked to be in control.

The conversation turned to our children and we chatted happily until the ambience was shattered by Debs' son bursting into the room.

'Ben pushed me off the slide and now my knee's bleeding,' he wailed.

Issi and Debs sorted out the squabble, and then Debs decided it was time for her to leave.

As Issi waved them off and closed the front door I picked up my coat. 'Thanks for lunch. I'm going to make a move as well.'

'Have you got a couple of minutes?'

There was something about her frightened eyes that made me panic. 'Of course. Let's sit down.'

We sat on the sofa and Issi fiddled with her rings, twisting them round and round. 'One of the reasons I invited you over was because I have something to tell you.'

The colour drained from her face and I grabbed her hand. 'Is everything okay?'

She shook her head. 'I found a lump in my breast last night,' she said quietly. 'It's only small, but with my family history I'm a little bit worried.'

I immediately tried to reassure her. 'It's probably a cyst

– it'll be nothing scary, you'll see. Have you phoned your doctor?'

Issi nodded and smiled weakly. 'I managed to get an emergency appointment this morning and I'm having tests next week, so I'll know soon enough. Listen,' she said, standing up, 'I don't want anyone to know, so keep it to yourself.'

'Of course,' I replied, giving her a hug. 'I'm here for you. Let me know what I can do to help. I'll have the children any time.'

On the drive home I thought about my friend's news. I could understand her concern and I hoped it would prove to be nothing. It made me feel thankful that the boys and I were healthy and it put all my own worries into perspective.

*

'Charlie! Jack!' I yelled, my stomach flipping over and over. I pushed my way through the throng of people at the Arrivals barrier, desperate to see my sons. I was nearly sent flying as they launched themselves at me.

'I love you, Mum!' Charlie yelled, his arms gripping my neck tightly as I bent down to hug him.

'Me too!' Jack shouted, arms clamped round my waist. 'We've had a great time, Mum.'

'It was brilliant,' Charlie shouted. 'But we missed you,' he added, causing tears to stream down my face.

I looked up to see Darren's mum and dad smiling. I disentangled myself from the boys and kissed both my in-laws. 'It sounds like you've had a good time.'

'It's been wonderful,' Janet replied. 'The boys have been great.'

I tried to take the boys' suitcase from Darren's dad, but Jack and Charlie each grabbed one of my hands.

'We'll manage, love.' Derek smiled at me. 'You catch up

with your boys.'

We skipped through the terminal building, the three of us talking at once.

'Dad and Shelley took us to a water park,' Jack told me.

'And Grandad nearly drowned,' Charlie added, turning round to wave to his grandparents, who were struggling behind us with the luggage.

Little knots formed in my stomach as they talked about Darren and Shelley as a couple, but I just swallowed hard and smiled, not wanting to let the boys know how much it hurt.

Darren's mum and dad stayed overnight with us before driving home to Yorkshire, and they enjoyed telling me all about the holiday once the boys were in bed. I mentally winced each time they mentioned Darren, but they were sensitive enough not to talk about Barbie and I was thankful for that.

'We'll email some photos to you,' Derek told me.

I knew he'd only send pictures of the boys, and I was grateful for this, too. Seeing photos of Darren and his floozy at their home would have been too much to bear.

As we sat chatting I thought how exhausted they looked from the journey. How would they cope with flying backwards and forward to California as they got older? I braced myself again for any mention of the baby, but they were kind enough not to say anything.

Chapter Six

Humpty Dumpty
Sat on a wall.
The nasty mums laughed
When she took a fall.

'Ooh, I didn't think we were going to make it on time,' I told Kate breathlessly as the boys ran into their classroom.

'It's hard getting back into a routine after a break, isn't it?' she agreed.

'How was your half-term?' I asked as we wandered out of the playground.

'It was good to be at home,' she muttered, 'not having any clubs to rush off to.' She frowned. 'But something horrible happened with Lucy's friends.'

'Oh. Everything okay?'

'I don't suppose you've time for a coffee this morning?'

I thought quickly. I was overloaded with work, but I'd never seen Kate looking down like this. 'Of course.' I smiled at her. 'I'd love to.'

We walked slowly back to Kate's house, with Connor stopping every few minutes to pick something up. I learned that Kate's husband was a fireman, and she learned that mine was a shit.

We arrived at her house, which was a small link-detached in immaculate condition both inside and out. Kate put the kettle on and smiled apologetically.

'I'm sorry – I know you're busy, but I just have to get this off my chest.'

'I'm a good listener.'

'Thanks,' she replied. 'Have a seat.'

She handed me a mug of coffee and sat next to me with a sigh. 'You know Lucy's friendly with three other little girls in her year – you've probably seen me chatting with their mums.'

I nodded.

'They're nice really,' she continued, 'but sometimes they seem to be deliberately hurtful to people. I don't know why.'

I raised my eyebrows. 'What did they do?'

'Well, we had planned to hold a Halloween party at Alison's house during the holidays – the three of us, plus Diana, another mum. We had been discussing the arrangements for a few weeks.'

'That sounds nice,' I interrupted.

Kate rolled her eyes. 'It should have been. Lucy had been busy planning her outfit and I bought a cookbook with recipes for Halloween biscuits and cakes.' She stared down at her drink before continuing. 'The week before half-term the girls had a falling out – I'm not sure what it was all about. They're only five, for goodness sake, but I know Lucy was said to be too bossy.' Kate took a gulp of coffee and I realised she was trying hard not to cry. 'Anyway, as half-term approached I hadn't heard what the arrangements were, and each time I asked I was put off with some story or other.'

'That's dreadful,' I said, frowning. 'Why?'

'I don't know. And if the party went ahead, we didn't go.' She sighed heavily. 'On the evening of Halloween, I answered the door to find the six of them, mums and daughters, all standing there in costume, asking for treats.'

'That's so thoughtless,' I said. 'How did Lucy react?'

Kate shook her head slowly. 'She was so upset. How do you explain to a five-year-old why she's been left out?'

I nodded in agreement, thinking about Charlie's cancelled tea with Josh.

'The thing is, I'm going to have to get over it, because Lucy wants one of their daughters to come back to tea this week.'

'It's tough,' I agreed. 'Why would the mums do that?'

Kate shrugged, and I automatically reached across and squeezed her hand. 'You can always rely on me as a friend.'

'Thanks.' She smiled back. 'That means a lot.'

We chatted for a little while about our children, and as I left she suggested we swap phone numbers. 'So we can call each other if we need to let off steam.'

'That's a good idea,' I replied as I took my phone out of my bag. It was sensible in case one of us was running late, but as I entered her number I doubted I would have anything more to let off steam about as far as the playground was concerned.

*

'Who's that, then?' I asked Kate as I tried not to stare.

'I'm not sure,' she replied, sneaking a glance herself. 'I saw him this morning – his son went into our children's classroom.'

'Yes, I noticed that too. They must have moved into the area.'

The new dad was tall and about my age, with sandy-coloured hair. Not especially good-looking, but not unattractive, either. He had a lovely smile, which lit his face up when his son came running out.

Kate and I speculated all week as to why it was him and not the child's mother in the playground.

'He's always so smartly dressed,' Kate said one morning. 'So he can't be unemployed.'

'No. Perhaps he works shifts?'

'Mm. Or works from home?'

Our guessing carried on for a few more days and one evening I casually quizzed Jack and Charlie about the new boy in their class.

'He's nice,' Charlie told me. 'I played with him in the home corner.'

'He's foreign,' Jack added. 'Because he talks in a funny way.'

They were dispatched to find out more information, and a few days later I tried again. 'Have you found out what country the new boy comes from?' I asked them over tea.

'Yes,' said Charlie excitedly. 'Sheffield.'

'Really?' I decided I would talk to his dad the next day. After all, the playground could be a daunting place when you didn't know anyone.

The following morning the dad was chatting to Rob Phillips and I wasn't sure who to look at first. Kate caught my eye and I looked at her guiltily. 'I was thinking of talking to the new dad.'

She raised both eyebrows as she smiled at me.

'I was just going to be friendly. Charlie told me he's from Sheffield, and that's where I went to university.'

'He might be single, you never know,' Kate teased.

I blushed. 'I wasn't thinking of him in that way.'

'Whatever you say…' she replied, suppressing a grin.

It was a cold grey November day, but there was no sign of rain at home time. I ditched the playground coat in favour of my favourite blue cardigan, knowing it enhanced my eyes, and arrived in the playground early. Helen and the "gossiping mums" were already standing at the gate and in full flow. It was entirely possible that they'd been there all day.

The new dad was already there. I suspected he would be, as he always arrived early. I casually walked over to him and introduced myself. 'Hello, I'm Becky. I think your son's in the same class as my boys.'

'I'm Martin.' He smiled at me. 'We only moved down here from Sheffield in the half-term holidays.'

'Oh, Sheffield,' I said, pretending to be surprised. 'I spent three years there at Uni. It's a lovely city.'

'I think so,' he replied, grinning.

'So did you move here with your job?'

He nodded. 'The company I work for relocated to Maidenhead.'

'And how are you finding life in the south?' I rolled my eyes. 'A little more expensive?'

'Er…just a bit.' He shook his head. 'It's been rather a shock.'

I laughed, and as we chatted he beamed each time he mentioned his son, Thomas. Definitely a hands-on dad. He wore a wedding ring but he didn't mention his wife, and I didn't like to appear too nosy, although I would have liked the full story.

The children all piled out of school together and Thomas grinned when Charlie whispered something to him.

'Can Thomas come and play?' he asked me.

I looked at Martin. 'Would he like to come round to tea one day?'

'Can I? Can I, Dad?' Thomas hopped up and down excitedly.

'Today!' Charlie shouted.

Martin and I smiled at each other.

'Thursday?' I suggested.

'That would be great.'

*

I hadn't slept very well because I was worried about Issi, and I rubbed my temples as I waited for her to arrive.

I had looked after Andrew, Emma and Ben the previous evening, while Jonathan took Issi for her test results. When they collected the children later Issi had shaken her head, her body rigid with shock.

'It's a malignant tumour.' Her voice was barely audible and I strained to catch the words.

I held her tightly as Jonathan ushered the children into the car. I'd gone into shock myself and hadn't known what to say. 'Oh, Issi,' I whispered. 'I'm so sorry.'

'I can't believe it's happening, Becky,' she replied, pulling away. 'I can't talk at the moment.'

I had texted her later, telling her I loved her and asking if I could call round to see her today. She had replied that she wanted to carry on as normal and would come to me, because she wanted to get out of the house but couldn't face L'Olivo.

The doorbell jolted me out of my thoughts, and as I opened the door I automatically pulled Issi towards me, hugging her so tightly she had to push me away.

'Sorry about yesterday,' she said as we walked into the kitchen. 'I felt numb with shock.'

'Of course you did – and don't apologise.' She looked pale and tired and I held her hand, not wanting to let go. 'What did they say, exactly?'

Her face dropped. 'It's not good,' she said, avoiding my eyes. 'It's a malignant tumour and I have to have it removed.' She inhaled slowly and deeply. 'I'll start a course of chemotherapy afterwards, just to be on the safe side.'

I grabbed her other hand and held them both tightly. 'There have been massive advances in treatment since your mum died. You mustn't worry. I'll support you all the way through.'

She smiled weakly. 'I know. Jonathan is more worried than

I am. He's switching roles at work so he can be home more.'

'If you need anything, you only have to ask. I'm here for you. I'll look after the kids, do your washing, ironing – anything.'

'Thanks, I appreciate that, but actually I feel no different.' She looked down as if contemplating what she was about to go through. 'Ironically it's the treatment that will make me feel sick.' She shook her head as if to rinse out the thought, and then smiled at me. 'I just want to carry on as normal.'

'Of course.' I nodded, swallowing hard.

'Sorry I didn't feel like going to L'Olivo,' she said, clearly not wanting to discuss her illness further.

'That's fine.' I shrugged. 'We can go another time.'

'I was looking forward to seeing the waiter in there,' she said, rolling her eyes.

'Me too.'

We stared at each other for a moment and then burst out laughing.

'Okay,' I told her. 'I don't mind a little bit of competitive flirting. This is war.'

By the time she left an hour later she had regained some colour, but I found it difficult to concentrate on my work. The next few weeks and months were going to be hard for my friend.

*

Kate and I waved at Martin and he started to walk over, but his path was suddenly blocked by the hordes of children who had just been let out. He shrugged and smiled, looking round for Thomas.

'See you tomorrow, Becky,' Kate shouted. 'I've got to run because it's Lucy's ballet night.'

I walked home slowly with Charlie and Jack, who had

thrown their bags at me as well as their coats, despite it being so cold.

'Here, put these on,' I told them both, holding the jackets out for them to take.

'I'm okay,' Jack replied, running ahead.

Charlie slipped his hand in mine. 'Mummy?'

'Yes, sweetheart? Aren't you cold?'

He shook his head and frowned at me. 'Why aren't I going to Josh's party?'

'I didn't know it was his birthday. Have you not had an invitation?'

'No. He's given some to the other children.'

'Maybe he'll give you yours tomorrow.'

'No, he won't.' He stopped walking and a tear trickled down his cheek. 'I asked him where mine was, and he said his mummy doesn't want me to come.'

I bent down and put his coat round him, hugging him. 'I'm sure that's not the case,' I said breezily. 'Perhaps he can only invite so many children and he found it hard to choose which ones.'

'But I'm his bestest friend,' he replied indignantly.

I hoped with all my heart that Josh would give him an invitation tomorrow – I refused to believe that any mother could be that spiteful.

*

Over the weeks I'd started to get to know a few of the mums who stood outside the Reception classroom, and if I'd had a solitary day working at home I looked forward to some of the jovial banter that passed between us. There were two mums I particularly liked.

Mandy was a large attractive brunette, with a vibrant personality and an infectious laugh. She was also a single mum and an ardent Arsenal fan. Because I enjoyed football myself, she and I had a lot in common. Charlie was sweet on her daughter, Alicia, and as they often played together after school, Mandy and I were getting to know each other fairly well.

My other favourite was Angela, who was rather eccentric. She was tall, with wispy brown hair that fell into its own unique and natural style. She dressed in clothes that looked like they'd been thrown on in a hurry, without any consideration for matching up the styles. The colours nearly went together, but not quite.

As well as being a full-time mum to Sara, Saskia and Harry, the latter having recently become Jack's best friend, Angela was also studying for a degree in English Literature. She loved books, particularly the classics, and once she had discovered I was a writer, she wanted to know my opinion on every book she was reading. I enjoyed this, but it made me realise how little time I made for myself, simply to read a good book.

I had just walked into the playground when Angela came bounding up to me.

'Morning, Becky.' She grinned at me. 'I'm considering setting up a book group. What do you think?'

Angela always spoke without preamble, and I wasn't sure if she was inviting me to be part of the group or simply asking my opinion. 'It's a great idea.' I smiled back.

'Good. I'll ask a few people I know will be interested. Perhaps you could choose the first book?'

As she walked off to find more participants I couldn't help but feel pleased. This was something I would really enjoy, and a part of my life that had almost been put on hold. Darren used to sulk when I sat in bed and read, saying the light disturbed him. At least now I would have time to read and make notes without being made to feel guilty.

Mandy disturbed my thoughts. 'Cor,' she said under her

breath.

Kate and I followed her gaze, the three of us falling silent as Rob Phillips walked past.

'Isn't he gorgeous?' Mandy whispered.

I willed myself not to blush. 'Mm,' I replied as nonchalantly as I could, not wanting to risk being teased.

'My friend, Beth,' Mandy continued, 'works as a teaching assistant in school and she says Miss Whittaker fancies him.'

I felt a stab of disappointment. 'Well, she is very pretty.'

'Are they going out, then?' Kate asked.

Mandy shook her head. 'Rumour has it he was jilted at the altar, and—'

'No!' Kate gasped.

'Apparently,' Mandy confirmed, revelling in her knowledge.

'So he doesn't feel able to date again?' Kate asked sadly, her attention riveted on Mandy.

'Ladies,' I interrupted. 'This is all rumour. Let's not gossip about the poor guy.' But as I walked away I couldn't help wondering.

I saw Martin a few times in the playground, just to wave to, but on Wednesday morning we met up to confirm the arrangements for the following day.

'Here's my phone number and address,' I said, handing him a piece of paper.

He read it and smiled. 'That's just round the corner from me. That's handy.'

'Great. I'll collect Thomas from school. Do you want to pick him up from me around six thirty?'

'That's perfect.'

The bell rang and we shouted the boys over. They all resisted hugs, and as soon as the doors opened they were gone without glancing back.

On my way out of the playground I walked past the

"chatting mums", who were once again gathered by the school gate. I was tempted to talk to Helen about Charlie not being invited to Josh's party, but she was entitled to invite whoever she chose. She would be pleased to know it had upset me. I gave her a cheery ironic wave, receiving a half wave and a smile-cum-grimace in return.

When I arrived home I rang Issi to find out how she was feeling following her lumpectomy.

'Not too bad,' she said brightly.

I was surprised how upbeat she sounded.

'I'm going to start a course of chemotherapy next week. The nurse has told me I might feel a little nauseous and tired, but that's all quite normal, apparently. She'll give me some tablets in case it gets too bad.'

'You poor thing.' I found it hard to know what to say, and I paused. 'Let me know what I can do to help.'

'Listen, Becky, I know this is hard for you too, but I'm still me, Issi. I don't want sympathy from anyone – I just want to be treated normally. Can we forget I've got cancer?'

It was difficult to reply because I was fighting back tears. 'I'm so sorry – I just hate to see you suffering,' I sniffed down the phone. I took a deep breath. 'Right. When are we meeting up for coffee?'

*

I collected Jack, Charlie and Thomas from school, feeling tired and fed up with the gloomy weather.

'Have you found your jumpers?' I asked Jack, annoyed they were both missing. 'It's cold, put your coat on.' I thrust it at him, with a look that said I wasn't taking no for an answer. 'We'll have to ask Miss Whittaker if she's seen them.'

We all wandered back into the classroom, where Miss Whittaker directed me to a plastic crate full of screwed-up clothes. I delved through the pile of sweaty PE shirts, odd socks, polo shirts and jumpers, eventually finding two of Jack's. I tutted loudly, ready to tell him off, but as I turned round Rob Phillips was leaning against the door frame, talking to Miss Whittaker.

She kept lowering her glance as she talked, twirling her hair round her finger. Mandy must be right about her fancying him – and maybe they *were* an item? They would certainly make an attractive couple. It was ridiculous, liking him myself. What would he see in me – a middle-aged, frumpy single mum?

I said thank you to Miss Whittaker and gathered the boys together, trying to leave the classroom without talking to Rob for fear of embarrassing myself.

'Mrs Dixon.'

I turned towards him and his brown eyes looked straight into mine. I hoped I wasn't going to blush.

'I just wanted to say that Jack's been doing really well in assembly.'

'That's great.' I smiled in relief. 'Thanks for all your help.'

'Not a problem.'

He resumed his conversation with Miss Whittaker and I scurried out of the classroom.

I took the three boys home and despite a few minor scraps, they played well together, taking it in turns to be tied up and shot. I sat with them while they ate their tea, enjoying their childish chatter. I had slaved over a spaghetti bolognese so Thomas didn't tell his dad I had only cooked chicken nuggets. I wanted to present myself as an accomplished working mother, who had no difficulty rustling up a wholesome, nutritious meal while simultaneously writing great copy.

Throughout tea I was desperate to quiz Thomas about his life, but my conscience got the better of me. It wasn't fair; I would wait and quiz his dad.

Martin arrived a few minutes early and I was surprised by the bunch of flowers he gave me as I opened the door.

'Oh! Thank you.'

'It was kind of you to invite Thomas.'

'Not at all.' I blushed. 'Have you time for a cup of tea?'

Martin followed me into the kitchen and the boys shouted in delight when I said they could carry on playing. The conversation with Martin flowed easily, and I was soon telling him my sorry saga about Darren.

'It's not easy being single, is it?' he said. 'My wife Jackie died two years ago.'

'Oh, I'm so sorry.' I waited to see if he wanted to tell me anymore.

'She had cancer,' he said after a few moments.

'I'm sorry,' I repeated.

'So I grabbed the chance to move down here. A new start and all that. My employer lets me work flexible hours, but it's still not easy.'

'No, I know.'

The boys wandered in for a drink and Martin looked up at the clock. 'Gosh, it's half past seven. We'd better make a move.' His pale blue eyes smiled into mine. 'Thanks again.'

*

The next day Martin came rushing over to me as we walked into the playground. 'Thomas enjoyed himself so much yesterday. It's really helped him to feel more settled.' He smiled warmly.

I glowed. 'Any time.'

'By the way, I've enrolled him into a football team that's just started up, and I wondered if Charlie and Jack fancied it as well?'

'That would be great – it's something I've been meaning to

look into for ages. When is it?'

'Saturday mornings, ten till eleven.'

'That's perfect.' I ruffled Charlie's hair as he came to grab his bags. 'The boys love football, so I'm sure they'll want to.'

'Okay.' Martin smiled as the bell sounded. 'If you ask them and let me know, I'll give you all the details.'

'Great.' As I smiled back, I caught Helen's eye. She scowled and turned her head away.

*

'Did you have a good weekend?' Mandy asked as we stamped our feet to keep warm.

'Yes, thanks. Quiet, but nice. How about you?'

'Same, really. Arsenal had a good win, so that cheered me up.'

'Morning, ladies.' Angela interrupted our conversation. 'Becky, I've spoken to a few people and we're all keen to start the book group.'

'Great.' I smiled at her.

'There'll be a few friends of mine and a few mums from school – it'll be good for you to meet new people. Did you choose a book?'

Angela always spoke without pausing for breath, and sometimes I felt exhausted just listening to her. 'I thought we could start with everyone's favourite – *Pride and Prejudice*.'

'Brilliant. It'll be at my house – I'll let you know the date.'

I grinned at Mandy, excited by the thought of doing something simply for pleasure.

'I could never get into that book.' She shook her head. 'All those swishy dresses.' She swished her own imaginary dress before wandering off to find Alicia.

Kate was threading her way through the mass of children and parents, frowning crossly, and I presumed she was still having problems with the mums of Lucy's friends.

'Hi,' I said gently. 'Everything okay?'

She pulled me to one side. 'I'm really sorry, but Helen's been at it again.'

My stomach somersaulted. 'What now?'

'Oh, Becky, I'm only telling you so you know what she's been up to. *Please* ignore it.'

'Go on.'

'I've just overheard Alison and Diana bitching about the décor in your boys' bedroom.' She lowered her eyes, clearly embarrassed at having to tell me this. 'And all about how your bathroom is looking a bit out-dated.'

I stared at her open-mouthed, unable to take in what she was saying.

She grabbed my arm roughly. 'You know it isn't true, so don't listen to it.'

I nodded, trance-like. I then had the vague feeling that people were looking at me and I had to take several deep breaths before I could speak to Kate. 'I remember her going upstairs to tell Josh to tidy up. She must have had a good look round then.' Anger rose up from my toes until I could almost taste it.

'She's obviously jealous of you,' Kate said, screwing her face up. 'Nasty cow.'

I frowned. 'Jealous? Why would she be envious of my house? She doesn't even seem to like it.'

Kate rolled her eyes. 'Not your house. At first it was because you have a great career; now it's because you've become good friends with Martin. I've seen her scowling at you a few times.'

I nodded slowly. 'Yes, I remember seeing her looking over in my direction when I've been chatting to him.' I shook my head sadly. 'It's not all to do with that, though.'

Kate put her arm round my shoulders. 'Do you want to

talk?'

I let out a long, slow breath. 'We used to work together – and I had to report her for turning up to a meeting too hung over to make much sense.'

'What happened?'

'She was sacked.'

'Wow.' Kate blinked several times. 'No wonder she doesn't like you. But that's no excuse for what she's doing now,' she added defensively. 'You can talk to who you like.'

'I can,' I agreed. I started to giggle, releasing some tension. 'At least I know what – or rather, who – the gossiping at the gate has been about recently.'

Kate shook her head. 'What are you going to do?'

I narrowed my eyes. 'I'm bigger than this, and I refuse to be intimidated by Helen and her cronies.' I turned and glared at Helen. 'If my talking to Martin annoys her, then I shall just have to do it all the more.'

Chapter Seven

Ring a ring of roses,
A pocket full of posies,
Atishoo, atishoo,
Oh, how you'll fall down.

I was furious. How dare this woman come into my home as a guest and then tell what seemed like the whole world about my boys' bedroom? Yes, it needed decorating, but the three of us had created that room together, with love and laughter. The boys had both chosen Star Wars duvet covers and we had put posters and stickers up to hide the flowery wallpaper. How dare she bitch about it?

I grabbed the phone and started to dial the school's number, but stopped, imagining the conversation.

'Hello, Mrs Jenkins. This is Mrs Dixon and I'm ringing to tell you that Mrs Stevens has been mean and nasty to me in the playground.'

'Oh dear, Mrs Dixon. What would you like me to do about it?'

I rang Issi instead. 'Do you feel well enough for an emergency coffee?'

'Of course,' she replied without hesitation. 'L'Olivo. Twelve o'clock.'

I threw myself into the leaflet I was writing for a client, but I was so angry I didn't produce my best work.

I arrived early at L'Olivo and sat down to wait for Issi. I ordered a skinny latte and looked round for the waiter, wishing I had taken more time with my appearance. The door suddenly flew open and he breezed in, his expensive-looking black suit highlighting his broad shoulders. He held the door open for a blushing Issi and she sauntered over to my table, grinning broadly.

'We just happened to arrive at the same time.' She shrugged, adding, 'Ooh, he smelled *so* good.'

I scowled at her in mock jealousy, but before I could speak the waiter appeared at our table carrying my latte and a cappuccino for Issi.

'May I join you, ladies?' His Italian accent sounded incredibly sexy. My stomach flipped several times and it was all I could do to mutter, 'Yes, of course.'

'My name's Nico,' he told us, flashing that smile again. 'And this is my café,' he added, waving his hand round the entire room.

'Oh – you *own* it,' I said, immediately feeling embarrassed that it should matter whether he owned the café or worked there.

'We love it here,' Issi gushed, ruffling her hair, which annoyingly looked particularly glossy.

'Thank you.' He grinned at each of us in turn. 'And you are?'

'Becky.' I smiled, suddenly sixteen again.

'Issi.'

'I want to get to know all of my regular clientele.'

I stared at his taut and tanned body. Oh, you could get to know me better.

'Yes, I have three children,' Issi was telling him. 'Andrew, Emma and Ben.'

'And you, Becky?'

'Two boys – Charlie and Jack.' As I replied I pushed my hair behind my ear with my left hand, hoping he'd notice the absence of a wedding ring.

'How about you, Nico?' Issi smiled at him. 'Do you have children?'

'Sadly not,' he replied. 'I'm very busy with my businesses.'

Issi tilted her head to one side. 'Are they going well?'

'Yes. Thank you.' He smiled broadly at us both. 'When I moved here from Italy, I wasn't sure how it would work out—'

'What part of Italy?' I asked, keeping my eyes riveted on his.

'Milano. My family…'

I was captivated by his accent and listened intently to his life story, but I was suddenly jolted back into reality when his mobile phone trilled.

'*Scusi,*' he said. After a brief conversation he smiled at us both. 'I am needed somewhere else, so for now, I must go.' He kissed both of our hands in turn. '*Ciao*, Becky. *Ciao*, Issi.'

We watched him disappear into the back, and as we both stared dreamily after him he suddenly reappeared clutching a black briefcase. He waved as he rushed past us.

'Mm,' I sighed heavily.

'Know what you mean,' Issi replied.

How was it that someone as vile as Helen could ruin my morning, yet the sparkle of Nico's eyes could leave me feeling on such a high?

'Right,' Issi said, putting her cup down. 'What's the crisis?'

'That can wait. Tell me how you've been feeling.'

'I've resorted to the sickness tablets and I'm in bed by eight.' She sighed. 'But other than that, I'm not too bad.'

I leaned over and kissed her on the cheek. 'I'm here for you and you know I'll help in any way I can – just tell me.'

'Thanks, I appreciate that.' She took a sip of her cappuccino.

'My dad and Maureen are brilliant, but I'll shout if I need anything.'

She put her cup back down and smiled. '*Now* tell me about your crisis.'

I explained all about Helen and how upset I was feeling. Just talking to Issi helped, and I resolved to not let that loathsome woman dominate my day. I then told Issi all about Martin, about how we had got along so well and how I wasn't sure what my feelings towards him were.

'Just give it time,' she advised. 'If there's anything there, it will develop naturally.'

We chatted generally before finishing our drinks and deciding it was time to leave.

'I need to do some work before school pick-up time,' I said as I stood up. I squared my shoulders and smiled brightly. 'Thanks for listening. I'm not going to dwell on Helen Stevens again today.'

'Good. She's not worth losing valuable time over.'

'You're right,' I agreed as I hugged my best friend.

*

During the following few days I found it difficult walking into the playground, wondering what else might have been said about me. I had to walk past Helen at the gate each day and I always looked straight ahead with my shoulders back, implying through my body language that she hadn't rattled me. It was difficult because the hatred directed towards me felt almost tangible.

'Hi, Becky,' Mandy said cheerily one morning. 'You get later and later.'

'It's the dark mornings,' I muttered, not wanting to admit that I was leaving home a little later than usual in case I had to stand alone. Normally I didn't mind if my friends were late or chatting elsewhere, but I was feeling vulnerable at the moment and could imagine Helen laughing at "Becky No-mates".

'We were running late as well this morning.' She grinned. 'I stayed up late to watch Arsenal's win in Italy. Did you see it?'

'I didn't know you two were into football.' Martin had walked up behind me, interrupting before I could reply.

Mandy gave him a look of feigned horror. 'Is that because we're women?'

Colour spread across his cheeks and I helped him out. 'Mandy's a staunch Arsenal fan and I just enjoy football in general.'

He smiled proudly. 'I support Sheffield Wednesday.'

Mandy stared at him and then burst out laughing. 'Sheffield Wednesday? Oh, you poor thing!'

Martin looked deeply offended and turned to me. 'Talking of football, did you ask the boys about Saturday training?'

'Oh, yes. They would love to join, thanks.'

His smile returned. 'Okay. We'll see you on the sports field at ten.'

Mandy caught his arm. 'I was only joking. Remember the two 1993 cup finals between Arsenal and Sheffield Wednesday?'

'Didn't Arsenal—' I stopped in mid-sentence, suddenly aware that Helen was striding purposefully towards us, closely followed by her cronies. I felt my face flush and hoped they were heading for someone else.

Helen stopped directly in front of the three of us, putting her hands on her hips. 'Sorry to interrupt you,' she said without any trace of sincerity. 'Oh, hold on.' She turned to one of her posse. 'Here comes another.'

Kate arrived breathlessly and stood next to me. 'Just made it in time.' She looked at Helen. 'Is everything all right?'

Helen smiled at her patronisingly. 'I've taken over the

running of the PTA…'

I shuddered involuntarily, recalling the conversation with Issi's friend Debs about how the PTA ruled her playground.

'…and I need to tell you all about the school Christmas Fair,' Helen continued.

'Oh.' Kate glanced round at us. 'It's only November.'

Helen glowered at her. 'These events take a lot of organising.'

Kate blushed and shrank back.

'I want you all to be involved,' Helen informed us. 'Bake a cake – or better still, bake two cakes.'

The posse laughed at her little joke and Mandy's cheeks reddened. 'I don't do baking,' she said, taking a step towards Helen.

'Well, you've plenty of time to learn,' she snapped at her. 'We're raising money for the school, for goodness sake.' As she turned to leave she spoke a little too loudly to one of the posse. 'My God. When I ran a busy advertising company I'd have sacked people like her in an instant.'

The posse scurried after her and Kate exhaled slowly. 'She's definitely head honcho around here now.'

I burst out laughing. 'Helen the Head Honcho. I like that.'

Martin and Mandy resumed their conversation, with Martin moaning about Arsenal's last minute winner back in 1993. I smiled. For every Helen in the playground, there was a Mandy and a Martin to keep you sane.

*

'Are you ready, boys?'

'We've been waiting for *ages*.' Charlie scowled at me.

'Yes, Mum. Hurry up,' added Jack.

I smiled at them both, proudly kitted out in new football shirts and boots. I'd only been able to afford cheap ones from a sports warehouse, but the boys had been thrilled.

'It's still only quarter to ten,' I said as we set off to the sports field. 'We'll be early.'

'I don't care,' Charlie said, running ahead.

'Neither do I,' yelled Jack, catching him up.

It was a cold morning, with the sun low in the sky, and I was glad I'd put a thick jacket on. The boys threw their sweatshirts at me and then tore across the field shouting to Thomas, who was waiting with Martin.

'Hi, Becky.' Martin walked over to meet me. 'I'll introduce you to Rob, the coach.' He pointed to a man setting out cones. 'You may recognise him, he's one of the teachers at school.'

I was amazed to see Rob Phillips. As we walked towards him my pulse rate quickened and my stomach did several flips. 'Hello,' I said, smiling brightly. 'Jack and Charlie haven't played before, but they're very keen.'

Rob smiled back before turning to the boys. 'I can tell you're both going to be good at football – and you've got great shirts.'

He had a lovely manner with the children, and I couldn't help but like him.

Martin smiled as I turned round. 'I've brought a flask of coffee for us,' he said. 'We can stand over there and get a good view of how the boys are getting on.'

I was in heaven. I knew I'd enjoy standing with Martin, I was looking forward to watching the boys, and best of all, I could stand and watch Rob. I was already finding it difficult to drag my eyes away from his muscular thighs.

Martin handed me a cup of coffee. 'Here you are.' He fished around in his pocket. 'I thought we might need sustenance against the cold.'

I took the chocolate biscuit I was being offered. 'That's so thoughtful. Thank you.'

He looked attractive in his jeans and casual jacket, but it

was his gentle manner that made me like him so much. He seemed interested in everything I had to say, and having discussed football we started to reminisce about Sheffield.

'Darren and I used to walk a lot in the Peak District,' I told him.

'Beautiful, isn't it?'

I nodded. 'Chatsworth House is one of my favourite places.'

'Jackie and I used to take Thomas there for picnics.' He stared beyond me as if lost in thought. 'She loved it, too.'

I waited before handing the cup back to him. 'Do you plan to go back much?'

Martin shook himself out of his trance. 'Both Jackie's and my family live there.' He paused and pursed his lips. 'But I have to get on with things and make a new life.'

We chatted comfortably, getting along well, and I had to stop myself from looking at Rob, feeling almost guilty. At the end of training we walked over to the boys, who were tired out but exhilarated.

'Oh, Mum, it was brilliant,' Jack panted.

'Yes,' joined in Charlie. 'Can we come again next week? Please?'

Rob nodded. 'Of course. They did really well.' He picked up his bag of balls and cones, slinging it over his shoulder. 'Bye, boys. You were all fantastic.'

I watched him walk over to where his car was parked, disappointed that he hadn't wanted to make conversation with me. I smiled at Martin. 'Thanks for the coffee. See you during the week.'

He waved to me as Thomas started to tell him all about the training, but on the walk home I wondered about Rob as I listened to Jack and Charlie's excited chatter. He had smiled straight into my eyes, but hadn't shown any other obvious signs of liking me. I shrugged and hoped.

*

'Hi, Dad!' Jack yelled into the phone. 'I scored two goals today.'

I smiled as Charlie hopped up and down by his side, desperate to tell his dad all about training.

After a lengthy conversation, Charlie handed the phone to me. 'Dad wants to talk to you.'

'Hi, Becky.'

The sound of his voice still made me melt inside and I sighed silently, suddenly feeling sad.

'The boys really seem to have enjoyed their football,' he was saying to me. 'Well done for organising it.'

'Yes, they can't wait for next week.'

'Jack seems to have particularly enjoyed scoring the goals.'

'I know. Martin and I thought his celebrations were hilarious.'

There was a silence before Darren spoke, and I presumed it was the time delay. 'Who's Martin?' His voice was flat.

Martin's name had just slipped out. 'Oh, he's the dad from school who told me about the football.'

'You've not mentioned him before.'

'There's not been any reason to,' I replied coldly.

'And do you see a lot of him?'

Suddenly I was angry. I didn't have to justify myself. 'Look, Darren, I don't have to tell you who I'm friends with.'

'*Friend*? He's just a friend, then?' His tone was almost accusatory.

'Yes, he's just a friend.'

There was a click as he put the phone down. I stormed upstairs and lay on my bed, thoughts tumbling through my head. How dare he put the phone down on me? Was he jealous of Martin or did he just want to control my life? He couldn't have it both ways. He couldn't leave me, get his girlfriend pregnant and then dictate who I saw.

I thumped the pillow. I shouldn't be going through this anyway. Dads took their sons to football – that's how it was. I was having to be both mum and dad, and he had no right to interfere. I would tell him so the next time we spoke.

Once the boys were in bed I continued reading *Pride and Prejudice*. I was so lost in the slow-burning romance between Elizabeth Bennet and Mr Darcy that the bleep from my mobile phone startled me. It was a text message from a number I didn't recognise. I opened it to find it was from Martin, complaining about Sheffield Wednesday's two-nil defeat that afternoon. I remembered I had given him my number when Thomas came round to tea. I sent him a reply back and smiled to myself. Were we flirting?

*

'How was your weekend?' I asked Kate, pulling my coat closer against the biting wind.

'Great, thanks. We took the kids to an animal farm.' She pulled her gloves out of her pocket. 'How about you?'

'Yes. Ours was good too. We—'

I was interrupted by the classroom door flying open as the children poured out. Miss Whittaker stepped outside with them, looking round the playground for someone. Eventually she waved and started walking over to Helen.

'Mrs Stevens,' she said in full earshot of everyone. 'Could you just spare me a few moments before you leave?'

Helen stared at her for a minute, then without replying she followed her back towards the classroom.

Kate and I were rooted to the spot, watching the drama unfold. As Miss Whittaker and Helen approached us I turned to Kate and spoke loudly.

'The walk of shame. Wonder what Josh has been up to?' It sounded spiteful and I was immediately cross with myself for allowing Helen to make me feel this way.

'Lucy says Josh has been badly behaved for weeks,' Kate whispered. 'Perhaps it's about that?'

Helen kept her eyes focused ahead of her as she walked past us, but Miss Whittaker stopped suddenly.

'You go into the classroom, Mrs Stevens,' she said. 'I just want a quick word with Mrs Dixon.'

I froze. Miss Whittaker had obviously heard my catty remark and was about to give me a dressing down. I composed myself, ready with my excuse.

The teacher positioned her petite frame in front of me. 'Mrs Dixon, Jack and Charlie gave a lovely account of their weekend to the class this morning.'

'Oh. Yes.' I smiled in relief.

She pushed her hair behind her ears. 'They particularly enjoyed the football on Saturday,' she continued, smiling warmly.

'Oh, yes. They loved it.'

'Apparently Mr Phillips organised it—'

'Yes,' I cut in, my mouth going into involuntary overdrive. 'He's just started the club up.'

Miss Whittaker nodded thoughtfully. 'And that's at the sports field?'

'Yes. Every Saturday.'

She smiled and turned towards the classroom. 'I'm often out that way walking my dog,' she said, glancing back. 'I may wander over – to cheer the boys on.'

'What a supportive teacher,' I said to Kate when she'd disappeared into the classroom. 'I must buy her something thoughtful from the boys for Christmas.'

As we walked away I couldn't stop myself from glancing through the classroom window. 'Look at Helen,' I whispered to Kate, not wanting the children to overhear. 'She seems very angry and defensive.'

Her arms were folded across her chest and she appeared to be shouting at Miss Whittaker.

'Yes,' Kate agreed. 'From the way she's standing it looks like Miss Whittaker's receiving a tirade of abuse.'

'With both barrels,' I agreed.

*

Martin and I were deep in conversation on the sports field when Thomas yelled out excitedly. 'Hello, Miss Whittaker!' He stopped dribbling his ball through the cones and shouted over to Charlie and Jack. 'Miss Whittaker's here!'

As she waved at them, the black and white border collie that had been obediently walking by her side ran onto the pitch. I giggled as all the children stopped what they were supposed to be doing and tried to catch the dog. After three attempts, Miss Whittaker managed to call the dog back, and clamped his lead on. 'Sorry,' she shouted over to Rob.

He looked up, but his lack of response didn't tell me whether he was annoyed or had found it funny.

Miss Whittaker walked over to us. 'Hello,' she said breezily.

'This is a surprise,' Martin said to her. 'Do you live this way?'

'Yes. I was telling Mrs Dixon that I often walk my dog over here.'

'Becky.' I gestured towards Martin. 'And Martin.'

'Louise.' She smiled back at us.

I was hoping she might talk about Charlie and Jack because I was keen to know how they were doing at school, but I didn't like to initiate the conversation on her day off. 'You've a lovely dog,' I said instead, bending down to stroke him.

'Hm?' She was watching the training intently and turned her head to me. 'Oh, thanks. This is Bailey.'

'How old is he?' Martin asked.

'Seven.' She smiled and refocused on the boys.

Feeling guilty for chatting, Martin and I stood silently until Rob blew his whistle.

'That was great,' Louise said to us. 'I want to be able to talk to the children knowledgeably on Monday.' She headed over to Rob, and as he gathered up the balls and cones she stood chatting to him.

'She's a very dedicated teacher,' Martin said as we walked across to meet our children.

'Yes,' I replied thoughtfully. I was disappointed; I had made a special effort with my hair and make-up, but now I wouldn't get the chance to talk to Rob.

'I'll text you later,' Martin said. 'Once the results are all in.'

'Mm?' I refocused my thoughts. 'Oh yes. That'll be great. Have a good day.'

Chapter Eight

One potato, two potato,
Three potato, four.
I'll start a nasty campaign against you
If I think you've got more.

'I think lunch is called for.'

'I couldn't agree more.' I grinned at Issi. 'Christmas shopping is over-rated.'

'I'm exhausted, my credit card is exhausted – and my feet are sore.' She rolled her eyes and laughed. 'L'Olivo?'

We found a table and dropped our bags underneath it, sinking into our seats. I'd just slipped my shoes off when a waitress appeared carrying two cappuccinos.

'From Nico,' was all she said, and we were too tired to question her further.

We both glanced round to thank him but he was nowhere in sight.

'It's bursting at the seams in here,' Issi said. 'We'd better not disturb him.'

'No,' I agreed. 'What do you fancy to eat?'

She glanced down the menu. 'House salad and an orange juice will hit the spot.'

'Good idea.'

Once the waitress had taken our order, I took a good look at Issi. 'How are you feeling?'

'I'm okay.' She smiled at me.

'I hope the shopping hasn't worn you out.'

'No...' She paused as our orange juices arrived. 'I'm still feeling fine from the treatment but...' She ran her finger round the rim of the glass before looking up at me. 'I've been giving a mastectomy some thought.'

I took a sip and put my glass down, giving Issi my full attention. 'Oh, okay. Why?'

'Well, the consultant was confident at the outset that he wouldn't have to perform one, but I wish I'd had it done now, just to give me peace of mind.'

I nodded slowly. 'Have you talked it over with Jonathan?'

'Yes, and he's very supportive.' She took a small sip of her drink. 'We went back to see the consultant yesterday.'

'And what did he think?'

'He agreed it would be a good precaution to take, so I'm booked in for just after Christmas.'

It was obvious how nervous she was, and I grabbed hold of her hand. 'Then it's the right thing to do, and you'll be well looked after.' I started to giggle and Issi frowned at me.

'What?'

'He could rebuild you as one of those famous page three models.'

We both burst out laughing, surprising the waitress as she delivered our salads.

As we tucked in we discussed how many more presents we had left to buy.

'I hate this time of year,' I grumbled. 'Not only do I have Christmas, but I've also got the boys' birthdays to buy for.' I bit my lip as I thought about the state of my finances. I was struggling through each month, but only just.

Issi leaned forward. 'You know I'll always help out if—'

'Thanks,' I said quickly. 'That's really kind, but I'm okay.'

'Any idea what the boys would like from me?' she asked.

'I think you could just walk into ToysForKids and pick anything in their age range.'

She shook her head. 'I know my way around *that* shop.'

'Me too.' I put my knife and fork down and sighed. 'I'm just going to do one huge, expensive shop in there and that will be it. Which reminds me...' I searched around in my bag and produced three party invitations.

'Thanks,' Issi said as she took them. 'Oh. Manik Monkeys.' She pulled a face and I burst out laughing.

'Yes, I know. Two hours of screaming sweaty kids, but it makes it easier for me.'

Issi shuddered theatrically. 'I took Ben there last year. He was in the ball pit when he suddenly shouted that he needed the toilet.' She winced at the memory. 'He wasn't tall enough to wade through the mass of balls in time...'

'Oh, no,' I chuckled.

Issi shook her head slowly. 'I told the assistant, but she was more interested in texting her boyfriend.'

'I always thought there was a faint aroma of urine in there...'

'And you have to put up with lukewarm tea and over-priced snacks,' Issi continued.

'I know, I know.' I smiled at my friend. 'But they provide "monkey" burgers and chips – and that's far easier than me making sandwiches at home.'

'Good point,' Issi agreed. She looked down at the menu. 'Tiramisu or crème brûlée for dessert?'

'I think I'll go for—oh!'

I'd been so lost in our conversation that I hadn't seen Nico approaching. He pulled up a chair and joined us. 'Did you enjoy your salads?' He flashed his beautiful smile.

'Yes, thank you. Delicious. And thank you for the

cappuccinos.' I blushed.

He smiled again. 'Oh, I saw you come in struggling with so many bags and I took pity on you.'

'It was just what we needed to revive us,' Issi replied, smiling back.

'I'm sorry I haven't time to chat today,' he said, standing up. 'It's so busy. But maybe next time?'

Issi and I nodded enthusiastically before smiling at each other. We decided against a dessert and headed back into the town for another hour's shopping.

*

Once Jack and Charlie were in bed I cleared the sofa of toys and stretched out, pleased with the day's purchases. My mother always said she didn't "do Christmas", but I had bought her a beautiful necklace, hoping that this year, with Vicente's influence, things might be different. I reached down for *Pride and Prejudice* but only managed to read two pages before I fell asleep.

An hour later I was woken by the phone ringing. At first I thought it was part of my dream, but when I realised it was reality I dashed across the lounge, picking the receiver up on its final ring, a little out of breath.

Darren's tone was cool. 'Have I disturbed you?'

Anger flooded through me – I didn't have to justify what I was up to. 'Not really.' I left my reply open to interpretation.

'Oh. I see.'

'No, you don't, Darren.' I gripped the phone. How dare he patronise me?

'You sound upset.' Angry as I was, the gravelly tone to his voice made me want to forget about everything he'd done.

'I'm wondering if you're going to put the phone down on me again.'

'Sorry.' That was it – no explanation. 'How are you?'

'Fine, thanks, but if you do it again I'll refuse to take your calls.'

'Sure.'

I sighed, exhausted by this game we seemed to be playing. 'The boys are fast asleep.'

'I thought they would be – that's why I'm ringing now.'

'Oh.' I didn't understand why we were having this stilted conversation and I waited for Darren to come to the point.

'I thought I would fly over for the boys' birthdays.' The words tumbled out of his mouth quickly, as if he had practised the speech over and over. 'I'm landing on Friday the eighth of December and I'll stay for a week, returning after their birthdays on Friday the fifteenth.'

I was so shocked I couldn't speak for several moments. Once I regained my composure I spoke to him calmly, trying to keep my tone even. 'The boys will be pleased.' I hoped he couldn't tell from my voice how much my heart was hammering. I needed time to think and to reflect on what he'd just told me. 'Oh, Charlie is calling me,' I lied. 'I need to see to him. Bye.'

I headed straight for the kitchen and grabbed the bottle of wine I'd opened earlier. My hands were shaking slightly as I topped my glass up, and then I sank back onto the sofa, tears stinging my eyes. Why did he still have such an effect on my emotions? Why did I desperately want to see him when he'd hurt me so much? Did he still have feelings for me?

I rang Issi. 'Do you feel up to a chat?'

'Of course. I've been fine today. The sickness comes and goes.'

I was relieved for her, knowing how much she wanted to feel normal again. I explained what had just happened.

'Oh, Becky, I wish I had all the answers for you. You'll just have to wait until you're with him and see what your intuition tells you.'

'I know. I'm just so confused – it's a fine line between love and hate.' I sighed heavily.

'Where's he staying? Did he say?'

I almost stopped breathing. 'No. You don't think he wants to stay here do you? That would just be too much.'

'I wouldn't have thought so – it sounds like he has his trip arranged in every detail, so he would have mentioned it.'

'You're right,' I said in relief.

'Ooh, I've just thought – he's going to be here for Manik Monkeys on the ninth of December!'

I put the phone down with a smile and that night I dreamed Darren was whizzing down a huge slide into the ball pit. Martin was waiting at the bottom ready to pelt him with coloured plastic balls, and I was standing at the side with a bottle of spray disinfectant.

*

'Dad, is it Charlie and Jack's party tomorrow?' Thomas tugged at Martin's coat as he, Angela, Kate and I stood in the playground, huddled against the cold wind.

'No. Two more sleeps to go. You'll have to be a little more patient.' Martin stroked his son's fair hair, pulling his hood up over his ears as he smiled down at him.

I was enjoying watching this touching scene and as Martin looked up our eyes met, both of us still smiling. I looked away first, pulling my hat down over my ears to keep out the biting wind.

'Thomas is so excited,' Martin told me. 'It's his first party down here, so it's extra special.' He pulled his own hat down. 'Is it still okay if I stay for the duration? I'll give you some moral support – do the toilet run or something.'

I had forgotten Martin had offered to help me. I still hadn't told anyone that Darren was coming, but I was surprised the boys hadn't done it for me; it would have made things easier. I questioned again just why I was reluctant to share this news. By being with Darren, did I have to face up to the truth that I had a failed marriage? Was I worried that people would see us side by side and say, 'Oh, I can see why he left her, she's not attractive enough to keep a man like that.' Or was it because I'd finally moved on and I didn't really want him by my side? I didn't know the answer; my emotions were still too fragile, even after all this time.

I bit the bullet. 'By the way, Charlie and Jack's dad has decided to come over from America for their birthdays. He'll be at the party.' Rather than answer Martin's question directly, I spoke casually to the whole group while rearranging my scarf. There was a silence before Angela spoke.

'Oh, that'll be nice.'

I could see their thought processes working. Wonder what he looks like? Wonder if they'll be speaking to each other? Must make sure I arrive at the party early to observe. Thankfully the bell rang and the moment was gone.

As we all gathered in front of the classroom window to wave to our offspring, Martin touched my arm. 'How do you feel about Darren coming over?'

I smiled briefly and shrugged my shoulders. 'He's their dad.'

*

I woke up the next day with my stomach twisted in knots, and Jack and Charlie's hyperactive behaviour during breakfast didn't improve my mood.

'Daddy's coming today, Daddy's coming today!' they sang together at the tops of their voices.

'I know you're excited,' I said to them, 'but keep the noise down.'

They carried on singing, lowering their voices, and Charlie started pushing Jack's cereal bowl around the table.

'Hey!' Jack shouted, giving Charlie's bowl a hard shove in retaliation.

I watched the dish spin off the table and land on the floor, spraying milk and nuggets of cereal everywhere.

'I was up late washing this floor,' I screamed at them, instantly regretting it. I leaned against the worktop and breathed slowly. Why did I feel the need to impress Darren, which meant I was now cross with the boys?

I handed Jack a clean bowl. Darren would have to take me as he found me, which would be at my absolute best.

In the playground, Martin was standing with Mandy discussing football and I was grateful he was giving me some space. I had been worried he would question me about Darren's visit and I really wasn't in the mood. I stood with Kate and Angela and decided to talk about a subject I loved.

'I'm enjoying re-reading *Pride and Prejudice*,' I told them. 'And I've made lots of notes.' I smiled at Angela. 'I'm so looking forward to the book group meeting next week.'

She frowned at me. 'Didn't I tell you? We've postponed it until January because everyone's so busy with the run-up to Christmas.' She smiled apologetically. 'Sorry, I thought I'd mentioned it.'

Disappointment sapped what little energy I had left. 'Don't worry, January is fine. It was just with Darren being here, I thought he could babysit for me.' I shrugged. 'To be honest, I was just looking forward to a night out.'

'Right,' Kate said decisively. 'We'll just have to organise one then. Thursday?'

I nodded and Angela agreed enthusiastically. 'Come round to mine and we'll have a girly night in. It'll be great fun.' She turned to where Mandy was standing with Martin and shouted over to her. 'Thursday – girly drinking night – my house.'

Mandy gave her a thumbs up by way of reply and then we all looked at Martin, who was laughing.

'Don't worry. I wouldn't dream of gate-crashing a girls' night in. To be honest, it would frighten me to death!'

I tried hard to work during the day but my thoughts kept wandering. Darren had arranged to come round later in the evening, to spend an hour with the boys. Would he still find me attractive? Would he want to stay and have a drink with me and if he did, would the conversation be awkward, or would we reminisce about old times? Too many questions. Just take things one step at a time.

Darren had told me he was staying at the Gateway Hotel in Maidenhead, which was very up-market, and I had woken in the middle of the night wondering if Barbie was coming with him. I knew that would be more than I could bear, sharing the limelight with my ex-husband's pregnant lover at my sons' birthday party. It would be hugely humiliating in front of my friends. I went over the conversation with Darren in my mind – he had definitely said *I'm* staying at the hotel, not *we're*, but maybe he couldn't face telling me?

I managed to complete some work before collecting the boys from school, and then after a quick tea and even quicker baths the boys settled down in front of the television to wait for Darren. It was important to me that he saw what a great job I was doing, raising our boys alone, and I was determined he should see them at their best. Whether or not the boys could sense this, I didn't know, but they tried their hardest to be good. As a result, our home had an atmosphere of calm when Darren arrived.

He pulled up outside the house in a smart BMW and I watched him walk up the drive by peeping through the slatted kitchen blind. He still looked good: tall and well-built, with his dark wavy hair complementing his Californian tan. The doorbell rang and the boys raced to the door, fighting each other to open it first. They flung themselves at their dad and for the next few minutes he couldn't move from the doorstep while they clung onto him. When he emerged from their bear hugs I could see his eyes were moist.

He reached into a bag and handed them each a present. 'Not your birthday presents – you'll have to wait until Tuesday for those. These are just because I've missed you.' He was smiling as he turned to me. 'Hello, Becky, how are you?'

As his blue eyes penetrated mine, I took in his clean-shaven face, his damp hair and the smell of the aftershave I remembered so well. I swallowed hard. 'Great, thanks.'

He turned to the boys. 'This is for Mummy. She deserves a present too, doesn't she?'

As the boys shouted 'yes', he produced a small beautifully-wrapped box out of his pocket. 'I hope it's still your favourite,' he said, walking towards me and kissing me gently on the cheek.

Oh, God, he smells wonderful. My stomach flipped over several times and I tried to stop my hands from shaking. The boys insisted I open it there and then and I gasped when I saw what was inside. It was my favourite perfume, the one Darren had bought for me as a treat when he'd first started travelling. He used to enjoy spraying it over my naked body and then we would make love for hours. I shook these thoughts from my head and simply smiled.

'Thanks. Yes, it's still my favourite, but I don't have any at the moment.' I smiled at the boys, not adding that I could no longer afford such luxuries. 'Take Daddy into the lounge and I'll bring some drinks in. Coffee, Darren?'

I walked calmly into the kitchen and sat down, starting to shake. Why had he brought me a present? Why had he chosen that particular perfume? Did it hold memories for him too, or was he simply trying to be thoughtful? I needed Issi, but now wasn't the right moment to call her. I composed myself and checked my reflection in the oven door. I had taken an hour to get ready, wanting to achieve a look that said, 'I've not really gone to any trouble, I always look this good around the house'. I felt I had managed this by choosing a pair of smart, tight-fitting jeans and a fluffy zip-up sweater in baby pink, which always made me feel feminine.

I carried the tray of drinks and biscuits into the lounge to find Darren rolling about on the carpet with Jack and Charlie. I sat down and drank my coffee while they played, saddened by how awkward I felt, when this should have been the most natural moment in the world.

After a while I left them to it because I was conscious this was Darren's time with the boys. I sat in the kitchen reading *Pride and Prejudice,* so absorbed in the continuing romance between Elizabeth and Mr Darcy that I didn't hear Darren walk in.

'I've got to go now.' He ran his fingers through his hair and looked directly into my eyes. 'I'd like to take the boys to football tomorrow, so I'll collect them just before ten.'

I put my book down. 'Oh. Okay. We'll see you in the morning, then.' Of course he would want to take them, but I was hurt by the fact I wasn't included. I forced a smile. 'The party starts at four, so you'll need to be back here by three thirty.'

We waved him off and I smiled at the boys. 'It's bedtime n ow.'

Jack sat down on the stairs, clinging to the banister. 'I want to go with Daddy,' he sobbed.

'Me too,' Charlie yelled, banging his fists on the front door.

I sat down next to Jack, trying to soothe him, but he turned away angrily.

Charlie came over and joined us. 'Why did Daddy have to go?' he asked petulantly.

'Yes,' Jack shouted at me. 'Why doesn't he stay here?'

I swallowed hard and tried to sound reassuring. 'Daddy's staying in a hotel, but he's not far away.' I smiled brightly. 'He's looking forward to taking you to football tomorrow, so you need a good night's sleep.'

They reluctantly followed me upstairs, brushing their teeth and putting their pyjamas on slowly.

Charlie lay face down on his bed and started to cry. 'I miss my daddy,' he sobbed into his pillow.

Jack picked up some toys and hurled them across the room. 'All my friends have a daddy who lives with them. Why don't I?'

I fought back the urge to cry myself and calmly led Jack to Charlie's bed. I sat Charlie up and cuddled both of them. 'Although Daddy lives in America, he loves you both very, very much. He misses you, too.' I tucked them both into their beds. 'He'll see you in the morning, so get some sleep.'

Charlie sniffed and pulled the duvet over his head before I could kiss him, but Jack held my hand and I sang a lullaby as he dropped off to sleep.

I wanted to jump in the car and drag Darren out of his comfortable hotel room so he could see what he'd done to his children, but instead I made myself a strong coffee. Once I'd calmed down I rang Issi as she'd firmly instructed me to do. She was desperate to know how it had gone.

'I'm not sure about his motives for the perfume, Becky,' my friend advised. 'Just be careful – don't set yourself up to be hurt again.' She paused. 'Did he mention Shelley at all? Is she with him?'

I scowled. 'I didn't ask, and he didn't say.' I thought for a second. 'He had to rush off, so maybe she is?'

'Well, take things slowly.'

'Thanks for listening.' I massaged my left temple, trying to fend off a headache. 'I'm sorry. It's all been about me and my issues recently.'

Issi laughed. 'I'm loving your problems – they take my mind off being ill!'

I put the phone down and climbed into bed with my book. I dreamed that Shelley, dressed as a pregnant Barbie doll, was coming down the slide at Manik Monkeys and I was the one at the bottom ready to pelt her with the plastic balls. This time there was no disinfectant.

*

'Oh. Hi, Darren.' I was surprised to see him standing on the doorstep.

'Morning, Becky. Sorry I'm early.'

'That's okay. Do you want a coffee while the boys are getting ready?'

'That would be great, thanks.' He followed me into the kitchen and stood at the window, looking out at the back garden. 'You've got a nice place here. You did well choosing it.'

'There's a lot of work to be done,' I said as I handed him his coffee. I tried to keep the bitterness out of my voice.

'It'll be lovely once you've decorated,' he replied. 'You've got great taste.'

I had to turn away. If I'd had a paintbrush handy I'd have rammed it into his hand, suggesting he make a start. It had been hard finding a place that I could barely afford with two children in tow; it had been hard moving in, trying to keep the boys both safe and entertained while Sam and I unpacked. Pride had made me tell my brother I would be fine putting up the beds and curtain poles, but after I'd struggled for hours I'd had to admit defeat and call him, all the time feeling so desperately lonely. I put these thoughts to one side and smiled.

'Is Shelley with you?' I nearly choked on the words, but was determined to appear as if I had moved on.

'No.' Darren was unable to meet my eyes.

'When's the baby due?' I hadn't intended asking this question. The words had somehow formed themselves, surprising me.

He snapped his head away, staring at one of the boys' drawings I'd stuck on the wall. 'She's…' He turned back and smiled. 'Due in Spring.'

At that moment Jack rushed in, closely followed by Charlie. 'Come on, Dad, hurry up!' they shouted together.

'I'm ready.' He put his mug down and turned to me. 'Thanks for the coffee. We'll see you later.'

I had been tempted to go with them to the sports field, mainly because of Darren's arrogance in not inviting me. Instead I had decided to use the time to wrap the boys' gifts, but I was annoyed I wouldn't get to see Rob. Somehow, however, I didn't want to present a united front to the world. Darren would be leaving on Friday, and it would be a long time before we saw him again. I was also worried about Martin. Would he would be offended if I stood with Darren? It was simpler just to avoid the situation.

*

'Is it time yet? Is it time yet?' chorused Jack and Charlie for the third time in a few minutes.

'Nearly.' I was just putting the finishing touches to my make-up. I was wearing my favourite blue cardigan, even though it was hot at Manik Monkeys. It suited me, and wearing it gave me confidence. 'Daddy's decided to meet us there, so we'll leave in five minutes.'

We arrived at the warehouse and were greeted by an overpowering smell of sweaty children. As I booked us in I could hardly hear the assistant above the noise of the screaming, and when I turned round Jack and Charlie had already discarded their trainers and were somewhere inside the huge dome of soft play equipment. Thankfully, Issi appeared at my side and sent Andrew to find them.

'Where is he?' she whispered.

'Not here yet.' I looked around me and shuddered. 'I don't blame him, either.'

Both of us were laughing as Darren walked through the door. His smile turned to a look of horror as he entered the building, but swiftly changed to delight as Jack and Charlie rushed over to jump on him. The boys were each holding one of his hands as he walked over to Issi and me.

'Hello, Issi. It's good to see you,' he said, kissing her on both cheeks.

I left them chatting because the children had started to arrive and I needed to supervise the present-giving and receiving. We were still all gathered in the reception area and Charlie and Jack were ripping the paper off their presents as children arrived. I had no idea who had brought what – the thank-you letters were going to be interesting. Parents were arriving to drop children off, quickly throwing various pieces of information at me, such as who they were lift-sharing with and who was collecting who, before they made their escape. Lauren decided she desperately needed the toilet just after her mother had left, and several of the children had taken their trainers off, ready to run into the play dome.

Tension was rising through my body and my face was starting to flush. I regretted wearing such a warm cardigan and looked over to Darren for some help. He was still talking to Issi, but she had her back to me, unaware of what was happening. Before I could shout over to them, Lauren announced, 'I'm going to wet my pants, Mrs Dixon.'

'Here, I'll take Lauren to the toilet.'

'And I'll pick up all the presents.'

I was so glad to see Kate and Mandy and I smiled with relief. Just at that moment our Manik Monkeys Playmate, Sarah, arrived to take over.

'Hello, everyone. Sorry I'm late. Right, who wants a party?'

All the children cheered and shouted 'me' at the same time and I started to relax.

'Have we got all twenty children, mum?'

I did a quick head count and then consulted my list. 'There may just be one more, but it's probably a good idea to go through to our room. I think they're all keen to get started!'

The children trooped after Sarah and I turned to Kate. 'Josh hasn't turned up. He was the only one who didn't reply, and I'm guessing Helen did that out of spite.'

'That's not very nice,' she tutted.

'I know.' I sighed loudly. 'I saw her in the playground two days ago and asked if Josh was coming, because I needed to confirm numbers. She simply gave me a withering look and said she hadn't decided yet.'

'That's incredibly rude,' Kate said, outraged.

'I was so taken aback and cross, I couldn't think of a clever reply. I don't know why she has to be like this, particularly when it's the children who lose out.'

'I know,' agreed Kate. 'Rise above it. Your boys will have a great day, regardless.' She squeezed my arm.

I glanced at my watch. 'I'll give them five more minutes and then I'm going to join the party.' As I was talking I suddenly realised I had included Thomas in my head count, but I hadn't seen Martin. I frowned at Kate. 'Have you seen Martin at all? He said he was going to stay and help me.'

'He must have changed his mind. I saw him walking out

as I came in.'

'Oh. That's strange.'

'Maybe he had things to do? Talking of which, I'm going to go shopping for a while. Have fun.'

As I leaned against the sticky reception desk, Issi rushed past, being dragged towards the soft play area by Ben. She managed to halt him for a few moments. 'Sorry I was no help – Darren just kept on talking to me.'

'It's fine.' I shook my head. 'I think he feels a bit lost.'

'Well,' my friend replied fiercely, 'I made sure he knows how hard things are for you and how well you cope!'

'Thanks,' I said as she was dragged off again.

I gave up waiting for Josh and walked over to the room that had been put aside for us. I smiled as I stepped over a huge pile of trainers, none of which looked like they were in pairs, and an even bigger pile of presents. I wandered out onto the viewing area, where I could see Issi playing with Ben in the younger section. It took me a few minutes to spot Darren; he was on one of the upper tiers inside the dome, playing with his sons. Strictly speaking adults weren't allowed in unless they were rescuing a child who was stuck and refusing to move, but surely they made allowances for dads who only got to see their children three times a year?

An hour later, nineteen red-faced and sweaty children emerged for tea and juice. Sarah kept them amused with games and singing while they waited to be fed, and Darren, Issi and I were kept busy refilling cups and taking it in turns to do the toilet run. After tea, Sarah produced the two cakes I had bought: a Spiderman one for Jack and a Batman one for Charlie. I was bursting with pride as I videoed the tuneless singing of happy birthday to my children; I choked back tears as they blew out the candles.

Parents started to arrive and I was so preoccupied trying to ensure all the children went home in a matching pair of trainers, even if they weren't the right ones, that I missed Thomas leaving. I looked up just as Mandy came over to thank me and saw the backs of Martin and Thomas disappearing through the exit. I would text him later to check everything was all right.

Once everyone had gone home I handed Darren a slice of cake. 'Do you want to come back and watch the boys open their presents?'

'I can't. I'm driving up to Yorkshire to see my mum and dad for a few days.' He handed the plate back to me. 'I'll be back on Tuesday for their birthday – is it all right if I take them out for tea?'

I wasn't invited, and that stung. 'Sure – they'll be pleased.' I held his gaze for a moment. 'Are we all going out together?'

'Oh.' He thrust his hands into his pockets, looking down at the floor. 'I'd like to spend some time alone with them – if that's okay? You get to see them every day.'

As he looked up I gave him a long hard stare. There was so much I could say about him choosing to leave us, but I refused to start a scene at our sons' party. 'Don't forget it's their school nativity play on Wednesday morning,' I snapped.

Jack, Charlie and I arrived home half an hour later with a boot full of presents and two half-eaten cakes. I was so exhausted I flopped down in the lounge with a coffee and a huge slab of cake while the boys tore off paper and ripped into boxes with great excitement.

It took a lot of persuading to get them into bed that evening, but by eight o'clock they were fast asleep and I sat down with yet another piece of cake; too tired to cook.

I was absorbed in watching a mindless reality television programme when the phone startled me.

'Hello, Becky.' Martin's voice sounded casual, not his normal up-beat self. 'I just wanted to thank you for the party. Thomas had a wonderful time.'

'That's okay.' I still wasn't sure if I had upset him in some way. 'Sorry I missed you – it was all a bit hectic.'

A small silence ensued and I felt as if I had to fill the gap. I wanted to ask why he hadn't stayed, but I didn't want him to take it as a criticism; after all, he was entitled to do other things without mentioning it to me. I couched my question carefully. 'Did you manage to get any Christmas shopping done while Thomas was at the party?'

'No, I didn't fancy the crowds. I sat in the car and listened to the football.'

I was confused. Why would he sit in his car for two hours, rather than join in with the party as he had originally intended?

'Oh.'

'It was fine – I don't often get the opportunity to listen to Radio Five in peace – it was a real treat.'

I was offended by his response. I thought we were friends, but clearly he preferred his own company to mine. 'You should have stayed at the party – it was good fun.'

There was another silence before Martin spoke. 'It was difficult, you know, with Darren being there. I didn't like to intrude.'

'You wouldn't have done.' I was sharp in my reply. 'Listen, I have to go. Thanks for the call. I'll see you next week.'

I stared at the television, mulling everything over in my head. Why were men so territorial? I gave up trying to work it all out. Darren would be gone on Friday and my life could go back to the way it was. I didn't need these complications.

Chapter Nine

Liar, liar,
Tongue's on fire

'Wake up, Mum!' Jack yelled as he dive-bombed onto my bed.

'It's my birthday!' Charlie shouted as he hurled himself across my legs, pinning me down.

I forced my eyes open and waited until I was able to focus on the clock. Ten to six. 'Happy birthday.' I laughed, trying to wriggle out from under Charlie so I could give them both a kiss.

Charlie grabbed his brother's arm. 'Come on, Jack. Let's go and see what we've got.'

I followed them downstairs, where they let out whoops of joy when they saw their respective piles. I had wrapped lots of small inexpensive presents, so they each had a huge mound laid out in the lounge.

'Wow!' shouted Charlie and they both ran over to start ripping parcels open. Their faces were brimming with pleasure and I couldn't stop smiling myself. Once they'd finished, I made their favourite breakfast – sausage sandwiches with lashings of tomato ketchup.

As the boys were eating I opened their cards and read them

out, knowing they wouldn't be in the least bit interested.

'Oh look, Granny's sent you both some euros.'

Charlie and Jack frowned at me with their mouths full, as if to say, 'what are euros?' I explained how I would change it into English money for them to spend. I was disappointed. Surely Mum could have gone to a bit more trouble – maybe sending them a toy as well – but at least she had remembered this year.

I carried on reading out their cards, but the only other time I could attract their attention was when one of them contained an "I am 5" badge each, which they pinned to their pyjamas.

We set off for school late, having left home the first time without their bags of sweets to hand out to each child at home time. Both the boys had three birthday badges attached to their sweatshirts. They were so excited I wasn't sure how they were going to get through the day.

We arrived in the playground just as the bell was ringing so I didn't get the chance to chat to anyone. I was worried I still hadn't seen Martin since his phone call to me on Saturday – I wasn't entirely sure how things were between us. As I was leaving I walked past Helen standing at the gate, chatting to her usual group of friends. We looked at each other. An explanation or an apology for Josh's non-appearance at the party would have been nice, but Helen simply held my gaze and then turned to her friends with a smirk. I quickened my pace, hoping physical exertion would dispel my anger.

I tried to fit all of my day's work into the morning because the infant school nativity plays started at half past one. There was another performance the following morning and I had felt it would be better if I went to one and Darren to the other. That way the boys would have someone to wave to at both performances. In truth, I didn't particularly fancy sitting with Darren. It would be an emotional moment, seeing our boys on stage in their first school nativity production. I had no intention of playing at happy families, knowing that Darren would be gone again soon. Also, I didn't want everyone staring at us, wondering what was going on; I had been the subject of enough gossip for one term.

I had arranged to meet Kate outside school at one o'clock so we would be early enough to get seats with a good view. As we walked into the hall my phone bleeped with an incoming text message.

'It's from Martin,' I told Kate. 'He wants us to save him a seat because he's running late.'

'Oh, right, I told him we were coming early.' She stopped suddenly. 'Oh, no.'

I looked up from texting my reply. 'What's the matter?'

'Er, next time we decide to come early, let's make it twelve o'clock.'

The hall was three-quarters full. 'Did they all bring sandwiches?' I asked her.

Kate found three seats together in the middle of a row half way back, and I put my coat on the spare seat to reserve it. By half past one I was fed up with confirming, yes, it was indeed saved for someone. I glanced round, hoping Helen was going to Wednesday's performance, but I spotted her on the front row in prime position. I nudged Kate. 'I think she's been there since morning break.'

Kate giggled and checked her watch. 'Martin had better hurry up. It's about to start.'

'I know,' I agreed. 'It's standing room only now – he'll never find us once the lights go down.'

Mrs Jenkins, the head teacher, took her position at the front of the stage to welcome all the parents and to explain how hard the children and staff had been working on the three productions. She was in full flow, thanking the parents who had helped with the costumes, when a kerfuffle came from the back of the hall. Someone was pushing their way through the crowd of parents who were standing there, and the next thing I heard was,

'Excuse me, sorry, oh sorry, excuse me,' as Martin pushed past parents' knees, making his way along our row. He sat down with a red face and a beaming smile. 'Made it!'

I couldn't help but laugh until I realised people were turning round to have a look. My eyes met Helen Stevens', who appeared to be furious. I wasn't sure whether her anger was due to the fact I had been indirectly involved in the disturbance, or because I was sitting next to Martin.

Mrs Jenkins smiled and introduced the Year Two play as if nothing had happened. Rob Phillips led the children out from behind the stage and immediately thirty cameras started flashing. The children looked so proud of themselves and a couple of them gave little waves to the audience, despite clearly having been told not to. From my seat I had a good view of Rob and I fantasised about him throughout the entire production.

The Year One play provided a few laughs when one of the elves collided with another and burst into tears, and then it was time for the Reception class' rendition of the Christmas story. I sat upright in my chair, my chest physically swelling with pride as they all trooped into the hall, waving madly. Jack and Charlie were both shepherds and while I wasn't great at sewing, I had bought some brown material, which I had made into simple tabards. I had also bought two red stripy tea towels, which were tied to their heads with some old rope. I had been really proud of my first attempt at costume making and was mortified to see what other parents had produced.

Josh was the third shepherd and was wearing the most exquisite tabard, which looked like it had been lovingly hand-sewn. It was accompanied by a matching headdress, which had been secured by a piece of plaited, coloured rope.

Thomas had been given the starring role of Joseph, and again, he was wearing a hand-sewn stripy tabard with tiny stars embroidered onto it, which twinkled as they caught the light. I was astounded. The four angels were wearing matching tutus, with beautiful pink wings attached. They certainly hadn't been bought from Primark.

The production was very moving. All the children remembered their lines and their singing brought the house down. Several times I had to swallow hard to stop the tears from flowing.

At the end of all three plays Mrs Jenkins once again thanked everyone for their hard work and announced that the PTA had laid on coffee and tea in the canteen as a fundraiser.

Kate, Martin and I stood up and stretched our legs, agreeing how good it had all been.

'I couldn't believe the costumes. They were wonderful,' I said to both of them. 'Were you up all night sewing Thomas's costume, Martin?'

Martin beamed, but Kate looked a little uncomfortable.

'Josh's mum made it,' Martin told me happily.

'And Lucy's.' Kate spoke more to the floor than to me.

I was so surprised I couldn't reply.

'She just made them,' Kate said by way of an apology, 'and gave them to Miss Whittaker. I thought she'd done it for everyone – sorry.'

'It was particularly helpful to me,' Martin said, unaware of my problems with Helen. 'I'd had a go, but my effort was pretty bad.'

Helen Stevens was surrounded by a few mums, all congratulating her on her own wonderful "performance" as costume maker. She looked like the cat who'd got the cream. I knew why she hadn't offered to make Jack and Charlie's costumes – she had wanted to make me look stupid. Right. Little did she know my mum was a seamstress – oh, next year things would be very different.

Kate wandered off to chat to one of her friends and Martin asked if I'd like a coffee. We stood in the corner of the canteen trying to talk above the noise of people chatting.

'Thanks for saving me a seat,' he shouted above the din.

I couldn't hear very well and moved closer to him. 'Any time. Thomas was wonderful.'

Martin smiled. 'Sorry I didn't stay and help at the party.' He dipped his biscuit into his coffee. 'I feel a bit low from time to time, and particularly near to Christmas. It's only my second one without Jackie.'

I felt an immediate rush of sympathy and touched his arm. 'I'm so sorry. If you ever need to talk, just call me.'

'Thanks.' His eyes welled up as he smiled.

As we continued chatting I became that aware Helen was watching us from the other side of the room. There would be more gossip at the gate in the morning.

*

I collected the boys from their classroom and the three of us chatted all the way home about the wonderful performance, re-living it moment by moment. I was surprised to see Darren sitting on the doorstep.

'I had a good journey down from Yorkshire and arrived sooner than I thought.'

The boys hurled themselves at him.

'I tried phoning you to see if I could meet you at school,' he said over the top of Charlie's head.

'Sorry, my phone was still on silent.' I hadn't wanted to incur Mrs Jenkins' wrath with my Dr Who ringtone just as baby Jesus was being born. Thankfully, Darren saw the funny side.

'Come on, boys,' he said as he jumped up. 'Your presents

are round the side of the house.' The three of us followed him to find two brand new bikes – one blue and one red. Jack and Charlie grabbed one each and immediately jumped on, pedalling down the drive, only narrowly missing Darren's car.

'I think the back garden might be safer,' he told them. 'I'll have a coffee with your mum and then we'll go out for tea.'

I put the coffee machine on and started to unpack the boys' school bags and lunch boxes while Darren watched Jack and Charlie through the kitchen window.

'I think their presents were a hit,' he said.

I smiled briefly. 'It's very generous of you.'

I found Darren's presence unsettling. I alternated between enjoying seeing him with the boys and hating him for blowing their young worlds apart. I didn't want to spoil their birthdays, but I couldn't hold back any longer. 'So are you going to take them to the park every weekend with their bikes, or will that be down to me as well?'

He spun round and stared at me. 'You think it's easy for me?' He walked slowly towards me, stopping inches from my face. 'You think I wouldn't give my right arm to take them to the park?' He spoke slowly, the vein on his left temple throbbing, tears forming in his eyes.

'It was your choice to leave,' I replied, holding his gaze, challenging him to deny it.

'Was it? Was it really, in the end?' He picked up his coffee and took it over to the table.

I turned my back on him, watching the boys riding and laughing in the garden. 'Sorry,' I said after a while, turning to face him.

'Me too.' Neither of us smiled.

'I know this isn't a great moment, but would you be able to babysit on Thursday evening?'

'Thursday?' He looked up as if coming out of a trance.

'One of my friends has arranged a girls' night out, or rather, a girls' night in.'

'Yes, no problem. I don't leave until Friday morning.'

We both studied our mugs intently. 'How are your mum and dad?' I knew the answer because I had spoken to them the previous week, but my thoughts were elsewhere while Darren was talking. He would be leaving on Friday and we hadn't cleared the air. I wanted to scream in his face, 'Why did you leave me? Why wasn't I good enough? Do you still think about me?' Instead I smiled when he'd finished speaking.

'That's nice,' I said, without having any idea what he'd talked about.

Darren drained his coffee cup and stood up. 'I think I'll take the boys out now, before it gets too late.'

Could he read my body language? Was he making his escape before I asked any awkward questions? 'I'd still like us to go out for tea as a family,' I told him.

'Well, we don't always get what we want, do we?' he snapped back.

Tears stinging my eyes, I called the boys inside for a quick wash and a change of clothes before the three of them set off for their pizza. I waited until they were out of sight and then I slammed the door as hard as I could.

*

'Mum,' Jack bellowed up the stairs. 'Someone's here.'

I had just emerged from the shower and I ran downstairs dressed only in a towel, to find Charlie opening the front door. He stepped backwards without looking, straight onto my foot.

'Sorry, Mum,' he said.

Darren strode into the house. He was wearing jeans and a sweatshirt which was just tight enough to show that he still worked out. He laughed at the sight of me hopping up and down on one foot. 'I always did fancy you with wet hair.'

I stared at him, pulling the towel closer round me, suddenly incapable of responding.

Darren blushed. 'I'm so sorry. I had no right to say that.'

Neither of us spoke for a moment.

'I came early to entertain the boys while you get ready.' He walked towards the lounge. 'Right. Well, I'll do just that.'

I nodded and fled upstairs. I sat on my bed for a while with thoughts tumbling around my head. How dare he say something like that to me? He had his pregnant lover waiting for him to arrive home tomorrow; he had no right to flirt with me, if that's what he'd been doing. I was unsure now – maybe it had been meant as a joke and I'd taken it the wrong way. I took my time getting ready, nervous of spending too much time with him, confused by my feelings.

Kate arrived to collect me at seven and I kissed the boys goodnight, giving Darren several more last-minute instructions and promising not to be too late. We avoided eye contact with each other, and again I felt confused. I had taken care with my appearance and had liberally sprayed myself with the perfume he'd bought me. Was it because I wanted him to find me attractive? And yet I'd been horrified when I thought he'd been flirting with me. I picked up a bottle of wine and followed Kate to the car. I would just get drunk and then I wouldn't care about it all.

*

We arrived at Angela's large detached house, which wasn't too far from mine, although it was far enough away to be in a more exclusive district. I admired the stunning hallway as I walked in. It was similar to the house Darren and I had lived in – the house I'd had before he'd had an affair and I'd had to move down market, before I had to work hard to make ends meet. Oh, I needed a drink.

Angela was wearing a floral skirt in shades of pink and purple with a turtle-necked green sweater and black boots. Her ensemble made me look twice. It must be so liberating to have the confidence to dress in that way – or to simply not care. I spent far too long agonising in front of the mirror each day, which undermined my confidence. I vowed to be far more creative with my clothes in future.

Angela air-kissed Kate and me, showing us into the sitting room, where I sank into a recliner. I gratefully accepted the glass of wine she offered me.

A few minutes later, Mandy walked in and tripped over the cat, spilling the glass of wine she'd just been given. Angela scurried round with a cloth, saying it was no problem. For once Mandy was lost for words and I started to giggle, which then set Kate and Mandy off. My confusion and anger disappeared – I was going to have a good night with my friends.

The doorbell rang and Angela reappeared with a dark-haired lady, who was beautifully dressed in what I presumed was a designer outfit.

'Ladies,' Angela announced, 'this is my neighbour, Denise.' She proceeded to introduce Denise to each of us. 'Now,' Angela continued, 'I sent Jeremy to the local wine shop and he got a little carried away, so we have rather a large number of bottles in the fridge, which all need drinking!'

Angela refreshed our glasses and produced several plates of canapés, getting the evening under way. After ten minutes of small talk, Kate turned to Denise.

'Have you known Angela long?'

'Well, we've been neighbours for about a year, but actually, we went to school together, although we weren't that friendly.'

'Yes,' joined in Angela. 'We were reminiscing a few weeks

ago about people we could remember. We had a look on that website – the one that reunites school friends. It was a real hoot.'

Denise spluttered on her wine. 'Can I tell them?'

Angela blushed and nodded.

'When I looked at Angela's profile, it seems she's now a fully qualified neuro-surgeon, working up in London.'

We all burst out laughing.

'Angela!' said Mandy, throwing her arms up in horror. 'On my profile,' she giggled, 'I own my own dental practice!' She turned to Denise. 'In reality, I'm a part-time dental receptionist.'

We couldn't stop laughing and Angela was dispatched to get her laptop from the study, to log on. We discovered that out of the five of us, Kate and Denise had been truthful but I hadn't changed my profile following my separation and was apparently still happily married. I shrugged and laughed.

'Who else can we look at?' Mandy asked.

We all thought for a while and then I smiled. 'Helen Stevens.'

'Ooh, yes,' said Kate. 'Type her name in.'

Angela found her profile and we all fell about laughing.

'I can't believe she's the "head of a thriving advertising agency",' Mandy snorted as she wiped away the tears. 'I can't wait to see her and ask about her latest ad campaign.'

'We'll have to have an amnesty in the playground tomorrow,' Angela said, laughing. 'Hands up all those who've lied on a website.'

No one could speak for the next few minutes as our laughter turned to hysterics, until Denise asked, 'So, who is Helen Stevens?'

We all started laughing again, and then I explained who she was. 'I worked with her years ago. She didn't like me then...' I giggled, '...and she likes me even less now.' I told her what had been going on in the playground.

Mandy rushed over and hugged me. 'I didn't know that – I'll kick her in the shins next week!'

'Get in line!' Angela said. She was perched on the arm of the sofa and looked like she could topple off at any moment.

'We've got women like that in our playground too,' Denise told us. 'My children still go to the school where we used to live, so I have no option other than to drive, but I don't get out of the car.' She drained her glass. 'I can't stand the bitchiness that goes on, so I park in the community centre car park next to the school and flash my lights when I see the kids walking towards me.'

I wiped my eyes and stopped laughing. 'What happened to make you do that?'

'It's a long story,' she continued. 'Basically, there were an awful lot of bitches in the playground, with little else to do but criticise other people's children.'

We all nodded knowingly.

'Why do they do it?' Angela asked as she filled everyone's glass up.

We all shrugged.

'Boredom?' Kate suggested.

'Helen doesn't like me because I got her sacked,' I said, way too much alcohol in my system to care about discretion.

'Nooo,' Mandy slurred. She shuffled closer to me. 'Tell us everything.'

'Crikey,' Angela said when I'd told them the story. 'I'll buy you a tin hat for Christmas.'

Everyone laughed as she passed another bottle round. 'Let's talk about something nicer,' she slurred. 'I think we need to sort out Mandy and Becky's love-lives.'

Mandy blushed and she and I studied our glasses intently.

'Come on. Is there anyone you fancy? We can't help you if you don't tell us.' Angela raised her fingers in a Brownie salute. 'It won't go out of this room. Girls' honour.'

'Well,' started Mandy cautiously, 'there's a guy who's been coming into the practice for treatment recently and he keeps smiling at me.' She paused.

'Go on,' encouraged Kate.

'He lost his two front teeth in an accident, so actually, he looks a bit weird.'

We all fell about laughing again until Mandy was able to continue.

'No, really, he's very nice – well, he will be once he's had his teeth fixed. I've got access to his phone numbers and I keep thinking about ringing him, although I'll probably get sacked for breaking data protection rules.'

We discussed the pros and cons of gaining a boyfriend but losing a job, and then Mandy suddenly said, 'There's someone else I like as well.'

I topped up everyone's glass. 'Come on, tell us.'

Even though I knew Mandy had drunk rather too much, she still appeared to be weighing up whether or not to tell us. The effect of the drink clearly won.

'Martin. There, I've said it.'

'As in Thomas's dad?' gasped Kate.

'I knew I shouldn't have told you. Don't you dare tell him.'

Fingers of jealousy jabbed at me, but Martin and I were just mates. Did I have deeper feelings for him? 'That's really sweet, Mandy,' I told her. 'You should tell him.'

She scowled. 'Just look at me – overweight, too loud. I'm not really his type. I'll settle for good friends.'

'What rubbish,' Kate shouted at her. 'You're lovely. You should ask him out.'

Kate was swaying as she spoke and I had no intention of letting her drive us home. I mouthed "taxi" at Angela, who nodded and went off to make a phone call. Kate moved closer to me and took my hand, mainly to steady herself.

'Now we need to sort you out. Who do you fancy?'

I thought for a moment about mentioning Rob. I tossed the thoughts around in my head; I would be hugely embarrassed if I told them, particularly if it leaked out, but there again, we did have a sort of code of confidence between us, and everyone had been supportive when Mandy had told her secret.

'Mm, well—'

I was interrupted by Angela. 'Is Kate all right?'

She had fallen asleep on the floor and we put a cushion under her head, leaving her there while we helped tidy up. Once the taxi arrived, Mandy and I lifted her into the back, praying she wouldn't be sick on the way home. A friend of Mandy's had dropped her round at Angela's and Kate had offered to drive her home, so she shared the taxi instead. We dropped Kate off first and were relieved to find her husband still up. We handed her over, feeling highly embarrassed that we were all a little drunk, and Kate's husband shook his head, pretending to disapprove.

'I'm never going to be able to get up tomorrow,' moaned Mandy. 'I'm out of practice at late nights during the week.'

'Me too, and Darren's going to be cross. I said I wouldn't be late.'

I was next to be dropped off and Mandy gave me a hug. 'I've had a great evening. We must do it again.'

I smiled as I walked up the drive. I remembered thinking that making friends in the playground meant enjoying coffee and biscuits during the day – I'd had no idea it meant getting drunk on a Thursday evening.

I opened the front door quietly, hoping Darren had fallen asleep without realising how late it was, but he came strolling out of the lounge to meet me.

'Hi. How was your evening?'

'Oh, great. Sorry I'm so late.' I thought I sounded completely normal.

'My God, let's get some coffee into you. How much have you had to drink?'

It was like being a schoolgirl getting told off by her dad. I felt myself swaying as I stared at him. 'That's none of your business – I can drink as much as I like, with whoever I like.'

He smiled and guided me into the kitchen by the elbow. I plonked myself into the nearest chair, hoping fervently I wasn't going to be sick in front him.

'The boys were fine,' he said as he put the coffee machine on. 'They didn't want to go to bed, so we played until late.' He stopped talking and looked at me. 'It was awful having to say goodbye to them. I miss them so much.'

'I know,' I replied. I was starting to feel dizzy and I didn't want to be having this conversation. I stood up, hoping that moving around the kitchen would help to clear my head.

Darren turned round with two coffee cups in his hands and looked straight at me. I stood still, somehow rooted to the spot and he put the cups down without moving his gaze from my eyes. Time seemed to stand still for me. He touched my hair, pushing it back behind my ears the way he used to; he touched my face gently, tracing my jaw-line with his fingers. Suddenly we were kissing; slowly at first, then more urgently, his body pressing against mine. His hands moved over me, igniting a longing I had long since forgotten. I wanted him so badly, but then suddenly my head was screaming 'no'. This wasn't what I wanted. I was slowly recovering from the hurt and the pain and I wasn't prepared to open myself up to it again.

I pushed him away. 'I'm sorry, you'd better go.'

'Becky, don't let's leave it like this. Can we at least talk?'

'It's not the right moment. I've had far too much to drink. You'll have to call me.'

'It's difficult over the phone.' Tears formed in his eyes. 'There's so much I want to say to you.'

I was staring at him fiercely, arms folded across my body. I was angry with him for making me want him, and cross with myself for giving in.

'Okay,' he continued gently, 'but I just want you to know I miss you – and I'm sorry.'

He moved towards me, but I took a step backwards and I saw the hurt flit across his face.

After he'd gone I checked on the boys and then flopped onto my bed. I thumped my pillows repeatedly in anger and confusion. Why did he still have this effect on me? Why had I allowed myself to let him in, albeit fleetingly? I rolled onto my back, wondering what he had wanted to tell me, suddenly wishing he was still here, lying next to me.

I got up and pulled the curtains apart. Maybe he was still outside? Disappointed at not being able to see him, I started to undress, but got in a tangle with my tights. I gave up and climbed into bed fully clothed.

*

I woke up with what felt like a bulldozer in my head, and I struggled to get out of bed. The boys were tired and grumpy due to their late night and so none of us had time for breakfast; just the thought of it made me feel queasy. I handed the boys a glass of milk to drink and gave them a handful of biscuits to eat on the way to school, feeling very guilty. I had no idea whether or not they'd brushed their teeth, but I wasn't in the mood to care. I checked I had some change in my purse.

'I'll give Miss Whittaker some money for hot dinners today because I don't have time to make your lunch boxes.'

'Yeah!' shouted Jack a little too loudly and I clutched my head. 'It's chips on a Friday.'

We managed to make it to school with a few minutes to spare and I saw Kate, Angela and Mandy standing in a group.

I joined them silently. No one was speaking. All four of us stood with our heads down. They must have felt like I did; raising your head only started off the hammering again. Martin crept up behind me and put both his hands on my shoulders.

'Morning,' he bellowed at us.

Four sets of hands immediately reached for four heads, and we all scowled at him.

'Ooh, you had a good night. Anyone for paracetamol?'

The bell rang far too loudly and we all grimaced. Once the children were inside the classroom and had been waved to through the window I walked home slowly, texting Issi on the way. *Need 2 c u. Meet L'Olivo 12.30?*

The reply was almost instant, making me jump. *Ok. c u l8r.*

*

I arrived at L'Olivo feeling slightly better for having gone back to bed for a sleep. Issi was already seated at a table, laughing with Nico who was taking her order. They both looked up and smiled as I approached the table.

'*Ciao*, Becky. Good to see you. Cappuccino?'

'Thanks.'

Issi grabbed my hand as I sat down. 'What's wrong? You look dreadful.'

As I started to tell the story to my incredulous friend, Nico appeared with our drinks. He hovered by the table for a couple of seconds but then told us he couldn't stop to chat as he had things to do.

'Complete bastard,' Issi said when I finished telling her about Darren's behaviour. 'You were vulnerable, and he took advantage.'

'I'm not sure.' I was staring down at my cup. 'He seemed

genuine.'

Issi was furious on my behalf. 'Of course he did – the chance of getting laid, who wouldn't? I bet he won't be telling his pregnant girlfriend.' She banged her spoon angrily on the table, making me jump. 'Maybe *you* should tell her.'

'No.' I shook my head. 'It crossed my mind fleetingly this morning, but I remember how I felt – far better to let her find out for herself what a rat he is.' I smiled for the first time. 'But you're right about him. Maybe I just wanted to think he still has feelings for me? Oh, I don't know what I think, really.'

'Oh, Becky.' Issi's eyes were full of compassion. 'I wish I knew how to help you.'

I squeezed her hand. 'Sorry – it's all been about me again. How are you feeling?'

She patted her head gently. 'I'm pleased the chemo didn't make my hair fall out.' She paused and looked away. 'But I'm nervous about the mastectomy.'

I reached across and hugged her. 'Of course you're anxious, but you'll be surrounded by people who love you – and you're having it done as a precaution.'

'I know,' she replied, brushing away a tear. 'It'll be fine.'

We chatted for a while and then I felt the need to go home. I was so emotionally drained I just wanted to sleep again. For once I didn't object when Issi insisted on paying the bill, and as we were putting our coats on Nico came over. He took both of my hands in his and kissed my cheek.

'*Ciao*, Becky,' he said softly. 'Come talk to me if you need to. I'll open a nice bottle of wine for us.'

I smiled at him gratefully. 'Thank you. Maybe I will.'

Issi and I walked out into the cold December air and she pulled me into her arms. 'I know it still hurts, but you can do better than Darren.'

Chapter Ten

Roses are red,
Violets are blue.
Revenge is sweet,
Especially on you.

Waves of nausea washed over me. Darren would be home by now, and I was dreading him phoning. What would I say to him? Should I ask if he'd meant what he said, or should I just pretend it had never happened? If he said he really did miss me, how would that make me feel? Did I want him back or did I just want him to want me, as some sort of revenge? I lay in bed mulling these thoughts over, eventually deciding that I was going round and round in circles. I showered and then went to wake the boys up.

'Good morning,' I said as cheerfully as I could, drawing back the curtains. 'There's no football practice today because Mr Phillips has to be at the school fair.'

'Ooh,' Charlie said, sitting up and rubbing his eyes. 'I can't wait to go there.'

'Yes,' added Jack sleepily. 'Miss Whittaker said to bring lots of money.'

I smiled at them both. 'It starts at eleven o'clock, and we're going to meet Thomas and his dad inside the hall.'

'Yippee!' Charlie started jumping on his bed, quickly copied by his brother.

'Okay,' I said, trying not to get cross. 'Let's get some breakfast.'

*

'Wow,' gushed Jack as we walked into the school hall. 'It looks really different.'

It had been transformed into a market bazaar, with stalls arranged around the room selling what seemed to be anything from scented candles to books and home-made cakes. I glanced at the cake stall, spotting my offering at the back. I prayed it wouldn't be the only one left at the end.

Martin had suggested we meet for moral support as neither of us had been to a school fair before. While we were waiting for him I caught sight of Angela on the book stall. She waved and beckoned us over.

'There are some great books here.'

'Yes,' I said, picking up a couple.

'Have a rummage through and see what you fancy.' She smiled at Charlie and Jack. 'The children's books are twenty pence each.'

They didn't seem too impressed but looked through a few anyway.

'How's it going?' I asked.

'Trade's a bit slow at the moment, but it'll pick up.' She frowned. 'I'm a bit annoyed, really.'

'Why? Because you haven't sold much?'

She shook her head. 'No, because I wanted to run the Tombola – it's much more fun.'

I was confused. 'So why didn't you?'

She lowered her voice. 'As chair of the PTA, Helen Stevens organises who does what.' She nodded to her left and I glanced up to see Helen, smartly dressed and strutting round the room with a clipboard. 'She gives the best stalls to her friends,' Angela whispered. 'If you peek underneath their tables you'll see bags full of goodies, if you get what I mean.'

I frowned, not understanding.

'Oh, you new mums,' Angela said in mock horror. 'You'll learn. They pinch the best stuff before it's even put out.'

I wanted to laugh at her conspiracy theory; this was a school fair, after all. Thankfully I was saved by a hand on my shoulder.

'What have you bought?' Martin was smiling at me.

'Nothing yet, but I think I'll buy a book each for the boys.' I handed my money over and turned back to Martin. 'Ready for a wander round?'

We promised to visit Angela's stall again later and set off round the school with the boys to see what else was happening. We all laughed at Martin as he tried to hook a duck out of a paddling pool full of water. I smiled at Charlie's distress when he won a tin of hotdogs on the Tombola, rather than the selection box he had been hoping for. I was really enjoying myself when I realised I was being scowled at from across the room. Helen Stevens was glaring at me, and in defiance I took Martin's arm and guided him to the hoopla stall, where we all had a go.

We continued browsing and I was disappointed I hadn't seen Rob, although I knew he must be around somewhere. Martin suggested the boys visit Santa's Grotto, and they gasped as they saw the fairy lights surrounding the make-shift grotto in the corner of one of the classrooms.

'Miss Whittaker,' gushed Thomas. 'You look beautiful.'

Martin's cheeks turned crimson and he blinked several times. As he moved to one side I had a good view of our children's teacher and I looked back at Martin, raising my eyebrows. Louise was wearing a tight-fitting and rather indecent pink t-shirt, which showed off her breasts, a short pink tutu, pink glittery tights and high-heeled silver sandals. She was also wearing a pair of silver wings and her hair was flowing down her back, topped off by a sparkly tiara. I realised I was gawping and quickly ferreted in my purse for some change.

Louise looked down at three adoring faces. 'Are you all going to see Santa and tell him what you'd like for Christmas?'

The boys nodded in unison.

'Great,' she continued. 'You can pay fifty pence to stand next to him, or you can pay a pound and have a photo taken as well.'

Louise looked up and smiled at Martin and me. 'One of our PTA dads has offered to take digital photos of the children with Santa and print them all off during the afternoon.'

'That's a great idea for a fundraiser,' I agreed as we handed over our money.

While we queued up I peeked inside the grotto, and I recognised Rob immediately. I had to stifle my giggles at the way he looked, because one of his stick-on eyebrows was a little askew, giving him a quizzical look. His beard was slowly travelling down his chin as the glue wore off in the heat.

Thomas went in first and told Santa he would like a new bike for Christmas. 'One just like my friends Charlie and Jack,' he said eagerly, not recognising who Santa was. He was thrilled to have his photo taken, and I smiled at his naivety as I pushed Charlie forward.

'I've already got a new bike,' he told Santa, 'but I'd like lots of Lego.'

'I'll see what I can do,' Santa said, and Charlie smiled excitedly for the camera.

Jack went in next.

'Ho, ho, ho, Jack. And what would you like for Christmas?'

I wasn't sure whether Jack was frightened or overcome with excitement because he froze, unable to reply. I leaned into the grotto and prompted him.

'Jack, you said you'd like a Power Ranger action figure.'

Jack nodded and grinned briefly for the camera before rushing back to the sanctuary of the classroom.

'And what would you like for Christmas?'

Santa was looking directly at me and his smile set off a fluttering in my stomach. I felt my face flush. 'Oh, er, I'm not sure.'

'Whatever it is,' he said, 'I hope you get it.'

As I walked out of the grotto Louise gave me a side-ways look. The mistletoe attached to her tiara made me wonder again what her relationship with Rob was.

Martin smiled at me. 'Do you fancy a coffee?'

I fancied a stiff gin, but settled for a coffee in the school hall. We visited Angela's book stall, which was now doing a roaring trade. She winked at me and whispered, 'I've bought a few books I think you'll enjoy. I'll give them to you later.'

'Isn't that abusing your power?' I teased.

'At least I paid for them,' she replied indignantly, stopping as Helen walked towards us, closely followed by two of her posse.

'Take all the notes from this stall,' she said, handing a cash bag to one of the women. 'I hope you've done well,' she said to Angela, 'because your layout could have been better.' She turned to me. 'Perhaps you could offer your services next time. We're always short of helpers.'

I looked at her evenly. 'Of course – if you look after my children.'

Helen stared at me for a split second before glancing coldly at Martin. 'I'm sure your friend will help out.'

She left us speechless, and our moods didn't improve until Martin showed me Thomas's win on the Tombola, which was an out-of-date tin of corned beef.

After another round of the stalls Martin looked at his watch. 'I'm going to head home. Could you collect Thomas's photo with yours?'

'Of course. I'll give it to you next week.'

Charlie and Jack had found a friend each, and both of the mums said they would take the children round one last time. Left alone, I wandered back to the grotto area, smiling at the thought of seeing the boys' photographs. Helen and her cronies were huddled in a corner, sorting through the photos, and my stomach churned as I steeled myself for some catty comment.

As I walked towards them Rob came flying out of the grotto, still dressed in his Santa outfit. Louise asked him how long he'd be and he replied over his shoulder as he continued walking quickly in my direction. Realising he was about to collide with me I moved to my left, tripping over a plastic crate full of Christmas lights. Not wanting to land on the queue of waiting children, I somehow twisted my body, ending up face down on the floor with my legs straddled over the box.

According to the onlookers, Rob had seen what was about to happen and had reached out to grab me, but had stood on his Santa trousers, which were too long, causing him to fall more or less on top of me. I was vaguely aware of a flash and I looked up to see Helen with the school camera in her hand.

The next thing I knew I was being hauled up by anxious parents, and someone pushed me onto a tiny chair.

'Are you all right?' Rob was kneeling down next to me. 'I'm so sorry. I was just rushing off for a quick toilet break, and wasn't concentrating.'

'I'm fine,' I replied, rubbing my left arm and leg, which I suspected would be black and blue in the morning.

'I'll take you for a cup of tea,' said one of the mums I often chatted to, helping me up.

After two strong sugary teas I decided I must collect the photographs because the boys would be ready to go home shortly.

I returned to the grotto where Louise had thoughtfully put my pictures in an envelope. 'Are you okay?' she asked.

'Yes, thanks.' I blushed, smiling as I looked at the photos.

As I started to walk away, Helen and her posse laughed loudly behind me. 'Look at her face,' one of them was giggling.

'One for the school website,' another cackled.

I turned round and my eyes met Helen's, who snatched a photograph from her friend and strode towards me; a look of pure malevolence on her face.

'Mrs Dixon,' she said loudly. 'Don't go without *your* photo.'

I took it from her and glanced at it before stuffing it into my handbag, fighting back the anger as I walked away as calmly as I could.

I left the fair and took the boys to the park, sitting on a cold bench while they played. The wind whipped round me, biting the tips of my fingers, and I stuffed my hands in my pockets, thinking morosely about how Helen seemed to enjoy humiliating me.

Against my better judgment I took the photo out of my bag, forcing myself to look at it. There I was, splayed across the floor, my mouth open in surprise, with Rob across my legs. It belonged in a Bridget Jones film. I ripped it into as many pieces as I could, tears burning my eyes. I marched over to the bin, shivering as I dropped my torn-up embarrassment inside.

I turned and saw Mandy and Alicia heading towards us, so I quickly wiped my eyes and blew my nose.

'Hi,' Mandy said cheerily.

'Hi there,' I replied, trying to raise a smile.

'Are you okay?'

I smiled and nodded. 'I'm fine – just freezing cold.'

We sat back down on the bench and Mandy pulled her jacket hood up. 'You're not kidding – I hate this weather.'

I nodded. 'It might snow later.'

She peered at me. 'You need cheering up. Do you want to hear some gossip?'

I shook my head, thinking how much I hated gossip, but Mandy didn't seem to notice.

'We missed most of the school fair because Alicia had a dance class,' she told me, 'but we rushed in at the last minute and went to see Santa.'

My heart sank, wondering if she'd heard about the photograph.

'We were the last people in,' she continued, starting to giggle, 'and as we came away I saw Miss Whittaker spray herself with perfume and head into the grotto.'

I stared at her.

'I told you she fancied Mr Phillips,' Mandy said matter-of-factly.

'So what happened?'

'I don't know, but Mr Phillips came rushing out, looking rather flustered.'

I stared across the deserted park, thinking that my love-life was as barren as the trees, stripped of their autumn colour. I couldn't compete with the beautiful and young Miss Whittaker. I had made a fool of myself in front of Rob, and my depression deepened.

*

I couldn't sleep that night. I kept replaying what had happened, distraught that it had been witnessed by both Rob and Helen. And that damned photograph. How humiliating had that been?

Rob had seemed so genuinely concerned when I fell – and I was pretty certain he'd held my hand as I sat on the chair. Maybe he was just a natural flirt? It was clear that Miss Whittaker liked him.

Maybe he did like me? This sent a tingle through my stomach. It wasn't beyond the realms of possibility. I would talk to him about the boys when I next saw him, and I would try to judge.

The clock said two fifteen – I really needed to sleep. I rolled over, willing myself to relax. Darren popped into my head and I groaned. Why couldn't I just fall asleep?

He was home now, but why hadn't he rung, even if only to speak to the boys? Home – with Barbie and her swelling stomach waiting to greet him. A wave of nausea forced me to sit up. How could he have played games with me like that?

I finally drifted off to sleep and dreamed that Darren was dressed as Father Christmas, walking towards me with some mistletoe. As I screamed, he turned into Rob and we had a long, lingering kiss, which was interrupted by Helen Stevens telling me my cake was the only one that hadn't sold.

*

'Wake up, boys! It's your last day of term and then it's the Christmas holidays!'

My enthusiasm couldn't entice the boys from under their warm duvets. I appreciated that they were tired after their first full term of school, but I was proud we hadn't been late once and I was determined today wasn't going to be our first time.

'Will Daddy be coming again on Christmas Day?' Charlie asked me sleepily.

I felt as if my heart was being crushed as I looked at his expectant face. 'No, sweetheart. But he'll call you.'

I hated Darren at that moment, and I wished he could see his son's face, but I also hated myself. I had become passive in a struggling marriage and I hadn't spotted the signs that Darren had been unhappy. I should have put more effort into it; I should have listened when he wanted me to forgive him.

I kissed both my sons gently. 'Come on, it'll be fun today – lots of playing games.'

We arrived at school just in time, and then I rushed home to work on a new project. The time flew by and I arrived in the playground at home time in a much better mood, which continued when Kate suggested we get together over the holidays. Angela and Mandy agreed it was a great idea, and I was pleased I had something to look forward to. I loved my boys, but I wasn't too keen on spending the majority of the holidays with two over-excited five-year-olds as my main source of company.

I looked round for Martin and was surprised to see him at the far end of the playground, chatting to Rob. He walked over to join us just as the children charged out of the door.

'Hi everyone, have a good Christmas,' he said happily.

'Yes, you too,' I replied. 'Enjoy yourselves in Sheffield. Happy Christmas, Thomas.'

'Thanks,' Martin replied on his behalf. 'We'll see you on New Year's Day. I'll call you.'

Kate was looking back and forth between the two of us. 'What's this, an arrangement without us lot? I'm offended.'

I laughed. 'You can come if you want to. The derby game between Sheffield Wednesday and Sheffield United is being screened live on Sky. Martin has invited us round to watch it with him.'

Kate pulled a face. 'Yuk. No thanks.'

As we said our goodbyes again, Helen walked past with two of her cronies. She scowled at me, raising her voice. 'Smug mums are at it again,' she said.

'Makes you sick,' agreed her ally.

There was something different about Helen. Her hair looked as though it hadn't been washed in days, and she wasn't wearing any make-up. I dismissed it. This was such a busy time of year, maybe she hadn't had time. I had better things to think about, because I was intrigued as to what Martin and Rob had been talking about. I hoped it wasn't the "Santa Incident" and I decided I would quiz Martin on New Year's Day.

*

During the holidays, Sam minded the boys while I caught the train up to the Royal Marsden Hospital to visit Issi. I found her private room and tiptoed in, just in case my friend was sleeping. She beamed when she saw me.

'Oh, some company. I'm so glad to see you.'

'How are you?'

'Okay, I guess.' She smiled, sitting up carefully. 'Jonathan's coming later with the kids, but I was just starting to feel fed up.'

I kissed her cheek and settled down in one of the chairs next to her bed, depositing a pile of presents on the other chair. 'Magazines, fruit, chocolates – I wasn't sure what you'd fancy.' I reached forward and took hold of her hand. 'How did the op go?'

'Fine – I'm just feeling very sore.' She smiled briefly. 'They're looking after me well. Jonathan's insisting I have the best possible care.' She turned her head away from me, reaching for her beaker of water. 'I've got to have another course of chemo, though.'

My stomach twisted. 'Why? I thought this was just a precaution?'

Issi sipped her drink slowly and then put the cup down.

'The consultant did a scan before the op – and things aren't going as well as he thought.'

'Oh, Issi.' I instinctively stood up, leaning towards her with my arms outstretched to hug her but I suddenly realised it would hurt her, and sat back down. We both sniffed and smiled.

I grabbed both her hands instead and squeezed them tightly. 'When will it start?'

'About two weeks' time. I'll be having nine weeks of chemotherapy, together with radiotherapy, so I should be fit and well by Easter.'

'We'll have to plan something nice to do together.' I grinned at her. 'Maybe a health spa weekend?'

'That sounds wonderful.'

'I'll get some brochures and we can start planning.' I had a sudden thought. 'Or maybe we could go for your birthday?'

'Ooh.' Issi's eyes brightened. 'I should be well enough to go by March.'

'Of course you will,' I replied assertively. 'I'll get it booked.'

She nodded and leaned back against her pillows. 'I've been dying to hear about your Christmas. I can't believe Darren bought the boys a PlayStation.'

I shook my head. 'I was furious at first – splashing out on expensive gifts when I can't afford to. But...' I grinned at her. 'It's meant I've had lots of time just to sit and read.'

Issi laughed. 'Maybe he was thinking of you, then, when he bought it?'

'Hmm – I doubt that.'

She frowned at me. 'Has he been in touch?'

'He's spoken to the boys a few times, but he didn't ask to talk to me. Thankfully,' I added.

'Don't let him hurt you again, Becky.'

'No,' I replied quietly.

There was a moment's silence, and then Issi gestured over to the pile of presents I'd brought. 'I suddenly feel chocolatey. Shall we indulge?'

I ripped the cellophane off and had the box open in seconds. 'Bagsy the Caramel Square.'

Issi hovered over my favourite one. 'All right, then.' She picked out two and crammed them into her mouth. 'What else did you do over Christmas?' she asked with difficulty.

'We had Christmas dinner at Sam's, which was great fun, and then we've been out and about with the friends I've made in the playground – just to the park, really.'

Issi patted my hand. 'I'm glad you're happy.'

Her voice sounded drowsy. 'Issi,' I said gently, 'are you tired?'

She nodded and I fluffed up her pillows. 'Get some rest. I'll see you soon.' As her eyes started to close I gently stroked her hair and kissed her forehead.

*

On New Year's Eve I was happy to stay at home with Charlie and Jack, despite receiving several invitations to join friends' celebrations. The boys stayed up later than normal and we cuddled up on the sofa, watching Toy Story 3 on DVD with a family-sized bag of Maltesers. After I'd put them to bed I fell asleep on the sofa, to be woken up by the phone ringing at eleven o'clock.

'Hello, Becky. Happy New Year!'

I could tell my mum had been enjoying the celebrations. 'Happy New Year, Mum, although we've still got an hour to go.'

'What? Oh, yes – I always forget about the time difference.'

I laughed – my mum would never change. 'How are you

both? I did leave several messages on your answer phone over Christmas.' I constantly surprised myself by how upset I felt when she didn't call back.

'I'm so sorry,' she said quickly. 'Vicente and I went away. He told me to let you all know, but it was just such a rush. He's cross with me now.'

I smiled into the phone. 'Can I speak to him?'

'*Feliz ano nuevo*, Becky,' his voice boomed at me.

'And to you, Vicente.'

'Your mum – I have told her she is very naughty.'

I smiled again. 'Well, thanks for trying to get her to phone us.'

'I shall call you myself next time.'

I felt guilty when I put the phone down. I had been feeling sorry for myself, wrongly thinking that Mum didn't care.

*

The boys and I spent a lazy New Year's Day indoors, and then we walked round to Martin's house later. He had called me on Christmas Day to wish us all a happy Christmas, and to suggest we come round well before kick-off for pizzas.

The boys shot upstairs with Thomas to look at his Christmas presents and I handed Martin a bottle of wine.

As he took it he leaned forward and kissed me on the cheek. 'Happy New Year.'

It felt nice.

I followed him into the kitchen, glancing round at his small but smartly-kept house. He appeared to cope well with his difficult circumstances, but I wondered if his trip back home had been painful for him. 'How was Sheffield?' I asked gently.

'Cold. We had two days of snow, so Thomas and I went sledging.'

'That must have been fun.' I laughed at the image of it in my head.

'Yes. My mum and dad live on a steep hill, which was just perfect for it.' He smiled at me. 'Pizzas are in the oven; let's open a bottle of wine for you and a beer for me and watch the build-up to the match.'

Once the pizzas were ready, the five of us ate in front of the television with the boys sprawled on the floor. It felt cosy.

'Okay, kick-off time,' Martin announced. 'Are you boys watching or going off to play?' He looked as if he was hoping for the latter, and beamed when they ran upstairs. He topped up my glass and flipped the lid off another beer. 'Score prediction?'

I thought for a moment. 'Both teams are mid-table, but I think home advantage will shade it. Two-nil to United.'

Martin spluttered. 'Not a chance. We've great away form. One-nil to Wednesday.'

I enjoyed this easy banter and we continued ribbing each other throughout the first half, which ended nil-nil.

'Another glass?' Martin suggested.

I shook my head. 'Two's enough, thanks. Could I have a coffee?'

'Here you are,' he said a few minutes later, coming back from the kitchen and handing me a mug. He sat down next to me on the sofa. There was no awkwardness between us, and I half wished he'd put his arm round me.

It was a great game – fast and furious, the way a true derby should be. Wednesday equalized with five minutes to go after United had taken the lead. Martin and I were on the edge of our seats for the remaining minutes, and were emotionally drained by the end of the match.

The boys reappeared to see what all the shouting was about and Martin rooted through the freezer, finding some ice-cream which they ate at the kitchen table. Once they'd finished, Thomas turned to his dad.

'Can we have all the torches and go and play Murder in the Dark upstairs?'

'Please,' chorused Jack and Charlie, and Martin searched around in the cupboard under the sink, only able to find two that worked.

'Here you go – you'll have to share.'

Jack and Thomas grabbed one each and the three boys ran off, shouting loudly.

I made myself another coffee, and as I opened the fridge to put the milk back Martin brushed past me to reach for a beer. My pulse rate quickened as we touched.

Martin put his beer down and stepped towards me. He looked straight into my eyes, tenderly stroking my cheek, and then he moved forward to kiss me.

It was urgent and passionate and I felt his tongue exploring my mouth. He pushed me against the fridge, his hands frantically un-tucking my blouse, and as I pulled him into me we heard Thomas thundering down the stairs.

'The battery's run out, Dad,' he wailed.

Frustration flooded through me and I was just about to make a joke, but Martin's expression stopped me. He was staring at me as if he were seeing me for the first time. In that split second I understood how much he was still grieving for his wife.

He sat down at the table as if he was in shock, and I found some sweets in my handbag, which I thrust at Thomas, hoping it would distract him from the torch. He ran off happily and I sat down opposite his dad.

He looked at me, his eyes staring, but not really seeing. 'I'm sorry,' he mumbled.

Was he was apologizing to me or his wife? I winced at the pain he must be feeling at having endured another Christmas without her. 'It's okay,' I said, stroking his arm. 'I understand how difficult it must be for you.'

Tears sprang in my eyes and then Martin started to sob. He slumped forward, resting his head on his arms, his shoulders heaving from the release of so much bottled-up pain. I just let him cry.

After a while I rubbed his back and kissed his cheek gently. 'Thomas can come and stay at mine for a sleep-over. We've got spare pyjamas – I'll call you in the morning.'

Martin didn't reply; he simply took a deep breath and continued to cry, his whole body racked with grief.

*

I was taking a quiet moment to finish reading *Pride and Prejudice* while the boys were absorbed in a PlayStation game. I hadn't phoned Martin because it was only ten thirty and I wanted to give him plenty of time to himself. Selfishly, I was also enjoying my own quiet time. Mr Darcy was just about to declare his love for Elizabeth when I was propelled back into the twenty-first century by the doorbell. I was annoyed by the interruption and opened the front door quickly, with the book still in my hand to let whoever it was know I had been disturbed.

Martin was smiling at me. He looked fresh-faced and clean-shaven, as if he had slept well and woken up refreshed. I felt pleased for him.

He looked at the book in my hand. 'Sorry. I should have phoned.'

'No, no,' I said, feeling guilty. 'I've read it lots of times. Come in – the boys are in the lounge. Three guesses what they're playing.'

Martin popped his head round the door, but Thomas told him he didn't want to be disturbed. Martin shook his head and we wandered into the kitchen, where I switched on the coffee machine.

'Becky.' He stood at the far end of the kitchen, staring down at the floor.

I rushed over to him and took his hand. 'There's nothing to say. I completely understand how difficult it must be for you.'

He smiled weakly.

'For what it's worth,' I continued, 'I think you cope remarkably well.'

He pulled me into a hug and I heard him sniff. 'I really like you – and I thought I was ready,' he mumbled. 'I haven't slept with anyone since…' He paused and took a deep breath. 'Since Jackie died – and I'm just finding it all difficult.'

I freed myself and looked directly into his eyes. 'Of course you are – that's natural. There's no time limit on these things.'

He sighed and sat down without replying.

I grinned at him. 'Fancy some Christmas cake with your coffee? I promise I didn't make it.'

He smiled back and I knew our friendship was intact.

'I know what I wanted to ask you,' I said through a mouthful of cake. 'I saw you chatting to Rob Phillips at school. Was it about football training? Anything I should know?' I tried to sound as casual as possible.

Martin put his coffee cup down. 'Ooh no, much more exciting than that.'

My stomach tightened, thinking about that damned photograph again.

'He's asked me if I'll consider being a parent governor for the school.'

'Governor?' My mouth dropped open, spilling crumbs everywhere. 'Sorry,' I said, sweeping the mess off the table. 'That's great. Are you going to accept?'

'I wasn't sure at first, but he sold it to me by insisting that we *must* go to the pub after every meeting.' He shrugged. 'It will improve my social life – get me out a bit more.'

'That's brilliant.'

'There's a process to go through. I have to put my name forward along with any other candidates, and then people vote.'

'Oh, I'll definitely vote for you. You'll make a good governor.'

'Well, the reality is that no one else has shown any interest, so Rob doubts I'll be opposed.'

'I'm really pleased for you,' I told him, glad he was starting to rebuild his life.

Martin and Thomas ended up staying for lunch and then we took the boys to the park. Mandy was already there with Alicia and beamed when she saw us walking towards her.

'It's good to have some adult company,' she said as she shuffled along the damp bench. 'How were your New Year celebrations?'

We exchanged stories, and as I sat in the cold, watching the children laughing on the play equipment, I felt a calmness I hadn't experienced in a while.

*

'Thanks for having the boys today.'

'Thomas is so looking forward to it.' Martin smiled. 'What are you going to do with your free time?'

'I'm going to visit my friend in hospital. I'll call you when I'm back.'

Issi and I had been speaking on the phone daily, but I was desperate to see her again in person. When I arrived she was fast asleep, so I settled into an armchair by her bed and picked up one of the daily newspapers.

I was absorbed in one of the stories when I heard a croaky voice say, 'Why didn't you wake me?'

I peered at her over the top of my paper. 'Because I never get chance to read the paper somewhere quiet.'

She burst out laughing and propped herself up. 'The infection's finally cleared up and I'm going home tomorrow – so make the most of it.'

I threw the paper onto the table and hopped up beside her, putting my arm round her shoulders. 'That's brilliant news. I bet you can't wait.'

A nurse poked her head round the door and offered to bring us both a cup of tea, and we settled back against the pillows as if we were having a sleep-over.

'Tell me some gossip to cheer me up,' Issi instructed. 'It's deadly boring in here.'

I told her about Martin, not sparing the details.

'Nearly-sex. That must have been frustrating.'

'I can't tell you how much,' I replied. 'Thinking about it now, it was a ridiculous thing to attempt with three children upstairs.' I looked away wistfully and sighed. 'It's been a long time.'

Issi patted my arm. 'You'll find someone.'

She stopped talking as our tea and biscuits arrived. The nurse looked at us and laughed. 'Room for another?'

'Poor Martin, though,' Issi continued once the nurse had gone. 'He must have thought he was ready to move on, but he clearly isn't.'

'No, but at least we're still friends.'

'Would you go out with him? If he asked you?'

I shrugged. 'I really like him, but he was telling me that Rob's asked him to be a school governor, and all I could think about was that he would be able to give me the low-down on Rob.'

'You mean find out if he's single or not?'

I laughed. 'Yes.'

'Just see what happens, then.'

I pursed my lips. 'Also,' I said quietly, 'I know my friend Mandy likes Martin – I've felt racked with guilt ever since New Year.'

'Hey.' Issi grabbed my hand. 'It wasn't pre-meditated, it just happened.'

'I know, but doesn't it make me awful? Sluttish, even?'

Issi burst out laughing, spilling tea everywhere. 'I think it makes you an attractive woman who is just getting over being hurt, and who should be enjoying herself.'

I smiled at my bestest friend.

We finished our tea and chatted until we were interrupted by the door flying open. I just managed to grab Ben as he launched himself at his mum. I hopped off the bed and sat him on my lap while Issi kissed Andrew and Emma, who had followed Ben in. Andrew had blonde hair and blue eyes, like his mum, but Emma and Ben had inherited Jonathan's brown hair and dark skin.

Jonathan strolled in and kissed me on the cheek. 'Hi, Becky. Good to see you.' His face looked strained; he had a day's stubble and his eyes were sunken. His tall broad frame, which was normally so erect, seemed slumped.

'Are you okay?' I asked quietly as I stood up to hug him.

He winked and nodded, before moving across the room to kiss his wife. 'Finally my turn,' he said, laughing as he took Issi's hand in his.

I saw the unspoken love that passed between them and felt choked. 'Would you like me to take the kids home for tea?' I asked them. 'I need to collect Charlie and Jack shortly and they'll be glad of the company.'

Jonathan's eyes regained their sparkle. 'That's the best offer I've had all day.'

'They could sleep over, if you like,' I continued. 'Then you can collect Issi in peace tomorrow.'

He wound his fingers round Issi's. 'No, *that's* the best offer

I've had all day. If I play my cards right, she might let me sleep over, too.'

*

'Come on, let's go to the park.' I handed coats and hats to all five children, hoping they would let off some steam. Charlie and Jack, having being spoiled all day yesterday by Martin, were then allowed treats at home as well because I wanted Issi's children to feel welcome. The resulting sugar over-load had left them hyper this morning.

It was a bitterly cold January day, and as the children played I sat on a bench, staring at the lifeless trees, silhouetted against the grey sky. Everything seemed stark and bare, which seemed to be a reflection of my life.

When Ben asked me to push him on a swing I jumped up, forcing life back into my frozen feet. I was happily singing nursery rhymes to him as a man jogged past. He had a hat pulled down over his ears and when he stopped and stared at us I automatically felt for my phone. There was no one else around and I felt unnerved as he started to jog towards us.

'Hello there,' he said breathlessly. 'You look like you've got your hands full.'

As I gave him my hard go-away stare he took his hat off and I realised it was Rob.

'Oh, hi,' I said, hoping the end of my nose wasn't bright red from the cold. 'You're out jogging.' My brain seemed to have switched itself off in the cold.

'Yes.' He patted his non-existent stomach. 'Just running off all those mince pies.'

His eyes looked deeply into mine and time stood still for a split second.

'You look cold,' he said. 'There's a garage over there. Do you fancy a hot drink?'

'That would be wonderful.' I grinned at him. 'Thanks, Mr—' I paused, not sure what to call him.

'Rob.'

'Becky.'

He returned with two polystyrene cups filled with steaming coffee, and as we sat on the bench I prayed that the children would amuse themselves for a while longer.

'I didn't know you had five.' He laughed, nodding his head towards the noisy mob pushing each other on the roundabout.

'No – my friend's ill and I'm just looking after her three.' I didn't go into detail because I still found it hard to talk about.

He nodded, respecting this, and we sat side by side, sipping our drinks.

'Are you by yourself, Becky?' he asked suddenly.

I wasn't sure if he meant today, or in general. 'I'm just going through a divorce,' I said quietly.

He glanced at me and our eyes locked for a second. 'So was that your ex who brought the boys to training the other week?'

'Yes – he was over from America.'

'Oh. I wondered if he was back on the scene.'

Charlie came running over, interrupting us. 'Hello, Mr Phillips,' he said, as if it were perfectly normal to see his teacher sitting on a park bench. 'Can we go home now, Mum? I'm cold.'

'Okay.' I zipped his coat up for him. 'Go and get the others.'

Rob drained his cup and stood up. He looked at me for a second before lowering his eyes. 'I've been meaning to apologise for the incident in the grotto.' He spoke quickly and his embarrassment was obvious. 'I'm not in the habit of falling on top of people.' He looked up and grinned apologetically, his boyish smile adding to his sex-appeal. 'Were you badly bruised?'

'A little.' I smiled back. 'But nothing was broken.'

As he jogged away I shouted, 'Oh, thanks for the coffee.'

'Any time,' he yelled back, waving to me.

I stared after him, wondering if he meant that.

Chapter Eleven

Sticks and stones
May break my bones,
But words can really hurt me.

'Wake up, Mummy!'

Jack's shout, inches from my left ear, catapulted me from a deep sleep. I sat bolt upright, looking around me for a few seconds as I wondered where I was. Charlie, who had climbed into my bed during the night, stirred and mumbled something incoherent. He often joined me during the early hours, telling me he was having bad dreams.

I squinted at the clock. 'You're up early, Jack – are you excited about going back to school?'

'Oh.' His face fell. 'Can't I just play with my toys again today?' He clambered over me, yanking the duvet back to poke his brother.

'It'll be fun seeing all your friends again,' I said brightly as Charlie pushed him away.

'Get off!' Charlie yelled, hitting out at his brother.

'Leave Charlie alone,' I said, pulling them apart. 'You can go and play with your Lego for half an hour.'

Charlie followed him and I snuggled under the duvet to grab a few more minutes of sleep. It took two cups of coffee, half an hour later, to get me back into the school-morning routine, but we made it into the playground on time.

I had two new projects to start and by the afternoon I had emailed a sample copy to both clients in the hope that they liked my ideas. I needed a good income in January to cover the cost of Christmas.

The words were flowing freely when the phone made me jump. I was tempted not to answer it, but I always worried in case the school was trying to get hold of me.

'I know you'll be busy working—'

'Issi!'

'But I just fancied a chat.'

I beamed in delight. 'You sound much brighter today.'

'I'm feeling a lot better,' she replied. 'Just very sore still. I need cheering up with gossip.'

'What would you like to know?' I teased.

She lowered her voice. 'Anything happened with Darren? Has he been in touch since I saw you last?'

'He rang the boys last night, but he didn't ask to speak to me – and that's fine.'

'Oh, well. What about Martin?'

'We're still getting on as friends, but nothing more has happened.' I grinned into the phone. 'Guess who I saw in the park, though?'

I filled her in and she was excited for me.

'He must like you, otherwise he'd just have carried on with his run.'

'Maybe.' My friend's thinking was good.

'I could do with a good romance,' she said, laughing, 'even if it's someone else's.'

*

'Am I being talked about?' I asked Kate.

'Not that I'm aware of. Why?'

'I don't really know. It's just a feeling.' I glanced round. 'A few people have been chatting as I've walked past, but then they've stopped and stared and sniggered.'

Kate seemed distracted. 'I haven't noticed anything. Could you see Lucy in for me?'

'Sure. Everything okay?'

'I've got to rush off to the dentist.' She circled her finger round a swollen patch on her cheek.

'You poor thing – yes, of course.' As I looked up to find Lucy I made eye contact with Miss Whittaker, who appeared to be scowling at me through the window. I moved closer to where Martin was standing and whispered to him, 'Is Miss Whittaker staring at me? Don't make it obvious you're looking.'

Martin turned his head so he had a good view of her. 'Yep, it would certainly appear that she's looking in your direction.'

I chewed my bottom lip. 'I wonder what the boys have been up to.' I smiled briefly. 'Oh well, she'll let me know if it's serious.'

The doors opened and the children rushed in, but Miss Whittaker didn't appear, so I felt reassured. I couldn't shake off the feeling of paranoia as I left the playground, however, particularly when Helen and her friends burst out laughing as I walked past.

*

I was running late at home time and walked quickly through the playground, where I joined Mandy, Angela and Martin.

'Here she is, the scarlet lady.' Mandy smiled broadly.

'You're a dark horse. I thought we were supposed to share our secrets,' added Angela. 'You didn't mention anything at our book group the other night.'

Martin looked at each of us in turn. 'What are we talking about here?'

'I have no idea,' I said, starting to panic.

Mandy eyed me suspiciously. 'You really don't, do you?'

I shook my head.

'I take it you're not having a rather outrageous romance with Mr Phillips, then?'

I stared at her in disbelief, so shocked I couldn't reply.

'See?' Mandy continued, turning to Angela. 'I told you they couldn't have done *that* in the bike shed; it's far too small.'

She and Angela burst out laughing, but I felt hot and sick. Why was it always me? Angela stopped laughing and put her arm round me.

'Don't let them get to you. It's just Helen Stevens at it again.'

'How do you know?'

Angela stared down at the ground for a second. 'She and her cronies have been gossiping about some photo where Mr Phillips is spread-eagled on top of you.'

A second surge of nausea engulfed me, replaced by anger. 'I fell over, and...' I shook my head. 'It was nothing.'

'Don't let her get to you,' Angela said fiercely.

Martin's cheeks coloured, and he turned to stare at the notices in the classroom window while Mandy mouthed 'sorry' to me. I was thankful the children came out at that moment, providing the distraction I needed.

When we arrived home I was determined not to let the playground gossip spoil my time with Jack and Charlie, but once they were tucked up and asleep I lay on my bed and thought about Helen.

What did she get out of doing this to me? I dreaded walking into the playground in the morning, facing all those people thinking bad things about me. I threw a few ideas around – could I drop the boys off at the gate? No, they were far too young. I would just have to walk in with my head held high; after all, I knew the truth, and that was all that mattered. However, thinking this didn't stop me from losing my breakfast.

*

'Is it time to go yet?' asked Jack for the fourth time.

'Yes, Mum.' Charlie pulled his sweatshirt on. 'We can't be late for football.'

'In a minute.' I rushed to the toilet again. I hadn't seen Rob since the rumours about us had been circulating, and I wasn't keen on seeing him today. What if he had heard them too? What if he knew I fancied him and thought I'd started them? What if he fancied me? The thoughts tumbled round in my head all over again, but it would be unfair to make the boys miss their football, and I couldn't make them late either.

'Come on, let's get going.'

Martin had phoned earlier to say that Thomas had gone down with a stomach bug so he wouldn't be going training, and I had groaned to myself. Not only would I now have to face Rob without Martin to hide behind, I'd have to make my own flask of coffee as well.

I arrived at the field and deliberately avoided looking in Rob's direction. The boys ran off to join the rest of the squad and I wandered over to stand with a group of parents I knew vaguely. I made small talk with them throughout the session, peeking at Rob occasionally, and when the final whistle blew I stayed where I was, waiting for the boys to run over to me.

My stomach somersaulted as Jack and Charlie walked towards me, chatting to Rob, who appeared to be heading my way as well. He smiled as he approached.

'Mrs Dixon, I'd just like to say how well Charlie and Jack have done today – they're really starting to improve.'

Oh, what a beautiful smile he has. And weekend stubble. Is he going to mention the rumours? Panic set in and I didn't catch part of what he said. He stared at me for a minute and then carried on talking.

'Oh, and I just wanted to check Thomas was all right.' He looked at me expectantly, shifting his weight from one foot to the other.

My breathing regulated itself and I forced my mind to focus. 'Oh, he's fine. Just a stomach bug.' I returned his smile and as I held his gaze he took a deep breath.

He put a hand on each of the boys' shoulders. 'Could you do me a huge favour and collect all the cones up?'

Charlie and Jack ran off, leaving me with butterflies in my stomach for company. As Rob turned back to me his face hardened. This *was* about the rumours.

He poked his trainers in some mud before looking up at me. 'Miss Whittaker said she thought you were upset a couple of days ago.'

It was a statement, not a question, and I didn't know how to respond. 'I...er—'

'Her teaching assistant mentioned that there were some ugly rumours circulating.'

My chest tightened. 'Look, I didn't—'

He interrupted me again. 'Becky, I can't apologise enough for the embarrassment I've caused you.'

'Oh.'

'It was a silly accident, and I don't understand how things have got out of hand.'

'No,' I agreed.

He blushed furiously. 'I just hope you don't think I had anything—'

'Oh ,no,' I gasped. 'Not at all.'

He gave me his schoolboy grin and I smiled back.

'We've done it!' Jack ran into the back of Rob, almost

knocking him over.

'Oh. Well done, boys.' He smiled resignedly at me. 'I'll speak to you another time.'

Damn! I'd thought he was about to say something more. I chewed things over as we walked home. Did he apologise because he liked me? Or was it so that I didn't make a formal complaint? Oh, this was all too complicated.

Chapter Twelve

Pat-a-cake, pat-a-cake,
Baker's man.
Make up a story
As fast as you can.

I didn't manage to see Rob until Friday morning, when he was on duty in the playground. Our eyes met briefly through the horde of children and parents, but I looked away quickly, conscious that Helen Stevens might be watching. The whispering seemed to have stopped but I didn't want anything to start the rumours off again. It had been a horrible experience, walking into the playground knowing you were the main topic of conversation. I turned to talk to Martin instead.

'How did your first governors' meeting go last night?'

He broke into a huge grin. 'Really well, thanks. I'll tell you about it at football tomorrow, when we've got more time.'

As we said goodbye to our children, Mandy grabbed my arm and whispered to me. 'You're so lucky getting to spend time with Martin on a Saturday morning. I've tried to get Alicia to join the football team, but she refuses.'

I thought back to New Year's Day and was once again racked with guilt. I felt very sorry as I turned to face my friend and wished I could apologise. 'If you like him that much, then ask him out.'

Mandy blushed. 'He might say no and then I'd feel stupid.'

I looked at her sternly and raised my eyebrows.

'Okay, I'll do it – once I've lost some weight.'

I shook my head in exasperation.

*

I was looking forward to seeing Rob so that I could feel that little flutter in my stomach when he smiled at me. I had fantasised all week about him making love to me, and I wasn't entirely sure how I was going to stop myself from just grabbing him. Did he want to ask me out? I thought about the advice I had given Mandy only yesterday. Maybe I should ask him out? I toyed with the idea, but I wasn't even sure he was single. I would wait and see what happened.

I arrived at the sports field early. Several of the dads were already there, helping Rob to set out the cones. I had wanted to continue our previous conversation, but now I would have to settle for just watching him. He saw us arrive and waved across to me – or was it to the boys?

'Hi, you're early.' Martin grinned. 'Come to help put the cones out?'

'Just ahead of myself today.' I smiled in embarrassment.

'Hold the flask, then. I'll join you in a minute.'

I stood alone, feeling rather foolish, watching Martin and Rob chatting together. As Martin jogged back to join me Rob looked up and caught my eye, lifting my spirits.

I turned to Martin as we walked round the field to stand in our usual position. 'Tell me all about the governors' meeting, then.'

'Well, as you know, nobody stood against me so I was voted in, although I'm not sure how many people actually voted.'

'I did, and I tried to rally my friends, but not very successfully,' I mumbled. 'Angela and Mandy misplaced their letters and Kate forgot. Sorry.'

Martin shook his head, as if feigning disbelief. 'There was a complete mix of people,' he said, 'who were all very nice and welcoming. In fact, Rob asked me to join them in the pub afterwards, but I had babysitting problems.'

'Oh.' If Martin had gone to the pub he could have found out more about Rob, and in particular, whether or not he was single. 'I'll have Thomas for you next time – he can always sleep over,' I offered helpfully.

'Thanks, that's really kind.' Martin smiled and I instantly felt mean.

'So what actually happened at the meeting?'

'Well, we split into different committees and I was asked to join the marketing one, since I have some experience in that field.'

'That makes sense. So what do you have to do?'

'We talked about producing a leaflet for new or prospective parents, because Mrs Jenkins feels the school prospectus is a little wordy which puts people off reading it.' Martin lowered his voice again. 'I was amazed when the woman next to me told me that Thomas would be photographed for it. Apparently, all the pictures featured will be of governors' or PTA members' children.'

'Oh, I didn't know that went on,' I gasped, pretending to be shocked. 'I thought it was all equal opportunities for the children. I shall complain.'

Martin smiled. 'This is the funniest part, though. Mrs Jenkins came up to me at the end and took me to one side.'

'Oh, yes?'

'She told me that as a governor, I was in a position of power because I would get to know certain confidential information and I might find myself targeted by some parents in the playground.'

'Targeted?' I repeated incredulously. 'Are we talking Bracken Wood School or MI5?'

'I know,' Martin replied. 'I could hardly keep a straight face. She implied that people might want to curry favour with me in exchange for information, so we'll have to see what happens.'

We both burst out laughing, only to be told off by Thomas, who asked, 'Are you going to watch me train today, Dad?'

At the end of the session I wandered over to where Rob was packing away. 'Thanks for the training session – the boys are really enjoying them.'

'I get a lot out of it, too.' He stopped what he was doing and smiled back.

An awkward silence followed.

'See you soon, then.'

His eyes remained on mine. 'See you soon.'

When the boys were asleep that evening I had time to reflect on Rob, but after rolling it around in my head too many times, I gave up trying to make sense of it all. Maybe at thirty-four, with two young children, I had to accept that friendships with men would always be platonic. The good ones were probably taken by now, and the others would no doubt come with "issues". I wasn't sure where Rob fitted into this thought process.

Feeling a little low, I picked up *The Grapes of Wrath*, which had been chosen for our next book group meeting. However, I put it down again after two chapters – far too much misery and depression for a Saturday evening. I rang Issi for a chat, but Jonathan said she wasn't feeling too good following her chemotherapy.

'She's tired and has gone to bed,' he told me.

'Ok. I'll text her tomorrow and arrange to call round.'

'She'll like that.' His usually up-beat voice was flat.

'Are you okay?' I asked gently.

'Yeah – you know.' He let out a long, slow breath. 'Sorry, Becky.' He sniffed loudly. 'I just don't feel like talking.'

'I'm here for you both,' I told him, fighting back my own tears.

'I know,' he whispered.

I sat in the quiet for a long time, thinking about the impact of Issi's illness. Eventually, I flicked the television on to force the thoughts away, and made myself a strong coffee. I fantasised about Rob turning up out of the blue and declaring undying love for me, but when he still hadn't turned up after half an hour I climbed into bed.

Unable to sleep, I tossed thoughts around in my head about Issi, Rob and Martin, and eventually fell asleep dreaming that Darren was telling me I must stay single to protect the boys.

*

'Dad wants to speak to you.' Charlie handed me the phone before running off to find his brother.

I was surprised, because Darren didn't normally phone on a Sunday morning. We hadn't spoken to each other since his visit and I liked it that way.

'Hello?' I said cautiously.

'Hi, Becky. How are you?'

'Good, thanks.'

'Okay, well I just wanted to let you know I'll be back in the UK in February, so I'll call in to see Jack and Charlie.' His voice was casual and he clearly didn't want to discuss what had happened, any more than I did.

'Oh, right. If you give me the date I'll put it on the calendar now.' I was equally casual.

His visit was going to coincide with half-term for the boys. 'If you could entertain Charlie and Jack for a few days I could carry on working, which would be great,' I told him.

'No problem. I might take them up to Mum and Dad's.'

Our conversation was friendly enough, so I decided to be brave. 'Is Shelley coming with you?'

There was a short silence. 'No. I'll let you know the exact flight times next week.'

'Okay.' Oh dear, I'd touched a raw nerve. There must be trouble in paradise.

*

I drove over to Issi's house, stopping on the way to buy a selection of goodies for our lunch. When she opened the door I blinked several times at her short hair, stopping myself from gasping out loud.

'I know,' she said, touching it self-consciously. 'I'm still getting used to it too.'

I hugged her. 'It really suits you. Shows off those wonderful cheek bones.'

She smiled. 'I was lucky the first time round, but the nurse warned me it would start thinning and falling out soon, so this way it's less distressing.'

I held up two bags full of shopping. 'Lunch.'

Issi frowned apologetically. 'That's so sweet of you, but I really fancy leaving these four walls. Would you mind?'

I grinned. 'L'Olivo it is, then.'

I dropped Issi off by the front door of the café to save her the walk from the car park, and by the time I returned she was sitting with Nico, deep in conversation. He stood up as I entered.

'*Ciao*, Becky. Lovely to see you.' He kissed me on both cheeks. 'I've just been admiring Issi's new hairstyle.' He beamed at her. 'She's very brave,' he whispered. 'Now, ladies, I shall leave you to chat.'

I glanced at Issi as I sat down. 'Did you tell him?'

'It just sort of came out.' She blinked away a couple of tears. 'He was very sympathetic.'

I nodded and smiled.

'I've ordered us cappuccinos and cake. Hope that's okay?'

'Perfect.'

We spent a happy hour chatting about our children and life in general while eating chocolate cake, until Issi said she was tired.

I pulled the car up outside the café and she hopped in, clutching a small brown bag. I frowned at her. 'What's in the bag?'

'It's from Nico,' she replied, laughing. 'Apparently lots of chocolate cake is going to make me better.'

*

I was standing in the playground chatting to Kate, Mandy and Martin when Angela came rushing over.

'Hi, everyone.' She put her hand on my arm. 'How are you getting on with the book?'

'It's heavy going, but I'm enjoying it. It's very moving.'

'Yes, I know what you mean. We've had to re-arrange the date for our next meeting because Tina's double-booked, so you've plenty of time to read it.'

As we were chatting, an attractive mum with bleached blonde hair walked over to Martin, taking him to one side. Mandy noticed too, and grabbed my arm as we both tried to listen to their conversation. We just caught the tail end.

'So good luck with it,' the blonde mum was saying as she ran her fingers through her hair and smiled at Martin.

'Hold me back,' muttered Mandy under her breath. 'Look at her in her gym kit, with her tight-fitting leggings. I can't compete with that.'

Martin wandered back to join our group, still smiling.

'Who was that?' Mandy asked casually.

'She's called Sarah, and she was just wishing me good luck in my new governor's role,' he replied, trying not to laugh.

'MI5?' I giggled under my breath.

The children descended on us before I could explain, but as I caught Martin's eye I laughed again. 'Oh, how popular are you becoming?' I whispered to him.

*

'Come on, Jack, you're going to make us late for school!' I shouted for the third time.

'He can't find his other shoe, Mum.' Charlie ploughed through the closet, hurling odd shoes and trainers out.

'Oh, why does this always happen at the last minute?' I started throwing the shoes back in. 'Jack, I've told you to get organised the night before.'

It was ridiculous to ask a five-year-old to think ahead, but I was feeling tired and tense. I was worried about Issi and nervous about Darren arriving next week, unsure whether seeing him would throw my emotions into chaos. I was also sick of the damp gloomy weather.

'Right, I've found it.' I looked at my two boys' anxious faces and smiled at them. They were too young to have to take on all the stress I was feeling. I smiled positively. 'Only two more days of school, then it's a week off and Daddy will be here.'

The boys cheered and ran out of the house, leaving me to follow them, juggling their lunch boxes, PE kit and school bags.

We arrived at school in good time and I joined Mandy in front of the classroom window, giving Miss Whittaker a cheery wave.

'I'm looking forward to half-term,' Mandy stated. 'I've

enrolled Alicia in an activities club all week because I'm working for three days.'

'That's a good idea.'

'Yes, and the other two days I'm going to do nothing but relax.' She grinned. 'How about you?'

'Oh, Darren's over, so he's going to take the boys up north for four days – it means I'll have time to work, which is good. Like you, though, I'm intending to have some "me" time.'

Jack, Charlie and Josh Stevens ran past us, closely followed by Alicia, who was trying to catch them for a kiss. Mandy nudged me and moved closer.

'I know we hate it when people gossip, but I've got to tell you this because I'm worried.'

'Oh. Okay.'

'I was talking to one of the mums who had Josh round to tea last week, and she said how dirty he seemed.'

'Dirty?' I queried. 'How do you mean?'

'Well, just a little unkempt, and she said his polo shirt was grubby, as if he'd been wearing it all week.'

Mandy and I watched him closely as he ran past.

'He has got breakfast round his mouth,' I observed, 'but I suspect half the children in the playground do.'

'That's not all,' whispered Mandy. 'This mum said that when Helen collected him she smelled of drink.'

'Really?'

'Yes – and that fits with what you told us about why she lost her job,' she added slowly.

'It was a long time ago.' I shook my head and frowned. 'Surely she wouldn't drink while looking after her kids?'

Mandy shrugged. 'It does all make sense.'

I nodded. 'Sad, isn't it, if it's true?'

'It could be serious, Becky.'

'You're right. If it's impacting on Josh, do you think we should tell someone at school?'

'I don't know – it's only hearsay on our part. Perhaps I should mention it at parents' even—oh-my-God!'

I turned round quickly to see what the drama was. Martin was talking to the blonde mum again, and Mandy was furious.

'Look at "floozy mum" talking to him again. That's the third time this week – and have you seen what she's wearing?'

I looked closer and had to stop myself from laughing. The woman was wearing a short denim skirt and it was clear from the tilt of her head that she was making a play for Martin.

'That's it,' said Mandy despondently. 'She's blonde, slim and gorgeous; I don't stand a chance.'

'Oh, don't give up.' I tried to encourage my friend. 'She's probably a complete bimbo who'll have nothing in common with him. Besides,' I continued, 'she must be dim. It's February – her legs will be freezing.'

Mandy burst out laughing, but then stopped suddenly. 'There's Helen over there,' she whispered. 'What do you think?'

Helen was standing just to the side of her posse, almost toe-to-toe with one particular woman, who had her hands on her hips. Helen was jabbing a finger in the woman's face as she spoke.

'Gosh, she's upset about something,' I said. 'I wonder what's gone on.'

'It does seem a little heated,' Mandy agreed.

I chewed on one of my finger nails. 'I can't stand the woman – but I'm concerned about her children. I hope everything's all right, for Grace and Josh's sakes.'

'Leave it with me,' Mandy said decisively. 'I'll mention it at parents' evening.'

*

'Is he here yet? Is he here yet?' shouted Charlie and Jack on Sunday morning, slightly out of time with each other.

'He promised to come at ten o'clock, so keep a lookout through the window while I finish your packing.'

I was just zipping up two identical Spiderman rucksacks, which were crammed full of goodies and activities for the journey, when I heard a whoop and a cry from downstairs. I presumed Darren had arrived and checked myself one final time in the mirror before picking up the boys' bags and sauntering downstairs. I didn't want to give Darren the impression I was nervous about seeing him, so I took a deep breath and presented myself with an aura of serenity.

The boys had let their dad in and were busy trying to wrestle him to the ground when I appeared in the hallway. Darren looked up, did a double-take and then walked towards me.

'You look lovely,' he said softly.

My pulse rate quickened, but I took a step backwards, passing him the suitcase and rucksacks to avoid his kiss. 'Have you time for a coffee before you go?' I smiled brightly at him, trying not to give my feelings away.

'I'd better not. It's going to be a long drive, so I ought to make tracks. Come on, boys, give your mum a hug.'

They flung their arms around me and I held onto them tightly. I hated being parted from them.

They jumped into the car and I glanced at Darren. Should I kiss him on the cheek, or would that be misconstrued? He was hovering by the driver's door and he stepped towards me. I folded my arms across my chest. 'Have a safe journey.'

'Yes. I'll ring you when we get to Mum and Dad's.'

Our eyes met for a fleeting second and then I waved madly to Jack and Charlie until they were out of sight.

I walked back into the house and sat down at the kitchen table, suddenly tearful. Ordinarily I craved time to myself but now I had it I felt a little lost. I made a coffee and as I sat back down my thoughts drifted to Issi. She was now receiving radiotherapy as well as chemotherapy and the effect of both treatments was making her feel ill. She didn't want any visitors at the moment but Jonathan was letting me know how she was.

*

Four days later the tooting of a car horn made me jump. I saved the copy I was working on and ran downstairs to see if it was Jack and Charlie back from their trip. I opened the front door to find two beaming faces rushing towards me. Jack made it first, but shot past me shouting,

'I need the loo!'

I laughed and scooped Charlie up into my arms. 'Ooh, I've missed you. Have you had a good time?'

He hugged and kissed me. 'It's been brilliant. Can I go on the PlayStation?'

Jack reappeared at my side. 'Please, Mum. Granny and Grandad didn't have one.'

I was disappointed and frowned at Jack as I hugged him. 'Can't you tell me all about your trip first?'

The boys looked at each other before delivering their cutest smiles, and I laughed at their transparency. 'Go on then, just for a while.' I turned to Darren, who was standing in the doorway with a small suitcase and two rucksacks. 'Manipulated again. Do you want a drink?'

He dropped the bags and stretched his back. 'A strong cup of tea would be great. It's been a slow journey.'

I picked up the suitcase and carried it into the kitchen. Sorting through the dirty washing would be a good avoidance technique if Darren wanted to talk about his feelings again.

I put the kettle on and unzipped the case, aware he was

standing just behind me.

'If you're looking for dirty clothes, my mum did all the washing and ironing before we left.'

Damn. Now I'd have to talk to him. 'That was kind of her. Are they well?'

We continued to make small talk while I made two cups of tea. I opened a packet of biscuits and then we both sat down at the kitchen table.

'Becky.' He paused and my stomach dropped. 'The reason I'm over in the UK is...' He paused again, and as I dipped a biscuit into my tea half of it dropped to the bottom of the cup. I started to fish it out with a spoon and Darren snapped at me.

'Can't you just leave that for a moment?'

I was so startled I stopped what I was doing and looked straight at him.

'Sorry,' he continued more gently, 'but what I have to say is important.'

I put my cup down and gave him my full attention, fervently hoping the boys would come bursting through the door.

'The reason I'm over in the UK is for a job interview.' He spoke quickly, as if he wouldn't be able to continue if he paused again. 'That's why I was over here in December, too, but the company decided that particular role wasn't right for me.' He glanced at my shell-shocked face, clearly deciding to keep going. 'They contacted me to say they had a second, more suitable role, and if I was interested, the interview would simply be a formality, which it was. I'm now the UK Director—'

'What?' I spluttered.

'The UK Director—'

'No, no. I mean 'what', as in, you're moving back here? To Maidenhead?' The thought of Darren and Barbie living close by with their little prince or princess was more than I could bear.

'The job is based in Bracknell, so I won't be far away. I thought you'd be pleased.' He seemed crestfallen and I immediately felt guilty.

'Yes, that's great. Well done. Have you told the boys?'

'No. I'm going to wait until I've signed the contract. If all goes to plan I should be here by Easter.'

'They'll be thrilled,' I said genuinely.

'So am I.'

I stood up to make a fresh cup of tea. 'How does Shelley feel about it?' I asked with my back to him. When he didn't reply, I turned round slowly. He was staring into space. 'Darren?'

'She's...still getting used to the idea.'

After Darren had left I phoned Issi on the off-chance she felt well enough to talk.

'I'm feeling much brighter, thanks,' she told me. 'I could do with a good chat.'

She listened as I repeated the conversation I'd had with Darren. 'He's a bit arrogant thinking you'd be pleased that he and his girlfriend are setting up home not far from you.'

'Yes, you're right. I'm just going to try and see it from the boys' perspective. I need to join a dating agency and have a man in tow by Easter. That would surprise him.'

We discussed various ways for me to meet someone, reaching the conclusion that it was going to be a tall order to find a suitable boyfriend by the beginning of April. I felt much happier when I put the phone down, though – Issi seemed well, and she had agreed to have lunch with me sometime soon.

*

In the playground, the boys ran off to find their friends and I wandered over to join Mandy and Martin, who were deep in conversation. They didn't notice me at first and I felt a little awkward, as if I were eavesdropping on them, even though they were only discussing football. Mandy looked up first and blushed when she saw me.

'Hi,' she said, smiling.

Martin smiled as well. 'Morning.' A little silence fell between us until Martin broke it. 'Have you both put your names down for parents' evening?'

Mandy nodded but I looked blank. 'No. Was I supposed to?'

'Didn't you read the letter on Monday?'

'Letter?' I looked vacant again. 'I'm sure Charlie and Jack use them to make paper airplanes with in the cloakroom, because I never seem to know what's going on.'

Mandy shook her head. 'Right, you need to go into reception and sign your name against the teachers you want to see. In our case it's Miss Whittaker and Mr Phillips, because he's been teaching them Maths to cover for the teacher who's just left.'

'Yes, I know that,' I said a little defensively. I had read that particular letter, but I hadn't realised I would need to see Rob at parents' evening. 'If I go and sign up now, will you see the boys in?'

As I turned to leave, Kate came rushing towards us.

'Are you all right?' I asked.

'Oh, God,' she said breathlessly. 'You'll never guess what Connor's just done.'

Before she could explain, Helen and her side-kick Diana appeared from nowhere. Both were wearing long winter coats, but whereas Diana was in a skirt and high-heeled boots, Helen was wearing trousers and trainers, an ensemble which looked a bit odd.

'That was disgusting,' Helen shouted at Kate, and there was

a slight slurring to her voice.

Diana nodded at Helen as if dismissing her. 'Don't worry, I'll deal with it.' She gave Kate a long withering look. 'I'm sure I don't need to point out—'

'He's two, and he's toilet training,' Kate interrupted. 'I'm sorry he chose the nature garden to wee in, but it's a difficult time,' she muttered, lowering her eyes.

'Does anything need, er, cleaning up?' I asked Diana.

'No,' she snapped back. 'But the PTA put a lot of time and energy into making the garden and—'

Mandy stepped between the two of them. 'As Kate said, he's a two-year-old, and I'm sure she'll speak to him about his misdemeanour.'

Diana inhaled sharply and turned on her heels, tutting as she walked away.

'Thanks, Mandy,' Kate said to her. 'I tried to stop him, but when nature calls—'

'There's no place like the nature garden,' I finished.

We all burst out laughing, but Mandy whispered, 'Did you see what I meant about Helen?'

I nodded, feeling more than a little concerned.

I left them chatting and walked round to the school's reception, planning what I would wear the following week to parents' evening. I was just poised with the pencil in my hand, trying to co-ordinate both appointments, when a familiar voice said, 'Hi.' I spun round to see Rob rushing past me carrying thirty yellow exercise books. He mouthed 'can't stop', but gave me a lovely smile, sending me weak at the knees and throwing me into confusion again.

Chapter Thirteen

Mary, Mary,
Quite contrary,
How do your stories grow?

I wasn't sure what to expect at parents' evening and hoped everything Miss Whittaker and Rob were going to say would be positive, bearing in mind Jack's difficulties.

Sam had agreed to babysit, and she turned up early so I had time to get ready. 'Ooh,' she said, peering at me closely. 'You look tired – and grumpy. What's up?'

'Just the usual,' I said petulantly. 'Darren wants me to call him as soon as I get back.' I scowled at her. 'He can't have it both ways, Sam. He chose to move half way round the world. If he's as worried about Jack as he says he is, then he should be here.'

'Well, I'm sure he—'

'There's no 'well' about it,' I interrupted. 'It's always me who has to deal with everything – and sometimes it all feels too much.'

'Come on,' Sam said gently. 'You're doing a great job – and after Easter it will all be different.'

'I guess.'

'Go and get ready,' she said, 'and I'll bring you a coffee up.

And put plenty of foundation on,' she called after me.

I sat at my dressing table staring into the mirror. I could see what she meant. My tired face reflected my stress back at me. Issi's illness was beginning to hit me hard, because I knew I was powerless to help. Even when I had been at my lowest after Darren left I knew I just had to dig deep and things would slowly improve, but Issi's illness was outside my control.

I applied concealer over the dark circles underneath my eyes and then rummaged around in my drawer for some blusher and eye shadow. I chose a brightly coloured blouse and thought I'd made a good job of pretending to be cheerful.

When I came back downstairs Sam hugged me. 'That's better – you look great.'

Charlie glanced up from the television. 'You look pretty, Mummy.'

'Your face is all shiny,' Jack added.

I smiled at the three of them. I would make more of an effort in the future.

*

I arrived early and waited in my car, hoping to spot Kate because I felt in need of a friend tonight. After a quarter of an hour I gave up and went into the hall alone.

The teachers were sitting at desks spread with papers, and rows of chairs had been put in front of them so that parents could sit and wait for their appointments. I had a long wait between mine – I'd been so late in putting my name down I hadn't managed to co-ordinate both meetings.

I glanced round at the parents, who were mostly in couples, and felt I'd failed my boys in some way. I should be here with my husband, presenting a united front, but I hadn't managed to keep my marriage together. I sighed and reached into my bag for the romantic paperback I was reading to get some light relief from *The Grapes of Wrath*.

I'd only read a page when Kate sat down heavily next to me. 'Oh, what a nightmare I've had,' she said. 'Mark's working and the babysitter let me down at the last minute. I've had to ask my neighbour to pop in, but I promised I wouldn't be long.'

'You poor thing – it's not easy, is it?' I smiled wryly. 'I'll be here for ages – I could only get Mr Phillips's final appointment.'

The parents with Miss Whittaker finished their chat and Kate stood up. 'It must be me next,' she said.

Miss Whittaker looked up and smiled. 'Mr and Mrs Stevens, please.'

Helen walked past us and sat down at the desk alone. Her clothes looked a little crumpled, unlike her usual way of dressing, and her hair was lank and un-styled.

Kate turned to me and raised her eyebrows. 'She's not looking her best.'

'No.' I sighed. 'We all have days like that.'

After ten minutes Kate looked at her watch impatiently. 'They're only supposed to be five minute appointments. What do you think she's got to talk about?'

I shook my head, studying Helen's body language. She was waving her arms a lot as if the discussion had become heated. Eventually Miss Whittaker scraped her chair back and stood up, but Helen didn't move. The teacher looked in our direction and smiled at Kate.

'Mrs Jackson, please.'

Kate shrugged at me, but by the time she'd walked over, Helen had stood up. She lost her balance as she reached down for her handbag, grabbing the table to support herself. *Was* she drinking again? She turned and stormed past me, heading for the door.

Eventually it was my turn and I listened intently as Miss

Whittaker told me that both the boys were well-behaved, eager to learn and had good social skills.

'That's all we can ask for at this age,' she said. 'Jack's doing really well now, and although he still needs reminding about not shouting out, it's nothing to worry about.'

I thanked her and sat back down, quickly becoming immersed in my romantic novel so that I didn't hear Rob call my name.

'Mrs Dixon,' he shouted loudly, cupping his hands round his mouth.

I looked up to see I was the last parent in the hall, and I flushed with embarrassment. Rob was leaning back in his chair and laughing. As I sat down he rolled his shoulders and cricked his neck.

'It's been a long evening, but at least this one will be easy.' He smiled, looking down at his papers. 'Charlie is doing really well at Maths, and he's in the top group.'

I listened to him telling me how helpful Charlie was in class, but my heart was hammering. Would he be as positive about Jack? At home he seemed to struggle with sums, and I was dreading being told he had learning problems as well. Seeing his brother in a higher group would dent his self-esteem considerably.

'Now to Jack,' he said. 'He's in the top group, too. He's a clever boy – he just needs to concentrate and calm down at times, but that's all under control.'

Relief swept over me and without warning the tensions of the last few days and weeks caught up with me. Rob started to swim in front of me as my eyes misted.

He leaned forward, frowning in concern. 'Jack's problems are very mild. I'm so sorry – I didn't mean to upset you.'

'No, no,' I muttered, dabbing my eyes with a tissue. 'It's just…everything.'

Rob continued to look straight into my eyes, his kindness

making me want to break down and sob.

I stood up abruptly, feeling mortified. I looked like a mother who couldn't cope – not the image I'd wanted to portray.

I walked through the hall quickly and straight to my car, where I sat taking deep breaths. I closed my eyes, giving in to self-indulgent sobs, wishing once again that I had more support around me. My thoughts drifted to Darren, but I was interrupted by the sound of laughter as the school staff walked out together.

I quickly put the key in the ignition, not wanting them to wonder why I was still sitting in their car park. As I started the engine I saw Rob glance across at my car. He spoke to one of his colleagues and then strode towards me.

My heart sank. On top of everything else, he was now going to see me with swollen eyes and a red nose. I wound the window down and smiled as brightly as I could. 'Hi.'

He peered in through the darkness. 'Are you sure you're okay?'

'Yes.' I nodded, trying desperately to stop myself from crying again. 'I just needed a few minutes, but I'm fine now.' I smiled at him as I put the car into gear, and he stepped back without replying. Through my mirror, I could see him watching me intently.

*

'That was a good training session.' I smiled at Martin. 'It's great exercise for the boys.'

'Yes.' He smiled back. 'I'm sorry to dash, but Thomas and I are off to the cinema.'

'Enjoy the film,' I shouted after them, turning round to call the boys.

Rob was standing watching me and I felt my pulse rate quicken as he walked across. 'Boys,' he shouted over to Charlie and Jack, 'can you do me a big favour again and collect all the balls up?'

As they leaped into action, Rob motioned for me to sit down on one of the benches. 'Are you sure you're okay?' His brown eyes had such intensity, I felt light-headed. 'I'm a good listener.'

I suddenly poured my heart out, explaining all about Issi and my feelings of hopelessness about being unable to help her. I told him how she had been there to pick up the pieces when my marriage had fallen apart and how she had given me the confidence to carry on.

'Sorry.' I smiled weakly when I felt I'd said enough. 'I don't know where all that came from.'

'It's good to talk about it,' he replied. 'And it sounds like Issi is in good hands.'

'I hope so.'

'You can't do a great deal by worrying too much,' he said kindly. 'Just concentrate on keeping yourself well, so you're in the best position to help her.'

'You're right.' I smiled and shrugged. 'I just feel so upset all the time.'

He nodded slowly. 'I can understand that.'

We sat in silence for a few minutes until the boys ran over to us.

'We've done it,' Charlie shouted proudly.

'Thanks.' Rob grinned at them. 'Could you stack the cones as well?' He turned back to me and smiled shyly. 'Becky, I wondered if…'

My stomach tensed. 'Yes?'

'I just wondered if you'd fancy having a drink sometime?' The words came out in a rush, making me smile.

'I'd love to.'

'Great.' His face lit up and it was all I could do not to kiss him. 'I wanted to ask you ages ago, but I wasn't sure it was appropriate.'

'Because you teach Charlie and Jack?'

He nodded, breaking into a grin. 'I discreetly asked Mrs Jenkins, and she said it was fine.' He briefly took my hand in his. 'How about next Saturday? '

'That would be great.' My mouth was so dry I could hardly get the words out.

I walked home happier than I had been in months. He likes me. He wants to take me out. How was I going to get through a whole week?

*

That week I sauntered in and out of the playground as if I hadn't a care in the world, much to the irritation of my friends, who pestered me to tell them why I was so happy.

The words flowed effortlessly as I worked, I was approached by a new client, and Issi said she was feeling well enough to come round and have lunch with me.

'I can't wait to hear all about Rob,' she said over the phone.

'Well, there's not a great deal to tell.'

'He asked you out – that's a starting point,' she said. 'How about tomorrow?'

I understood my friend's need to get out of the house and be part of the real world. 'That sounds great. I was also wondering if you'd like me to have the children one weekend?'

'Ooh.' She giggled. 'A weekend away with Jonathan. I'll start looking at posh hotels.'

The good feeling lasted until Charlie announced that he'd been invited to Josh's house for tea the following day.

'You just have to arrange it with his mum in the playground tomorrow morning,' he told me.

My heart sank. If Helen was drinking, I didn't want

Charlie round there. Neither did I relish the thought of having a conversation with her, particularly when she was surrounded by her sneering cronies. 'Are you sure you want to go round, Charlie? I thought you said you didn't play with Josh anymore.'

Charlie thought for a moment. 'Well, he smells a bit, but he doesn't have any other friends.'

I looked at my innocent little boy. I would let him go, but would pop round on some pretence after an hour to check everything was okay. 'Of course you can go. I'll speak to his mum in the morning.'

I walked into the playground with trepidation, knowing I had to rise above all the bad feeling for the sake of Josh and Charlie. Helen was standing in her usual place by the gate and I wandered over to her. 'Hello, Helen. I understand Josh has invited Charlie for tea.'

She stared at me without replying, while the other two mums sniggered.

I started again. 'Is it all right if Charlie comes for tea?'

Helen studied me for a moment before speaking. 'No, I don't think you've asked me properly. Try again.'

The other two mums dissolved into fits of laughter and Helen grinned, clearly proud of herself. I clenched my fists and shook my head. 'Do you know what? I don't think I'll bother.' I stormed across the playground to where Kate and Mandy were standing, and started shaking. Charlie ran over and looked at me expectantly. I smiled at him. 'Josh's mum got mixed up with the dates. We'll try and arrange it for another day.'

'Okay, Mum.' He accepted my explanation and ran off to find his brother.

Mandy took me by the hand. 'What on earth has happened?'

I explained and the three of us turned to where Helen was

standing and glared at her.

'Nasty cow,' I said, close to tears. 'You know what though, I'm sure I could smell alcohol on her breath.'

Mandy sighed loudly.

'And that fits with what you were told,' I added. 'Did you say anything at parents' evening?'

Mandy nodded and explained to Kate, who raised her eyebrows. 'That's awful, but if school is aware, we'll have to leave it to them to monitor.'

'I'm so angry I'm tempted to ring Social Services.' I spat the words out.

'Don't do anything rash,' counselled Kate. 'Get your facts straight and then we'll see what happens.'

'You're right,' I replied, screwing my face up.

'This woman may need support,' she said kindly. 'I understand how hurt you feel – but don't sink to her level.'

Kate was right, but even after a brisk walk home I still felt cross. As I struggled to concentrate on my work my thoughts drifted to Rob, and I put the incident with Helen behind me, determined to regain my good mood.

Part-way through the morning the phone rang and my heart jumped when the lady announced she was the school receptionist.

'It's nothing to worry about, Mrs Dixon,' she told me. 'Mr Phillips asked if you would be free at lunchtime to call in and see him.'

'Oh. Yes, of course.' I smiled as I put the phone down. Gosh, he must be keen if he's making up excuses to see me.

I brushed my teeth and sprayed myself discreetly with perfume before walking to school. As I sat in the reception area I wondered what excuse Rob would use for seeing me. I was just fantasising about him producing a sumptuous picnic in his classroom when he appeared and walked over to me.

'Mrs Dixon,' he said formally.

'Mr Phillips.'

He didn't return my smile and I felt little flutters of anxiety in my stomach. These turned into huge knots as he lead me into the head's office.

'Becky,' he said, as he pulled out two chairs. 'This is a little awkward, but we received a complaint this morning.'

I stared at him, not believing what I was hearing. 'About me?'

He shook his head. 'About Jack, I'm afraid.'

'Oh.' I was completely thrown. 'I don't understand.'

He crossed and uncrossed his legs. 'Mrs Stevens, Josh's mum, has complained that Josh went home crying yesterday because Jack says he smells.'

I shook my head, anger filtering through every pore. Had this evil woman somehow heard that Rob had asked me out? Was this her way of spoiling it for me?

'I'm sorry,' I replied, unable to meet his eyes. 'I will, of course, speak to him.'

When Rob didn't reply, I looked up, straight into eyes full of compassion and understanding.

'There's something else as well,' he said quietly.

My stomach tightened as I continued staring.

'Miss Whittaker has told me there have been one or two spats between Josh and Jack over the past couple of days.'

I frowned at him. 'Neither Jack nor Charlie have said anything.'

He kept his eyes on mine. 'Well, as I understand it, Josh has been teasing Jack about…' He paused briefly. 'About not having a dad at home.'

My stomach lurched and I felt sick.

'Jack's been lashing out,' he continued, 'verbally and physically.'

I winced as though I'd been punched in the stomach. 'I had no idea.' I shook my head. 'Why didn't Miss Whittaker tell me?'

'She's been monitoring the situation, but she felt there was no need to call you in at this stage.'

'I've let Jack down,' I said, turning my head away from him. 'I'll have a long talk with both the boys tonight.'

As I sat there, aware that Rob was watching me, my whole body crumpled under a weight of great sadness. What a terrible mother I was.

I stood up, glancing over at Rob. 'Thank you for letting me know – I'm very sorry.' I paused, wondering if mentioning my worries about Helen would seem like a tit-for-tat response. I left it, knowing that Mandy had already spoken to someone.

Rob showed me out, pausing in the doorway. 'Jack will be fine, Becky. You're doing a good job.'

His kindness made me want to cry, but I held onto my tears until I got home. I dropped my bag in the hall and sat down heavily on the bottom stair, leaning against the banister. I cried for my boys, and also for myself. I guessed there would be no date on Saturday now.

Later that evening I bathed Charlie first before calling Jack up. I sat in my usual position on the bathroom floor, leaning against the radiator, and took a deep breath.

'Mr Phillips told me that you and Josh have been falling out a bit,' I said carefully.

He turned and scowled at me. 'Josh is nasty to me.'

'Then you must tell Miss Whittaker,' I told him firmly. 'Don't say anything back – or hit him.'

He concentrated on sinking his boat, before turning back to me. 'So why doesn't Daddy live with us?'

I smiled at him, even though my stomach was churning. 'Daddy and I both love you and Charlie, but—'

'Josh says it's because you hate him.'

I breathed in sharply, as if I'd been hit. 'No,' I replied, swallowing hard. 'Daddy and I are good friends; it's just that we don't live together anymore.'

'Why?' Charlie was standing in the doorway.

I wished I knew the answer. 'Because sometimes adults are silly and fall out with each other.' I smiled at them both.

Jack climbed out of the bath and I wrapped him in his towel, pulling him into me. I hadn't answered their questions properly, but I hadn't known what to say.

I started to rub him dry, but he snatched the towel from me, storming off to his room. Darren and I had really messed up our children's lives.

*

I avoided looking at Rob throughout training on Saturday, but afterwards he wandered over and spoke quietly to me while Martin was busy with Thomas. 'Would you prefer going for a meal tonight, rather than just a drink?'

'Oh.' I stared at him. 'I presumed that because of Jack—'

'I've thought long and hard about things,' he said, 'because the boys have to come first. But…' He looked up and waved at Martin, who was walking towards us. 'I'll talk to you about it tonight,' he said quickly. 'Shall I book a table at the Red Lion in Iscombe? Seven thirty?'

'That sounds great,' I replied. It was a country pub with an excellent reputation for high-quality food. 'I'll meet you there.'

I phoned Sam on the way home, telling her my night out was definitely on.

'Great,' she said. 'I'll pick up the boys for a sleepover as planned. What time is he collecting you?'

'I'm meeting him at there at seven thirty.'

'Oh. I thought—'

I knew exactly what she thought. 'This way there's no awkward moment when he drops me home,' I told her. 'I can decide how the evening ends.'

'Here's hoping,' she teased.

*

Sam arrived early and I made us a coffee.

'You look lovely,' she told me. 'Stunning.'

'Thanks – it's taken me ages to get ready.' I'd been up and down stairs while cooking the boys' tea, trying out different combinations of clothes before settling on a simple, yet hopefully stylish, dress. 'The boys are ready – we're just waiting for the muffins to finish cooking.'

'Muffins?'

I sighed. 'They made them at school yesterday and brought the recipe home.' I peered into the oven to check they'd risen. 'They wanted to make some more for James and Joe.'

Sam smiled. 'It's ages since I've cooked with my two. That's so sweet.'

I rolled my eyes and shook my head. 'Try doing it when you've just made yourself as glamorous as possible. I was terrified I was going to get flour all down my dress.'

Sam laughed and stood up to put the mugs in the dishwasher. 'By the way,' she said, 'Michael popped round yesterday evening.' She was grinning and I raised my eyebrows.

'With Sophie?'

'Yes. And from what Sophie told me I think there might be another wedding in the family this year.'

As Sam was talking the timer on the oven sounded and I opened the door to check the muffins were done, pressing a couple with my finger. 'That's great news,' I said over my shoulder as I reached inside to remove the tray.

I held it in mid-air as the realisation that I'd forgotten to put the oven gloves on hit me. An agonising pain spread through my hand and I dropped the tray, sending the muffins skidding across the floor.

Time seemed to slow down. I was aware of Sam running towards me and plunging my hand under the cold tap, and I had never been more grateful for my sister's medical training.

'Keep it under there for at least ten minutes,' she said calmly, 'while I get the boys organised.'

I watched the water running over my hand. How had I managed to be so stupid? The burn was blistering before my eyes and pieces of skin were being pulled off by the force of the water. I shouted to my sister. 'Sam, come over and look. It doesn't seem right.'

She calmly examined my hand and then spoke gently to me. 'We'll have to get you to the hospital. That's a nasty burn.'

'Oh,' I groaned.

'The boys are watching television but I'll put them in the car and drive us all there.'

I could feel the tears welling up behind my eyes, but I didn't want to worry the boys, so I bit my lip hard.

As we left, I thought about Rob. 'Could you phone the pub to explain what's happened?' I asked Sam. 'Tell him I'm at the hospital.'

'Okay. The Red Lion, wasn't it?'

'Yes, the one in Iscombe,' I replied, sighing deeply. Why did this have to happen? Didn't I deserve a night out?

It was a short drive to the hospital and Sam took me straight to the Accident and Emergency department, registering my details.

'It's very busy tonight,' she told me, 'so the best thing I can do is take the boys to my house and put them to bed. I'll be back here as quickly as possible.'

'Good idea,' I agreed, 'but don't worry about coming back for me – you've done enough. I'll get a taxi.'

'Okay. Call me later.'

I kissed the boys and was glad to see them leave because they were tired and becoming irritable. The last thing I wanted was for them to witness the drunks who would no doubt be in A and E on a Saturday night.

I was left alone feeling sorry for myself and in considerable pain, but Sam had reassured me that this was a good thing because it meant the nerve endings hadn't been damaged. I felt frustrated and stupid and passed the time watching the sliding doors, hoping Rob would come rushing in.

Eventually I was called into a cubicle, where a nurse gently examined my hand before calling the registrar.

'You've been lucky – you don't need admitting,' he told me. 'We'll put a gauze dressing on and see you as an out-patient every day for a week to have it changed.'

I thanked them and scanned the rows of chairs as I left, desperately hoping that Rob was waiting for me. Disappointed, I trudged along the corridor and shivered in the cold night air as I called a taxi.

I was relieved to be home at last and I collapsed into bed, tired but unable to sleep. How would I care for the boys? How would I be able to work?

*

Issi's dad pulled onto my drive and I leaped up, excited about seeing Issi. She had wanted to rush straight round when I had called her, but she hadn't felt well enough.

I automatically tried to open the door with my right hand, wincing in pain as I did so and then clutching my burned hand to ease the throbbing. I beamed at my friend, and Issi's dad looked from one of us to the other, shaking his head.

'Just look at the pair of you – it's like an episode of ER. Don't wear yourselves out chatting.' He kissed us both before smiling at Issi. 'Call me when you want collecting. Have fun.'

Issi was wearing a pretty pink hat to cover her now almost complete hair loss. 'Nice hat,' I said.

'Nice bandage,' she replied. 'Gucci?'

We burst out laughing and wandered into the kitchen, where I tried to clear the table with one hand.

'Here, I'll help,' Issi offered, moving my laptop. 'Have you been able to do much work?'

I nodded. 'Typing with my left hand isn't easy, but I can't afford to lose any clients.'

'Won't they understand?'

'Not in this business.' I laughed sardonically. 'They'll just go elsewhere.'

'You poor thing,' she said, putting the kettle on. 'Now, tell me all about Rob. Has he been round to see you with flowers and chocolates?'

My face fell. 'No, I haven't heard from him at all.'

'Oh.' Issi frowned. 'That's strange.'

'I know. Sam definitely phoned the pub and left a message.' I sighed heavily. 'Maybe he wasn't that keen after all?'

'Nonsense. He sounds lovely. Why don't you contact him?'

I pulled a face. 'I haven't had chance to see him because Martin's being doing the school run for me, and I can hardly leave a message for him with the school secretary.' I shrugged. I wasn't going to humiliate myself if he wasn't that bothered. 'Surely he should call me?'

'Mm, I can't understand why he hasn't been in touch, but you should give him the benefit of the doubt. Call school and leave a message for him to ring you – pretend Jack has a problem with his Maths.'

'I don't know.' I explained about being called into school. 'Maybe he just feels it's awkward. I'll wait a few days.'

Issi pretended to be exasperated. 'If you think that's best.'

She handed me a coffee. 'Have you been back to the hospital today?'

'Yes, George from next door has taken me every day to have the dressing changed – it's healing really well, so I should be back to normal in no time.'

'That's great,' she replied, taking a sip of her drink. 'Who'd have thought we'd have had so many hospital visits between us?'

'I know.' I patted her hand with my good one. 'The staff are lovely, but they're not pleasant places.'

'Particularly when you're by yourself. I wish you'd called me.'

'I didn't want to disturb you.' I stared down at my coffee. 'And of course I hoped Rob—'

'He'll have a good explanation – you just need to ask him.'

'I know,' I muttered.

Issi hugged me. 'How about some lunch to take your mind off things?'

'Great idea.' I smiled. 'I'm afraid it'll have to be pizza out of the freezer because I haven't been able to go shopping.'

Issi put our mugs in the dishwasher. 'I was thinking more along the lines of seeing Nico.' She raised her eyebrows and smiled. 'Do you fancy L'Olivo? I could call a taxi. My treat.'

Half an hour later Issi and I pushed open the door of L'Olivo to find Nico watching us with his arms folded across his chest.

'Becky, what has happened to you?' He threw his hands up in mock despair.

I flushed in embarrassment. 'Silly accident. I burned myself.'

He looked at Issi as he pulled out a chair for her. '*Ciao*, Issi. What am I going to do with you both?'

'Oh, I could think of a few things,' I whispered as he scurried off to get two cappuccinos without waiting to take our order.

I watched my friend laughing. She looked frail and tired, and I suddenly felt compelled to hold her hand. 'You okay?'

She smiled back. 'Just a bit tired. It's my last chemo session next week, so not much longer feeling like this.' She slumped forward, resting her arms on the table. 'Do you mind if we have our cappuccinos and go?'

Nico overheard her as he brought the drinks and gently touched her shoulder. 'I'll take you both home. Let me know when you're ready.' His expression said 'no arguing', and we gratefully accepted his generosity.

Chapter Fourteen

Tell-tale tit,
Your tongue will split.

'Thomas is here!' Jack shouted at the top of his voice. He'd had his nose pressed against the window for the last ten minutes.

I opened the door as Martin and his son were walking up the drive. 'Hi there.'

'Morning,' Martin replied with a grin.

'Thanks for taking them to football training.'

'It's not a problem,' he said. 'I enjoy their company – the three of them have been very entertaining on the way to and from school all week.'

I nodded, knowing what he meant.

'I've learned a lot about the other children in their class – Thomas doesn't normally tell me much.'

'Talking of school...' I grimaced. 'I'm still struggling to do things because I'm in so much pain—'

'Of course I'll take them again next week.' He shook his head, pretending to be cross. 'You don't need to feel embarrassed asking me.'

I was relieved. I had been dreading having to ask him again because I hated the thought that I was taking advantage of people. 'Thank you,' I said quietly. 'Once I'm better, I'll make it up to you. I would offer to cook a nice meal for you, but…'

Martin laughed. 'There's really no need. Right, boys, are we ready?'

I watched through the kitchen window as the three boys kicked a large stone down the drive. Should I have been brave enough to go along to the training session and face Rob? My hand was still very painful, and because I was trying to do everything left-handed I had fallen behind with my housework. I was hiding behind these facts so I didn't have to face the reality that Rob wasn't interested in me.

I busied myself around the house for the next hour and a half, and when Martin and the boys returned I hoped Rob had sent a message with them.

'Hi. How was training?' I tried to sound casual.

'Oh, just the usual stuff – they all did very well.' Martin looked at his watch. 'Sorry, I must dash because Jackie's mum and dad are on their way down to see us.'

'Okay. Have a good weekend – and thanks again.'

'See you on Monday morning.'

I was disappointed about Rob, so I tried again with the boys. 'Did Mr Phillips say you did well today?'

Charlie nodded and Jack looked up at me. 'Is lunch ready? I'm starving.'

*

I grinned as I walked into the playground and saw my friends waving at me. I rushed over to where Kate, Angela, Mandy and Martin were standing and the three women grabbed me for a hug.

'Oh, it's so good to see you,' Angela said. 'How's your hand?'

'I'm on the mend, thanks, but I haven't really been out of the house for two weeks – I feel like I've been in some sort of time warp.'

'Martin kept us updated on your progress. We all offered to help out, but he said it was under control,' chipped in Mandy.

'I know – and thanks for the flowers you sent.'

I watched as Mandy smiled at Martin, and as he beamed back at her it was almost as if I were intruding on a private moment.

'You haven't missed much,' Kate added with a grin. 'It's good to see you – it hasn't been the same without you.'

Tears pricked my eyes. I never imagined I would make such good friends in the playground, and I was really touched. 'It's great to be back,' I replied, my eyes shining.

Mandy nudged my arm. 'I've been keeping an eye on Horrible Helen. She's been rather quiet, actually, but that'll change now you're back.'

My stomach churned. That was the only thing I hadn't missed about being away from school – having to see Helen every day. I automatically glanced round to where she normally stood, to find her staring right at me. Our eyes met briefly before I looked away.

'Gosh,' I whispered to Mandy. 'She looks terrible – pale and gaunt.'

'I've been thinking that, too.'

'I'm worried. Has Josh been in school every day?'

'On and off, I think.'

The bell rang, and once the boys had run in I wandered home slowly. I was keen to catch up with some work now my hand was less painful, but I would phone Issi first to see how she was feeling. She'd had a bad reaction to her last chemotherapy session and although Jonathan told me this was normal, I was worried about my friend.

Issi answered on the first ring. 'Hi, Becky. How was your first day back?'

'It's great to be in a routine again, and it was good to see my friends, but more importantly, how are you feeling?'

'Oh, much better now I'm no longer being sick.'

'That's good.' I smiled in relief.

'I've got a scan booked for the beginning of the Easter holidays, so we should be able to get together with the kids at some point.'

'Yes, that would be great,' I replied. 'Once you've got the all-clear we'll book our spa day.'

'I can't wait. Sorry I don't feel like going for my birthday, as we'd planned.'

'We can go any time – it doesn't matter. Is it still all right if I come round on your birthday?'

'Of course it is.'

'I thought I might bring a picnic.'

'That would be lovely,' she replied. 'Not too much food, though, because Jonathan's taking me out in the evening.'

'That'll be nice – he'll have something romantic planned, I'm sure.'

'He will – I'm very lucky.' She fell quiet for a moment. 'Talking of romance – did you see Rob today?'

'No.' I sighed heavily. 'I looked round, but I couldn't see him.'

'So, did you pop into school?'

I sighed again. 'I've given up on him.'

'Why?' she demanded.

'Because he's had plenty of opportunity to contact me and he clearly isn't interested.'

'You don't know that.'

'Well, there's no more football training until after Easter, so I won't see him for a while anyway.'

'That's a real shame.' She paused. 'There'll be no man in tow when Darren comes back then,' she added.

'No, sadly. By the way, he's arriving on the sixth of April

and is renting a place just outside Bracknell – not too far away.'

'That's great for the boys. Do they know yet?'

'He told them last night, and it was all I could do to get them to bed.'

'I'm not surprised – it will be a huge change in their lives. Listen, I'm going to let you get on with some work. I'll see you next week.'

'Yes. I'll be over about lunchtime.'

'Great.'

'Ooh – I keep meaning to ask. Have you booked that hotel yet?'

'No.' Issi laughed. 'But Jonathan's definitely looking forward to it.'

'Get it arranged then!'

I put the phone down and thought about my friend. She must be feeling nervous about her forthcoming scan, and I was determined to support her in every way I could.

*

'I'm glad you're here early,' Martin said as I walked into the playground. 'I need to talk to you about last night's governors' meeting.'

My stomach somersaulted. Was it about Rob? Had he said something to Martin in the pub about why he hadn't been in contact? I fiddled with my scarf nervously.

'We had a meeting of the marketing committee and talked at length about producing a leaflet for new parents.'

'Oh.' I could hardly disguise my disappointment.

Martin ignored my lack of enthusiasm and carried on. 'Do you remember I spoke to you about it some time ago?'

'Oh, yes. Vaguely.' I hadn't really been listening to Martin; my thoughts had been elsewhere.

'Right,' he continued, 'the committee decided to produce a separate leaflet aimed at new or prospective parents, letting them know what to expect from school life. Everything from separation anxiety – theirs and their child's – to joining the PTA.'

I refocused on what he was saying, and I was taken by surprise by what he said next.

'We wondered if you would be prepared to write to it for us.' He grinned at me before continuing. 'There's a budget available, so if you could work out your fee we'll submit it to the finance committee when we have our full meeting next week.'

I couldn't believe it. I'd write it for free. Oh, how much I could get off my chest about what goes on in the playground. I doubted I could really include that, because it would put parents off school altogether, but I still felt I could produce a helpful leaflet by drawing on my own experiences. Thoughts were already flying around my head.

'Yes, I'd love to.'

'Great. I'll get it confirmed at the meeting, and then if it's okay with you I'll pop round one evening in the Easter holidays and tell you exactly what we're thinking of.'

*

I loaded the picnic hamper into the boot of my car, looking forward to the next few hours. I'd found a rug shoved at the back of the garage and had washed it with extra fabric conditioner to make it smell nice. I was determined everything was going to be perfect today.

I arrived at Issi's and was shocked to see how pale and thin she looked. I handed her a large bouquet of spring flowers and a tiny package. 'Happy birthday.'

'Oh,' she gasped as she opened the present. 'I love these

charm bracelets.'

'I've put five initials on it – one for each of you.'

'It's beautiful – thank you.'

Although the sun was shining, it was a cold March day and I spread the rug out on the conservatory floor where we would be warm and cosy. I grinned at her. 'Here, sit on these cushions and just enjoy yourself.'

'Okay.'

'We've got mini quiches,' I told her as I opened the hamper, 'your favourite little sausages, an assortment of sandwiches, strawberries and cream – and some naughty chocolates!'

Issi snuggled down on the cushions, nibbling on a sausage. 'This reminds me of when we were young.'

I nodded, passing her a glass of fresh orange juice.

'Remember how my mum always used to make a picnic for us on our birthdays?'

I smiled wistfully, thinking about Issi's beautiful mum, hoping this hadn't upset my friend.

'My picnics were always in the lounge, like this,' she said, smiling, 'but we used to race around in the garden for yours, as it was summer.' She looked at me and grinned. 'This was a lovely idea, Becky. We did have fun in those days, didn't we?'

'We still do.' I laughed, clinking my glass against hers.

She'd only picked at the food, so I passed her a bowl of strawberries, knowing how much she normally enjoyed them.

She ate a few and then pushed the bowl away. 'Sorry – I don't really feel like eating,' she explained. 'I'll be glad to get my scan out of the way and then I can concentrate on getting back to normal.'

'Have you got a date for it yet?'

'The letter came this morning – it's on the tenth of April, but let's not talk about that.' She smiled brightly. 'Jonathan picked up some health club brochures for us – let's have a look through them.'

We spent the next hour deciding where we were going to go and what treatments we would have, and then I told Issi about the leaflet I was writing for school.

'I can't think of anyone better to write it,' she replied. 'You're going to have a busy Easter.' She paused. 'How are you feeling about Darren coming home?'

I was silent for a moment. 'I don't know, is the honest truth. I've been trying not to think about it. I'll just see what happens.' I smiled at Issi. 'You look tired. Do you want me to go?'

'I could do with a sleep – if you don't mind.'

I hugged my friend. 'I'll be in touch soon. Concentrate on getting some rest.'

'I will, and thanks for a lovely birthday.'

*

'Come on boys, hurry up with your breakfast. Two more days of school left, and then you get two weeks off for Easter.'

'And Daddy will be home!' shouted Charlie.

'And we'll get lots of Easter eggs,' added Jack.

'Yes,' I said absentmindedly. I had put Darren's return to the back of my mind because over the past two weeks I hadn't really had time to think about anything except work and Issi. My thoughts automatically turned to her, as they did on and off throughout every day, and I texted her to see how she was feeling. I hoped she felt up to another visit and I was disappointed when she said she'd rather not.

We arrived in the playground and as I stood chatting to Mandy, Martin wandered over to join us.

'Morning, ladies.' He smiled at both of us and I noticed Mandy blush. 'Becky, thanks for your quote,' he continued. 'We're having a meeting tonight and then I'll come round and talk to you about it next week.'

'Okay, that's great.'

Mandy suddenly gripped my arm. As we'd been talking, "floozy mum" had wandered up behind Martin and placed a manicured hand on his arm, giving him a smile and a flutter of her eyelashes. 'Martin, I understand there's a meeting tonight,' she purred. 'I was just wondering…'

Mandy was hopping up and down on the spot. 'Right, that's it,' she muttered. 'If I don't act soon he's going to be snapped up by some predator. I'm going to ask him out.'

I stared at her in surprise. 'What, here? Now?'

Her resolve faltered. 'Er, no, not this minute. Over the Easter break,' she continued more decisively.

'Go, girl.' I was genuinely impressed and didn't feel in the least bit envious.

While Martin and the woman were chatting, Josh ran over to Helen. I couldn't tell what was being said, but when Josh came back to play with Charlie he was crying. I bent down and held his hand. 'Are you all right?' I asked.

It was still cold in the mornings and I was surprised he wasn't wearing a coat. He sniffed and wiped his nose on the sleeve of his jumper. He had a stale, unwashed smell about him.

'My mum didn't bring my lunch again today,' he said.

I was tempted to rush home and make a lunch box up for him. 'Make sure you tell Miss Whittaker and she'll sort it out.'

He nodded and ran off, but when I stood up I came face to face with Helen. She was standing inches away from me and her eyes were cold and hard. Her complexion had a grey tinge to it and her cheeks were flushed. 'Nosy bitch.' She spat the words out.

Chapter Fifteen

What's the time?
Ten to nine –
I'll hang your dirty washing on the line.

Charlie and Jack had their usual race downstairs to see who could be first to pick up the post. Charlie shoved his brother to one side and scooped up the letters, handing them to me.

'There you are, Mum,' he said, giving me his sweetest smile.

Jack followed us into the kitchen, rubbing his arm. 'He pushed me – it wasn't fair.'

I sent them out into the garden to run off some energy and sifted through the post. There was the usual scattering of junk mail and bills, but in amongst these was a hand-written envelope postmarked London. I ripped it open and read the letter, sitting down to re-read it more slowly. It was from Rob and was a little garbled, as if he had written it in a hurry.

Dear Becky,

I'm just off to Corfu and need to say some things to you before I leave. I've written this letter so many times, but I don't really know where to start. I'm at the airport now and this is my last chance.

I saw Martin at the governors' meeting last night and when we were having a drink afterwards he told me you'd had an accident doing some cooking. I waited for over an hour at the pub, feeling foolish. It never occurred to me that you'd been hurt, and now I feel ashamed of dwelling on my own misery – unfortunately I carry lots of baggage, but that's my problem, not yours.

The flowers I bought to give you have wilted, so please give me the excuse to buy some more. I booked this holiday with my friends to escape from my self-inflicted despair and now I wish more than anything that I was staying at home! Please could we try again when I get back?

So sorry, Becky – I still don't understand why you didn't tell me, but I'll call round when I get back next week so we can talk. Hope your hand is mending,

Rob x

My heart skipped a beat as I read his words and a surge of adrenalin rocketed through me, making me feel light-headed. He liked me. He clearly hadn't been given Sam's message and he wanted another chance. All that time I'd wasted thinking he wasn't interested in me, and I'd been wrong. He liked me.

I was grinning like a teenager in the first flush of love as I picked up the phone to call Issi.

*

I was still on a high when Martin came round on Thursday evening to talk about the school leaflet. As I put the kettle on he sat down at the kitchen table, and when I turned round with two mugs of tea he was studying me.

'You seem happy. Have you enjoyed the first week of the holidays?'

I didn't want to tell him about Rob, just in case his feelings changed while he was in Corfu. I still couldn't believe he wanted to see me. 'Yes.' I smiled back. 'We've seen Kate and Mandy, and I've even managed to get some work done. How about you?'

'I'm working all week. My mum and dad are here spending some time with Thomas and they're all having a great time.'

'They'll no doubt be spoiling him.'

'Yes,' he agreed. 'I'm taking next Thursday and Friday off when they go home – and it will be normal service resumed!'

I laughed. 'If you fancy getting the boys together, let me know.'

'Okay,' he replied. 'That sounds good.' He took a sip of his tea and then spread his papers out in front of him. 'This is what we had in mind – generally speaking, a parent-friendly guide to starting at the school.'

'Great. I was thinking of suggesting a new parent mentoring scheme, just until they find their feet. Perhaps introduce them to a few people so they don't have that awful "where do I stand?" feeling in the playground.'

'That's a good idea,' agreed Martin. 'I'll add it in. We also thought…'

I didn't listen to what he said next. I couldn't stop thinking about Rob – imagining him lying on a beach, wishing I was there with him; wishing he was here with me. Martin finished talking and looked at me.

'Is that all right, then?'

I refocused, squinting at the papers. 'Absolutely fine.' I smiled. 'I've a few projects on the go, but then I'll get started.'

He stood up as if to leave. 'Thanks. I'll push off now. Are you doing anything exciting for the Easter weekend?'

I paused before replying. I hadn't told anyone about Darren coming home because I was still trying to come to terms with it myself, but it would soon be common knowledge.

'Darren's coming home tomorrow.' I automatically folded my arms across my chest.

'Oh,' he said, sitting back down and frowning at me. 'Just for the holidays?'

I looked straight at him. 'No. For good.'

'Oh.'

'He's taken a new job over here, and he and his girlfriend will be living not too far away.'

He smiled at me sympathetically. 'I bet the boys are thrilled.'

'Yes.' I smiled back, knowing I was being selfish. 'It'll be great for them. They're so excited it took me ages to get them settled tonight. He's coming over tomorrow morning, by which time they'll be completely hyper.'

Martin laughed and stood up to leave, pausing in the doorway. 'By the way, I had a pint with Rob Phillips the other night. He was very concerned about your hand.'

I felt myself blushing. 'Oh?'

Martin raised one eyebrow and I could tell he was trying not to smirk. 'Whenever we have a drink, the conversation always turns to you. If I didn't know better I'd say he fancied you.'

I smiled coyly without responding.

Martin tutted loudly. 'I'm beginning to think the only reason he asked me to be a governor was to pump me for information about you.' He walked towards me and looked directly into my eyes. 'Are you two…?'

He let the words hang there and I couldn't tell if he was pleased or jealous.

'No,' I replied, 'but, well…' I shrugged noncommittally, and I couldn't read his expression as he left.

After he'd gone I sat alone thinking about Darren. I was nervous about seeing him again, but I hoped he wouldn't want to try anything now that Barbie was over here as well. I wondered if they would both be coming tomorrow.

I thought about Rob's letter and Martin's comments, causing my stomach to churn in excitement. I couldn't wait to see Rob. I had so many scenarios in my head – different things I would say, or he would say – but they always ended with us making love.

*

I was catching up with some work when Jack shouted from downstairs. 'Mum, Daddy's here!'

I checked my watch and smiled. He wasn't due for another hour – he must be so excited about seeing the boys. I ran downstairs and was relieved to find Darren standing alone in the hall, fighting off his sons.

I frowned at him. 'You're early.'

'Yes,' he said, offering no explanation.

'Charlie and Jack aren't dressed yet. Are you in a hurry?'

'No.' He blushed and lowered his voice. 'Actually, I came early so I could have a quiet word with you.'

I froze. I didn't know what he wanted to talk about, but it seemed important. Maybe it was to do with custody now he was back?

He turned to the boys. 'Go and get dressed – then maybe we'll go to Legoland?'

The boys let out huge whoops and ran upstairs.

I glanced at Darren. 'Do you want a cup of tea?'

He nodded and followed me into the kitchen. As I filled the kettle I tried to keep the conversation light to hide my worries. 'Good journey?'

He was staring out at the back garden and didn't seem to hear me.

I handed him his tea and we sat down opposite each other

at the table. He seemed uptight and took several sips of his tea before speaking.

'I'm staying in a rented house in Bracknell while I house-hunt,' he said, passing me a piece of paper. 'This is the address and phone number. Once I've bought somewhere I'll set up a proper bedroom for Charlie and Jack so they can sleep over at weekends.'

I was still worried that this was about custody, but I smiled at him. 'That's a great idea. They've missed having you around – it will be good for you to bond again.'

'I can't wait.' He sipped his tea without looking at me. 'I was a fool to move so far away.'

'Yes, it was selfish. It'll be great for me to have someone to share the load.'

He nodded, still unable to meet my eyes.

I felt a tinge of guilt; that last remark had been uncalled for. Darren was trying to make amends for being an absent father, but I couldn't quite get over the bitterness of his desertion.

'What about Shelley and the new baby?' I asked. 'I hope the boys are going to get an equal share of your time.'

There was a long pause before Darren spoke. He inhaled deeply, as if summoning up the courage to say something important. 'It was all a lie. There never was a baby.' He spoke quickly, glancing at me and then away again. 'She made it up because I told her I was still in love with you and I wanted to go home.' He stared down at the table. 'We've split up and I'm very, very sorry for what I've done to you and the boys.' He glanced up at me and I saw the pain in his eyes; I saw how truly sorry he was. 'Say something, Becky.' He was close to tears.

I was having difficulty taking it all in, and I certainly didn't know how I felt. I simply stared at him. 'I don't know what to say.'

He took hold of my hands. 'Take your time, Becky. I just

want you to remember how good we were together, and how good it can be again.'

I pulled my hands away. He was right, but what about Rob?

'It would be brilliant to be back together – as a family,' he whispered.

I stood up slowly, suddenly feeling dizzy. 'I need time to think.'

'Of course.'

'I'll just see to Charlie and Jack.' I went upstairs and sat on my bed, starting to shake. Was he serious? Did he really think he could just walk back into my life as if nothing had happened? I began to feel angry, and what made it worse was that I knew I'd give his suggestion some serious thought.

*

I woke up with a slight hangover, still feeling cross and confused. I'd been so agitated after Darren's visit, I had opened a bottle of wine later that night and drunk more than I'd intended.

I showered and managed to eat some breakfast, sitting down at the table with Charlie and Jack.

'Mum?' Charlie said as he poured cereal into his bowl, managing to spill most of it on the table. 'Will Daddy be living with us?'

I stood up, taking my bowl to the sink. Had Darren said anything to them?

'He's got a different house, silly,' Jack shouted at him. 'He's not allowed to live here.'

I felt sick. Why hadn't Darren and I tried harder to spare the boys all this uncertainty? I smiled at them both brightly. 'Dad's going to live not too far away. He'll always be welcome here, and we'll see lots of him.'

I sighed. Would my life be easier if Darren moved back? But I knew it wasn't that straightforward. It would be one thing having someone to help me with the boys, but it would be quite another spending my life with someone I wasn't sure I could really love or trust again.

I was clearing the dishes away when the doorbell rang. I hoped it wasn't Darren and I opened the door cautiously, gasping when I saw Rob standing there. My heart leaped with such force, he must have been able to see it thumping.

He was wearing jeans and a white t-shirt that showed off his tan. We just stared at each other before I broke into a huge grin. 'It's good to see you.'

He stepped forward and grinned back. 'You got my letter then?'

I nodded.

'Sorry it was so short,' he said. 'I did write several longer ones.' He paused and looked directly into my eyes. 'I poured my heart out about how stupid I've been, but they all got posted in the bin. I thought I'd tell you in person.' He looked towards my bandaged hand and stepped closer. 'I didn't realise what happened that night. I thought I'd been stood up, and I went home feeling stupid and devastated. If it hadn't been for Martin...' He frowned at me. 'Why didn't you tell me?'

I blushed in embarrassment. 'We were in such a hurry to get to the hospital, but I know Sam phoned the pub. I can't understand why you didn't get the message.'

He shrugged. 'There are lots of pubs called the Red Lion. Maybe she phoned the wrong one?'

'Yes. It was all a bit frantic at the time.' I glanced up at him and then stared down at the floor. 'I just assumed you weren't really interested when you didn't call me.'

'Not interested?' He moved closer still and gently brushed a strand of hair from my face. 'I fancied you the first moment I saw you.'

My cheeks turned crimson and I giggled like a sixteen-year-old. 'Likewise.'

'So where do we go from here?' he asked. 'Would you let me take you out for dinner again?'

'Only if you promise not to bring your holiday photos.'

We both laughed and I thought how comfortable I felt with him.

'Do you want to come inside?'

'I'd better not,' he said. 'I'd like to spend some time with you, but I don't want to confuse Charlie and Jack.'

'Okay. I'll give you my phone numbers and we can speak later.'

He entered the numbers into his phone and then just stood looking at me. Without warning he pulled me into him and whispered, 'You're so beautiful.' Suddenly we were kissing. Slowly, gently, melting into each other, the electricity between us pulsing up and down my body. Eventually I stood back, grabbing the door frame, my legs having turned to jelly.

'I can't wait to see you again,' he said kissing the tip of my nose. He sauntered down the drive, turning at the bottom to wave. His smile mirrored mine.

I stood for a moment taking in what had just happened, and then surprised the boys by singing loudly as I loaded the dishwasher.

*

Issi had invited us over. To prepare the boys for the shock of seeing her without hair, I explained that she had been unwell. As it turned out my worries were unfounded – Jack and Charlie glanced up at her and then ran off to find their friends without passing comment.

I hugged Issi, who was still looking pale and tired. 'If this gets too much for you, just say and we'll leave.'

Jonathan joined us, kissing me on both cheeks. 'Hi, Becky.' The stress of Issi's illness was clearly etched across his face. 'I'm off all week, so I'll keep the troops entertained. Issi's been looking forward to seeing you.'

'I'm so nervous about the scan tomorrow,' she said, biting one of her fingernails. 'I'm relying on you taking my mind off things.'

'That's what I'm here for,' I replied, laughing.

'Let's go into the conservatory, and then I want to hear everything, starting with Darren.'

I chuckled at my friend's direct approach. 'Okay,' I said, once we were settled. 'In a nutshell – Barbie was never pregnant. He's now dumped her and has declared his undying love for me.'

As Issi's jaw dropped open Jonathan popped his head round the door to check if we needed anything.

'We'll need coffee and cake,' his wife instructed. 'This is going to be a long session.'

I slowly related the whole story to my incredulous friend. When I'd finished, Issi shook her head.

'So what are you going to do?'

I shrugged. 'I don't know. I still have feelings for him and he's the boys' father – it makes sense to play happy families.'

'But?'

I beamed at her. 'I now need to tell you about Rob.'

'Good grief, Becky, I'm going to need a lie down after this.'

I paused as Jonathan appeared with a tray. He passed Issi a coffee and a sliver of cake, tenderly taking the throw off one of the sofas and wrapping it round her shoulders.

I ate some of my cake before continuing. 'I told you what he said in his letter.'

Issi nodded.

'Well, he just turned up on Saturday. Good job I looked

half decent.' I told her about his visit in detail, and by the end Issi's smile matched mine.

'Ooh, I feel all warm and tingly. What a lovely dilemma to have. My advice would be to go out with Rob and have some fun and romance in your life.' She wagged her finger at me. 'Darren caused you so much pain. You don't have to do the "right" thing.'

'I know,' I replied with a sigh. 'If it was just about me the decision would be easy, but the boys have to come first. I've got a lot of thinking to do.'

'I'm always here for you, you know that.'

'Thanks,' I said, taking her untouched cake from her. 'You look really tired now. Shall we go?'

'I wouldn't mind an hour in bed. I go back for my scan results on Wednesday morning, so I'll call you when I get home.'

'Are your dad and Maureen having the children?'

'They're coming over tomorrow, but Dad's not sure about Wednesday. Maureen has a hospital appointment as well, but they're trying to re-arrange it.'

'I'll look after them,' I told her. 'I want to do something. I'll come over here to save you dropping the kids off and then I'll cook us all something nice for lunch – to celebrate.' I hugged my friend. 'Thanks for listening to all my problems. I'll see you on Wednesday.'

*

I drove across to Issi's feeling anxious for my friend, knowing how worried she was. She was calmly doing a jigsaw with Ben when I arrived, but Jonathan was tense and jumpy.

'I don't know what time we'll be back,' he told me. 'Sometimes you have to wait for ages.'

'It's not a problem. I've brought some food – I'll make

lunch for the kids.' I looked round at the immaculate house. 'Can I do some ironing or put some washing on?'

He smiled for the first time. 'Maureen did it all yesterday. It's like living in a hotel – I'll almost be glad to get back to normal.' He glanced up at the clock. 'Shall we go, Issi?'

I put my arms round my friend. 'Good luck,' I whispered.

I spent the morning doing puzzles with Ben, and then baked fairy cakes with him and Emma while Charlie and Jack played with Andrew. My stomach was wound into tight knots as I listened out for the sound of Jonathan's car.

I was just in the middle of preparing the children's lunch when the front door banged. I waited for Issi and Jonathan to come rushing into the kitchen, but it was Jonathan who poked his head round the door. His face was ashen and his eyes were expressionless.

'Can you give us some time?' he asked.

I nodded, too stunned to reply, thankful the children were in the garden and hadn't seen them come home. I kept them occupied during lunch, desperately trying to stop myself from thinking the worst.

Eventually Jonathan reappeared, walking across the kitchen to hug his children. He glanced over at me. 'Can you pop up and see her?' His voice was tight and he looked as if he'd been crying.

My legs became leaden as I found my way to Issi's bedroom, as if on autopilot. I pushed the door open and saw her lying on their bed, staring up at the ceiling. She turned her head as I walked over to her and I could see her red-rimmed eyes.

'Issi?'

She turned over and buried her head in the pillow, her body racked with huge heart-wrenching sobs. I climbed onto the bed next to her and held her tightly until she found the strength to speak.

'It's not good, Becky.' Her voice was barely audible and I

strained to hear. 'The cancer has spread into my lymphatic system and is too aggressive to treat.'

I shouted, 'No!' holding her while we both sobbed and screamed.

The journey home, later, was a blur – I didn't remember any of it. I put a DVD on for the boys and phoned Sam.

For over an hour I cried while she talked, giving me practical advice on how to help Issi.

'I'll talk to the cancer nurses at work,' she told me. 'They'll have some information to help you cope, as well.'

'I don't care about me,' I said angrily, wiping my swollen eyes. 'I just want Issi to get better.'

'I know.'

'It's not fair.'

'It never is,' Sam replied gently. 'Why don't you search the internet for ways to help her? It'll give you a focus.'

I thanked Sam and steeled myself to prepare the boys' tea, even though I felt nauseous. Once I'd got them into bed I fired up my laptop, reading every site I could find. It was two in the morning before I fell into bed – to the tortures of a sleep filled with vivid and distressing dreams.

*

The next day I texted Issi a few times telling her I loved her and would help her get through this, but she didn't reply. I cared for the boys, but it was as if I were in a thick fog.

Martin rang to see if we fancied doing something together and I explained about Issi, telling him I wasn't feeling very sociable.

'I'll come and collect Charlie and Jack,' he said immediately. 'They can stay for the rest of the day, and I'll bring them home after tea.'

'Thank you so much, Martin,' I replied, my voice choked

with emotion. 'I really appreciate that.'

I researched more websites and then called in at the library, picking up as many books as I was allowed on positive thinking, how alternative treatments can help, and the power of organic food. I headed straight round to Issi's, hoping she would see me.

Jonathan opened the door and we hugged in silence. 'She's in bed, but not asleep. Go up, she'll be pleased to see you.'

Issi smiled weakly when she saw me and sat herself up. I joined her on the bed, putting my arm round her shoulders and holding her tightly. 'How are you feeling?'

'Still in shock. Can we not talk about it?'

I squeezed her hand, but try as I might I couldn't stop the tears from coming. I buried my head in the pillow and cried solidly until I had no more energy left.

'Sorry,' I said eventually, rummaging through my bag for a hanky. 'That's the last thing you needed.'

'Don't worry – I'm getting used to it happening,' she replied, handing me a box of tissues. 'Now,' she said brightly. 'What have you brought?'

I was amazed by her strength and immediately focused on the job in hand – getting Issi better. The two of us sat together, poring over books and websites, and when it was time for me to leave we had several plans in mind and I felt much more positive.

'We're going to beat this, Issi.'

'I know.'

'I'll order the vitamins we decided on, and buy the book you liked the look of.'

She smiled at me, her eyes suddenly losing their dullness. 'You keep me sane – everyone else has fallen apart.'

*

Darren picked the boys up on Friday night and I told him briefly about Issi. I didn't want to talk then, though, and he respected that. When he brought them home on Sunday evening he put them straight to bed for me. I was sitting in the kitchen when he came back down, searching through websites for yet more information. He made two coffees and sat down opposite me.

'Why didn't you tell me about Issi?' he asked. 'I could have supported you more.'

'Because you chose not to be part of my life.'

He winced as if I'd hit him.

'And because I just thought she'd have her chemo and get better.'

He reached across the table and held my hand. 'She will get better, though?'

I nodded assertively, smiling through fresh tears. 'Of course she will. I'm in charge of her recovery.'

I saw compassion and love flood through his eyes and he walked over, pulling me up into him, his arms enveloping me and rocking me like a small child.

'Take me back, Becky,' he whispered. 'I want to be here for you.'

Chapter Sixteen

Twinkle, twinkle
Little Star.
Who the hell
Do you think you are?

'Charlie, I know you're tired, but you need to eat your breakfast.'

'I don't want to go to school,' he said. 'I want to stay with Daddy.'

'Yes, well, Dad has to work today. Now hurry up,' I snapped at both of them.

I still wasn't coping well and felt permanently tired and weepy. I guessed the boys had been spoiled by Darren because they had been reluctant to do anything I asked them.

We managed to make it into the playground on time and I headed straight over to Martin to thank him for all his help. He was chatting to Mandy, who turned and gave me a huge hug.

'Anything I can do – you've only got to ask. Anything at all. Shopping, ironing, child minding...'

'Oh.' I was surprised she knew about Issi.

'I hope you don't mind Martin telling me. It's just that I helped him out with the boys on Friday.'

I looked at them both. 'I can't thank you enough…' I was so choked I couldn't continue, and I was grateful to Martin for swiftly changing the subject to football.

As I walked out of the playground Kate caught up with me. 'Becky, I was hoping I hadn't missed you. Mandy rang me over the weekend. I'm so sorry to hear about your friend. Can I do anything to help?'

I shook my head. 'Thanks, but I'm okay.' I hadn't known these people long, and yet they hadn't hesitated to offer their support. I was so lucky to have such good friends.

During the afternoon I was surprised when Martin texted to ask if he could come round.

'Sorry about intruding,' he said as I put the kettle on. 'I'm working from home today and…well…I've been wanting to say something to you for ages but I haven't found the right moment.'

I glanced across at him. He was sitting at the table, wringing his hands nervously, his shoulders hunched. I concentrated on making the coffees, my stomach churning. I didn't need this. I still found him attractive, but I was happy for us to just be friends – my life was complicated enough as it was.

I handed him a coffee and sat down, steeling myself to hear what he had to say.

'Becky,' he said slowly. 'The…er…kiss we had at New Year was lovely, but as you know, I didn't feel ready to start a new relationship.'

I nodded, dreading what was coming.

'I've spoken at length to my parents and Jackie's mum about it, and they all agree I should move on with my life.' He swallowed hard. 'I'll always love Jackie, but I have to accept she's gone.'

My eyes filled with tears and I focused hard on what he was saying, not wanting to cry.

'Anyway,' he said brightly, looking straight at me, 'I'm

now ready to take that step, and I feel we have a special friendship…'

He paused and I felt sick. How was I going to let him down gently after all the courage this must have taken?

'So that's why I want to ask you…'

I stared at him, my body tensed. 'Yes?'

'Do you think there's any chance Mandy might say yes if I asked her out?'

I exhaled slowly, relief flooding through me. 'Mandy?'

His cheeks flushed. 'Sorry. That must have sounded dreadful. I do find you really attractive; it's just that I've been seeing a lot of Mandy and we get on so well.' His cheeks reddened further. 'I'm making this sound really insulting now.'

I laughed and rescued him from his misery. 'I'm really pleased for you. And I'm a hundred per cent certain Mandy will say yes.'

'Really?' His face suddenly came alive and I couldn't have been happier for them.

As he left, he kissed my cheek gently. 'Thanks for being a good friend. It'll all work out for you, too.'

I walked back into the kitchen and picked up the untouched drinks. Why hadn't I told him about Rob? I guessed it was because I was enjoying my secret and I didn't want anyone to intrude on it for the moment.

I smiled as I thought about the daily phone calls that sent my pulse racing. I was grateful to him for being so understanding about Issi, patiently waiting for me to feel ready for our date, and I grinned as I thought about his reaction when I'd suggested Saturday.

*

'Hi, Darren,' I said as I opened the front door. 'The boys are nearly ready – they're so excited about sleeping over with you again.'

He nodded and smiled. 'Have *you* got plans?' he asked quietly. 'You could always join us.'

I looked away, feeling terrible that I was about to lie. 'I'm just going to have a long soak in the bath and catch up on some reading.'

'Okay.' He looked away in disappointment. 'Have you given any more thought to...' He turned back to face me. '... what we talked about?'

I shook my head, suddenly angry that he was pressurising me so much. 'I've a lot on my mind,' I said.

'Of course. I'll see you in the morning.'

I took my time getting ready, applying plenty of make-up to hide my tiredness. Pleased with the results I drove to the restaurant, butterflies zipping round my stomach at a hundred miles per hour.

It was a warm April evening and Rob was waiting for me in the car park. My heart skipped a beat as I walked towards him. He was still looking tanned and was smartly dressed in a light-coloured shirt and dark trousers. He had flattened his spiky hair, giving him a softer, more mature look – one that I found unnervingly sexy. We stared at each other for several seconds, our smiles spontaneous and genuine.

'You look stunning in that dress,' he said. 'Really pretty.'

I grinned at him. 'You look pretty good yourself.'

He took my hand and electricity shot through me as if I'd been plugged into a socket. He turned and smiled and I guessed he'd felt it too. Inside the restaurant we sat down and studied the menu, but I couldn't concentrate; I could feel him watching me, and when I looked up he was smiling broadly.

'Sorry.' His whole face was illuminated. 'I just like looking at you.'

We talked and talked throughout the meal, learning all

about each other's lives, and it felt so good to just be me, to be happy and carefree, simply enjoying the moment.

Hours later Rob paid the bill, refusing my half, and as we wandered out into the cold night I shivered. He put his arm round me and I snuggled into him as we walked to our cars. The kiss we shared was so tender, so passionate, I felt my whole body melt.

*

'Did you hear about Josh yesterday?' Mandy whispered as she pulled me to one side in the playground.

There was something about her tone of voice that made me feel concerned. 'No. The boys both went back to a friend's for tea, so I wasn't here. Is he all right?'

'Well,' she continued, 'Helen didn't turn up to collect him, but that's not unusual because she's often late these days, so I didn't think anything of it.'

I sighed heavily.

'When we got home I realised Alicia had forgotten her lunch box for the second day running and we popped back for both of them. The classroom door was locked so we had to use the main entrance, and Josh was still there waiting to be picked up.'

'That's awful,' I said. 'Poor boy.'

'I know,' Mandy agreed, 'but what makes it worse is that Helen arrived as we were leaving, and when I walked past her I could definitely smell booze.'

'That's dreadful. We need to tell someone.'

'Yes. Actually, when I got home I rang Mrs Jenkins and told her about my concerns again. She was very grateful, and obviously already aware of it.'

'Well done. Let's hope something gets done.'

'Thanks. Oh, there's Martin. I need a quick word with him

– I'll catch you later.'

Martin's face lit up as Mandy walked towards him and I smiled, wondering if he'd asked her out yet.

*

I called round at Issi's to be greeted with a hug from her dad.

'She's been asleep most of the morning, so she'll be glad of your company.'

'Okay,' I replied quietly.

'Go up and I'll bring you both some tea.'

He wasn't his normal sparkling self and I kissed his cheek. 'Are *you* all right?'

He nodded without replying, and I understood what terrible memories this would be bringing back for him.

I crept into Issi's room to find her sitting up watching television. She smiled broadly as she pressed the remote. 'Great – some company.'

'How are you feeling?' She looked washed-out and fragile.

'Not too bad. Jonathan arranged for one of the healers we found to come round. She's been giving me healing every morning, and then I've slept for hours.'

As I settled myself on the bed Issi's dad brought in a tray of tea.

'That smells nice,' I said to him.

'Yes, it's herbal – you've got one as well.'

Issi and I smiled at each other as he left the room.

'He's trying so hard,' she said, 'but do you know what I'd really like?'

'Cappuccino?' I suggested and my friend broke into a grin. 'Okay. One day next week I'll drive us to L'Olivo.'

Issi sipped her herbal tea. 'Right. Tell me what's been going on with Rob and Darren.'

I sighed. 'Darren's still having the boys every weekend,

which is great. He took them to football practice, which was a bit awkward for Rob but not for Darren, since he doesn't know about Rob.' I shook my head. 'It's a bit complicated – are you keeping up?'

Issi laughed and I continued.

'When he brought them home he wanted to talk about "us". He's putting a lot of pressure on me to make a decision.'

'That's not fair.'

'He says he's given up a lot to make another go of it, and I should think of the boys.'

Issi scowled. 'You haven't agreed to anything, have you?'

'No. I'm really enjoying seeing Rob.'

'And have you…?'

'No.' I laughed. 'He's being a real gentleman.'

'I'm so pleased for you,' she replied, smiling.

'I know it's a bit clichéd, but he makes me feel so valued. Although I haven't told him what Darren has said to me, he seems to understand how difficult the situation is.'

'He sounds lovely. I can't wait to meet him.'

'He is.' A slow smile spread across my face. 'But I'm just taking things slowly.'

Issi smiled sleepily. 'You'll wake up one morning and know your answer.'

I checked my watch. 'I'm going to have to pick up the boys from school now, but I'll be back in a couple of days.' I kissed Issi gently on the forehead as she snuggled down to have another sleep.

*

'I'm still worried about Josh,' I said to Kate and Mandy. 'Jack said he wasn't at school again yesterday, and there's no sign of Helen yet.'

'I've been thinking the same thing,' Kate replied, frowning.

'Should we approach Mrs Jenkins again?'

I would mention it to Rob when we spoke later, and I smiled involuntarily at the thought of our phone call. Although we were still being discreet about our relationship we phoned each other every evening, and I was always left with a warm glow afterwards.

Before I had chance to reply, "floozy mum" started chatting to Martin and I prodded Mandy. 'Do you want me to hold you back?' I teased.

'No. No need,' she replied with a smug smile.

Kate and I stared at her.

'I knew there was something going on.' Kate was jumping up and down, oblivious to all the stares she was receiving. 'Tell us everything.'

'I had a feeling, too,' I added, not wanting to let her know that Martin had told me. 'I'm so pleased.'

Mandy's smile lit up the whole playground. She'd clearly being dying to share her secret. 'It started in the Easter holidays when Martin was looking after Jack and Charlie.' She glanced at me, but I smiled, letting her know she hadn't upset me. 'He rang to see if we fancied doing something together, and we had a wonderful time.' She grinned manically. 'A week or so ago I decided to just go for it, and I told him how much I enjoyed his company and asked if he fancied a drink sometime.' She paused for a moment, enjoying the attention.

'Go on,' Kate said in frustration.

'Well, I prepared myself for a rejection, but before I could say anything more – *he* asked *me* out.' She beamed at us triumphantly. 'I can't tell you anything else because it's X-rated, but I will just say that with all the exercise I've been getting...' She winked at us. 'I've lost half a stone!'

The bell sounded and we ushered the children into school in record time so that we could resume our conversation. Kate and I had just grabbed Mandy and were hugging her when

Helen rushed past us, pushing Josh in through the door. She scowled at us as she turned to leave, dampening the mood. We exchanged worried glances.

'Were you thinking what I was?' Mandy muttered as we started to walk across the playground. 'Alcohol?'

Kate and I nodded, but then Kate stopped suddenly. 'Look over there,' she said, pointing to our left.

'It's Helen's posse,' Mandy said. 'God, they look menacing. Let's just wait and make sure there's no trouble.'

The group of mums strode towards Helen, their high heels clicking in unison.

'It looks as if Diana's taken over as head honcho,' I whispered. 'The others are all a few steps behind her.'

'I wonder what's happened,' Mandy whispered back. 'It's as if Helen's been ousted from the pack.'

The posse stopped, all folding their arms in an aggressive stance, but Helen scurried past them with barely a second glance.

'I almost feel sorry for her,' I said.

*

I couldn't wait to tease Martin and took great delight in making him blush.

'I'm sorry I didn't tell you I'd actually asked her,' he said, 'but we were enjoying having a secret. It was good fun.'

'I'm so pleased for you both – you're well suited.'

Martin grinned. 'I can't believe how well we get on. I feel on top of the world.'

At that moment Mandy and Kate strolled over and Martin kissed Mandy on the lips, much to our delight.

As we stood laughing we were distracted by shouting coming from across the playground, and we turned round to see Helen and one of the posse yelling and screaming at each other. Everyone stopped to watch, and I was taken by surprise when Charlie and Jack appeared by my side. Josh was standing outside the classroom door with Miss Whittaker, staring at his mum, who showed no signs of letting up on the other woman. Martin had clearly noticed Josh, too. He started walking over to Helen, glancing over his shoulder at Josh, but Miss Whittaker brushed past him, almost flying across the concrete.

'Mrs Stevens,' she bellowed. 'I need to see you in my classroom – now!'

Helen stopped shouting, slowly looking round at the crowd of people who were staring. She looked at Miss Whittaker's red face and followed her back to the classroom with her head down, avoiding eye contact with anyone.

Before any of us could move, Angela came rushing over. 'Ooh, I witnessed the whole thing, because I was standing over there. Shall I tell you what happened?'

I didn't want to hear about the details; it was bad enough that it had happened in front of Josh, but before I had time to reply Angela was in full flow.

'I heard Helen telling the other mum that Grace wanted her daughter to come back for tea, and the other woman said that no child of hers was going to Helen's until she'd got her drinking under control.'

Kate, Mandy and I exchanged glances.

'I got the impression they'd had this conversation before because Helen told her to get off her back. She replied that she was worried about Grace and Josh and then Helen just erupted, hurling abuse at her. It was awful.'

Angela disappeared to tell her story elsewhere, leaving us saddened and worried.

'At least the school will have to take some action now,' Mandy observed and we both agreed.

The boys and I walked home slowly in the April sunshine

and I was thankful they didn't mention anything about Helen.

'Will Dad be there when we get home?' Charlie asked.

'No. You've got time to have a quick sandwich and get changed,' I told them.

'I can't wait to see the movie,' Jack said. 'James in my class saw it yesterday and said it's brilliant!' He ran ahead and Charlie and I hurried to catch him up.

Darren arrived an hour later and told the boys he wanted a quick word with me. I knew what it would be about; I was dreading this conversation.

'I presume you got the same papers in the post as me this morning?'

'Yes.' I didn't tell him that I had cried when I saw the divorce papers, and how I couldn't bring myself to sign them.

'I haven't signed mine.' His eyes were cold and hard and he clenched his jaw. 'I'm still hoping we can sort things out.'

I shrugged, unsure what to say.

'Becky.' He took my hands in his. 'I know I've got a lot to make up for. Please will you think about what I've said to you? The boys would love us to be back together.'

'This isn't a great time for me,' I replied. I knew Darren loved me, but why did he make me feel as if I were part of a business deal? Surely getting back together, if that was what we were going to do, should be romantic? Exciting even?

Rob's ringtone on my mobile phone trilled as I waved Darren and the boys off, and I smiled as I said hello.

'I just fancied a chat,' he told me. 'Actually, I'm desperate to talk to you. I have some news.'

'Ooh, that sounds interesting.'

'It is.'

He was excited about something, and I suddenly wanted there to be no secrets between us. I wanted to tell him about Darren: the divorce, the non- divorce, everything. 'Could you squeeze me in for a consultation, then?' I asked coyly.

'I'll clear the desk,' he flirted back. 'See you in ten minutes.'

I walked quickly round to the school, suddenly losing my nerve. What if it put him off? What if he didn't want someone with all this baggage? I stopped walking. What if he told me it was a good idea to get back with Darren? I forced myself to keep going, determined to be honest with him. I needed to do that if our relationship was going to move forward.

As I walked up the school drive a car roared past me and turned sharply into the car park. It came to a halt with an almighty screech and ended up on the grass verge. I was amazed to see Helen jump out of the driver's seat and march into school. I ran after her, intuition telling me that something was wrong.

I couldn't see where she'd gone, and I headed for Rob's room. He was sitting with his feet up on his desk and smirked at me.

'Rob—'

'Mrs Dixon.' He smiled. 'Close the door. We have a lot to discuss.' Then he suddenly shot up and raced over to me. 'Becky? What's wrong?'

I hadn't moved from the doorway and was frantically looking up and down the corridor. 'I think Helen Stevens is drunk. She's just come storming into school.'

'Oh my God. Louise had a run-in with her earlier.'

He grabbed my hand and we ran to Miss Whittaker's room, where we saw Helen through the glass in the closed door. She was standing in the middle of the room waving her arms around, and from her contorted face we could tell she was shouting and screaming at the teacher. Louise wasn't reacting, but was sitting quietly at her desk, clearly trying to diffuse the situation.

'I need to get that woman out of there,' Rob said as he

grabbed the door handle. He pushed the door open just as Helen picked up one of the children's chairs and swung it towards Louise's head.

Chapter Seventeen

Two little dicky birds
Sitting on a wall.
I'd love to push you off
And see you fall.

I was dreading walking into the playground. I had hardly slept and had been unable to eat breakfast due to the tight knot in my stomach. I was still reeling from the shock of what I'd witnessed; I couldn't shake off the memory of seeing Louise's blood splattered up the classroom wall.

Rob had rushed over and cradled her in his arms, his body shielding me from the most sickening sight of all. I closed my eyes, trying to wipe away the memory of his ashen face as he told me to call an ambulance. Thankfully Mrs Jenkins had seen Helen run out of school and had come to investigate. She took over, instantly dialling nine-nine-nine on her mobile; I had been rooted to the spot in shock.

Rob had called me from the hospital and I had hardly dared ask how Louise was.

'She's conscious now,' he'd said with relief. 'She has two broken ribs and a nasty head wound.'

'Oh my God.'

'She should be allowed home in a couple of days though.'

He'd paused. 'I wish I'd been quicker.'

'You probably stopped it from being a lot worse.'

'Maybe. But how are you? Sue Jenkins told me you went into shock.'

'I had to sit down with a sugary tea, but I'm okay now. I gave a statement to the police, but I couldn't say why Helen had done it.'

'She accused Louise of being critical of her parenting skills.' He'd laughed wryly. 'Typical Louise – she was more upset about that than being attacked, because she had only ever spoken to Helen out of concern for Josh.'

I had filled him in on what had been happening, feeling guilty that I hadn't been more pro-active in expressing my concerns.

'None of us could have seen this coming,' he'd replied.

I had worried all night about Grace and Josh.

What I had witnessed was confidential and I was not intending to pass it on in the playground. At the same time I wanted to talk to my friends about the children and whether we should offer to help, so I thought I might confide in Mandy and Kate. I needn't have worried, though, because as I walked through the gates Angela ran straight over to me.

'Becky,' she gasped breathlessly. 'I've just been talking to Sally Collins, the children's classroom assistant, and I'm afraid I've got some terrible news.'

Angela related the story fairly accurately and I didn't feel the need to feign surprise or upset because it was just as bad hearing the news second-hand. Martin, Kate and Mandy joined us and Angela repeated it all over again.

'I'm worried about the children,' I said to my shocked friends.

'Me too,' agreed Mandy. 'Let's go and talk to Mrs Jenkins and see if we can help in any way.'

Martin put his hand on Mandy's shoulder. 'I've got to get

to work. Call me later and let me know how it goes.'

Kate knocked on Mrs Jenkins' door and we were ushered in quickly.

'Becky, how are you feeling?' she asked.

Kate and Mandy frowned at me and I explained what had happened.

'You poor thing,' they both said together, giving me a quick hug.

I smiled weakly and looked at Mrs Jenkins. 'We want to help with Grace and Josh if we can. How is Miss Whittaker this morning?'

The head teacher sat down with a sigh. 'Miss Whittaker, thankfully, is recovering well, although she is obviously very shaken up.'

We all breathed a sigh of relief.

'I'll buy a basket of fruit,' I said to the others, 'and take it to the hospital.'

'I'll organise a collection later,' Mandy added.

Mrs Jenkins smiled. 'She'll appreciate that.'

'And what about Josh and Grace?' Kate asked tentatively.

'I've been trying to get hold of Mr Stevens since last night,' she replied, rubbing her temples. 'I don't know what's happening at the moment.' She stood up, signalling that the meeting was over, and we walked out of her office in stunned silence.

*

I opened the front door and stared at Rob in surprise. 'Oh my goodness, how are you?' His grey complexion told me how much the stress of yesterday had affected him. I rushed towards him, enveloping him a huge hug. 'Have you time for a coffee?'

He stepped into the hall and kissed me on the lips. 'No –

I'm actually on my way to work. Mrs Jenkins told me to take a few hours off this morning.'

'She says Louise is recovering.' I smiled at him. 'I'm just about to go to the hospital to see her.'

'That's kind.' He checked his watch. 'Go on, then, I'll have a quick drink with you. Mrs J won't mind.' He sat down at the table. 'I was dying to see you yesterday,' he said as I pulled two clean mugs out of the dishwasher, 'because I have some news to tell you.'

'Yes, of course.' I had forgotten all about that. I handed him a coffee and sat down next to him.

He took hold of my hand, interlocking his fingers through mine. 'You know I told you that Mrs Jenkins is retiring next year?'

I nodded as I sipped my drink.

'And that it set me off thinking about headships.' He took a slow drink of his coffee, watching me all the time.

I frowned at him. 'Yes – you said you were going to apply for a few as experience.' My hand flew to my mouth 'No! You haven't?'

His eyes were dancing. 'I heard yesterday that as from September I will be the head teacher of Palmer Primary School, which is just outside Slough.'

'Rob,' I screamed, 'that's fantastic!' I put my mug down and flung my arms round his neck, kissing him deeply.

'Wow,' he said, laughing. 'I'll have to get promoted more often.'

'I'm thrilled for you – and Slough isn't very far away.'

'No, I won't have to move house, which is good news financially.'

I turned round in my chair so our legs were touching. 'Tell me all about the school.'

'It's in the middle of a council estate,' he said, already proud of his new empire, 'and there are lots of children with emotional and behavioural issues. That was the attraction.'

I kissed him again. 'You'll be brilliant at helping these kids.'

He told me more about the job as we finished our coffees, and then we had one last, lingering kiss on the doorstep. 'Now go and do some work,' I scolded him.

*

I found Louise's ward, approaching her bed cautiously and hoping she wouldn't mind my unannounced visit.

'Hello, Louise,' I said softly, putting the basket of fruit down. 'How are you?'

She sat up slowly, wincing in pain. 'I've been better.' She looked at the gift and smiled. 'Thank you – that was very thoughtful.'

'It's from all of us. Everyone sends their love.'

She nodded, immediately closing her eyes and putting her hand to her head.

'You must be in so much pain,' I said. 'Can I get you anything?'

'A drink would be good, thanks.'

I poured a glass of water and passed it to her carefully. 'Is there anything else I can do?'

'No – I've just been given some pain killers,' she replied as she sipped her drink.

I perched on a chair by the bed, unsure what to say. I felt awkward. She didn't appear well enough to make small talk, and I doubted it was appropriate to discuss what had happened.

'Well, I'll leave you to rest,' I said after a short silence, 'but we all hope to see you back soon.'

Louise put the glass down. 'Sorry – the shock and the pain-killing drugs have made me a bit woozy.' She smiled at me. 'I want to thank you and Rob for all your help.'

'I'm just sorry we weren't quicker.'

'I'm glad you were there.' She smiled. 'I'm also pleased he did as I told him and asked you out.'

I stared at her in surprise. 'You told him to?'

'I was worried about you when those spiteful rumours about the photograph were circulating.'

My cheeks flushed at the memory.

She slowly picked up her glass and took another sip of water. 'Rob was mortified when I told him, and I wheedled out of him how much he liked you.'

'Oh – and you didn't mind?' I blurted this out before I could stop myself.

She held my gaze steadily. 'No. I did like him at one point – who wouldn't?'

I nodded and looked away, embarrassed I'd asked the question. 'Thank you,' I said. 'He's a lovely guy.'

'And I've never seen him happier.' She paused, breathing slowly through a spasm of pain.

I leaned forward and touched her arm. 'Louise, why don't you rest now?'

'I think I will.'

I helped re-arrange the pillows for her. 'It's good to see you.'

'Yes, you too.' She smiled back. 'Thanks for coming – I'll see you at school in a few weeks.' She put her hand on my arm. 'Becky, there's just one other thing.'

The serious tone of her voice made me sit back down. 'Yes?'

'I'm worried sick about Josh and his sister. Would you do me a favour?'

'Of course. What is it?'

'I'm stuck in here, and all I can think about is Helen Stevens being drunk and neglecting her children – or worse.'

'But her husband will be there,' I reassured her. 'Or Social Services might be involved by now.'

She shook her head. 'Her husband travels a lot – and Social Services might not have done anything yet.' Her breathing quickened and she seemed on the verge of hysteria.

'Louise,' I said, holding her hand. 'The children will be fine.'

'Will you check on them – please?'

I took a deep breath. 'I don't think Helen will want me interfering. I—'

'Please, Becky.' She started to cry. 'If I give you my mobile phone number, will you text me to say they're all right? Then I can relax.'

I nodded, standing up to leave. However, I was not certain I could keep my promise.

I thought of nothing else on the drive home, finally telling myself that Louise needed to get better and Helen's children needed to be safe.

I steeled myself and pulled up outside Helen's house, but I sat for a while thinking things through. What I was doing here? How could this possibly help? Eventually I forced myself out of the car – Louise was so distressed, I couldn't let her down.

I walked slowly up the drive, hoping Helen wasn't home, but when I reached the front door the sound of raised voices told me otherwise. As I turned to leave, the door was yanked open and a tall overweight man stepped out.

'Yes?' he barked at me.

'I'm a...er...friend of Helen's.'

He stared back without responding.

'Could I see her?' I asked tentatively. This really hadn't been one of my better ideas.

'Go in – I'm leaving.' He pushed the front door wide open and yelled into the house. 'I'll collect the kids' stuff later.

They'll be staying at my mother's.'

'This is a bad moment,' I muttered. 'I'll go.'

'Did you hear what the stupid cow did?' he asked, his face contorted in anger.

'I...er—'

'She got drunk and attacked a teacher.'

'So doesn't she need your support?' I asked quietly, taking an instant dislike to this arrogant man.

'Support?' He clenched his fists and I could see that he was struggling to control his temper. I immediately regretted interfering.

He took two steps towards me. 'I work away most of the week and I need *her* support. My job isn't to prop my wife up – I've told her repeatedly to pull herself together.' He glared at me. 'After the disaster that was our family Christmas...' he rolled his eyes and snorted, '...I told her I'd had enough and I was leaving – and that I'd fight her for the kids,' he added angrily.

I stepped back, wishing I hadn't come round. Helen's husband jumped into his car and sped away, and I almost felt sorry for Helen, being married to him. I now understood why she had looked so unwell over the past few months – it couldn't have been an easy time.

I took two deep breaths and stepped into Helen's hallway, my stomach churning. 'Hello, Helen,' I called out.

There was no response, but I heard a movement in the kitchen and I pushed the door fully open. She was leaning against the worktop, a glass of wine in her hand, tears streaming down her face. Her hair hadn't been combed and her grey complexion and sunken eyes increased my sympathy for her.

'What the hell do you want?' she shouted, wiping her eyes with the back of her free hand.

'I, er, just wondered if you were okay.'

'As if you care.'

'I—'

'You've just come to snoop – to report back to your smug little group of friends.'

'No, Helen,' I said firmly. 'I've just been to visit Miss Whittaker and she's worried about the children.'

Helen sniffed loudly. 'Well, as you just heard, they're going to be fine.' She took a long slug of wine, draining the glass. 'How is Miss Whittaker?'

'In a lot of pain, but thankfully she'll recover.'

Helen suddenly choked on a sob. 'I didn't mean it to happen – I don't know what came over me.'

'Had you been drinking?' I asked carefully.

She turned and glared at me, and for a second I thought she was going to deny it. She closed her eyes briefly, nodding as she opened them again.

'You need help, Helen.'

'I think you're stating the obvious there,' she snapped back. 'The police have been round and I've been charged with assault.' She stared at me, narrowing her eyes. 'I know I've made a huge mess of everything.'

'It's clear you've had very little support from your husband,' I said. 'I'd like to help you.'

'You? The woman who got me sacked?'

'Oh, I think you managed that all by yourself.'

She turned her head away from me. 'I've gone beyond getting help.'

'No, you haven't.' I stopped myself from rushing over to her. 'If you want your children back you'll need some professional help.'

She snapped her head back, giving me a long hard stare. 'Want to come and hold my hand at an AA meeting, do you?' she mocked.

'If that's what it takes, then yes.'

My answer clearly surprised her and she blinked several times. 'I'll cope by myself, thanks.' Her voice was cold and hard. 'I wouldn't want to disrupt your perfect little life.' She screwed her face up and mimicked my voice. 'I've got such an amazing job, and so many friends. I—'

'Helen,' I shouted at her. 'My life isn't perfect—'

'Really?' She took a step towards me. 'I wanted Thomas's dad to notice me, but no – Little Miss Perfect had to go and throw herself at him.'

I glared at her, our eyes locked onto each other's, anger seeping through my every pore. I shook my head – there was no way I was going to tell her anything about my life. I didn't have to justify myself.

Helen broke the silence. 'If there's nothing more, I'd like you to leave.'

Driving home I felt overwhelmed by both anger and sadness. I hoped Helen would find help for her drinking problem, and my thoughts turned to Grace and Josh. I could have wept for the break-up of their family life.

*

'Dad's here!' Charlie screamed, tearing through the house so he could be first to the door.

'Daddy!' Jack yelled, giving his brother a hard shove as he raced after him.

I was glad Darren was taking them out. After seeing Louise and Helen, I was exhausted.

'Hello, boys.' Darren hugged them both. 'Ready for tea?'

'Pizza,' Charlie said, jumping up and down with his arms in the air.

'Burger,' Jack shouted louder, copying him.

'All yours.' I shrugged and smiled at Darren.

'They're a bit hyper,' he said as he walked over to me.

'Could I just have a quick word before we go?'

I immediately tensed. I just wanted them to leave so I could have some peace.

He put his hand on my shoulder, guiding me to the kitchen, and he turned to the boys over his shoulder. 'Put your shoes on while I speak to Mummy.' He stood inches away from me, the smell of his aftershave overwhelming. 'Becky, I know I've been asking you to make a decision, but I've been thinking.'

I frowned in confusion. Was this good or bad news?

'Why don't we start dating again?' He grinned at me. 'You know, you get a babysitter and we'll go out for meals or to the cinema.'

'Oh.' I hadn't seen this coming.

He kissed me on the cheek. 'Have a think about it.'

After they'd gone, tiredness engulfed me and I slumped into the nearest chair. Should I give it a go?

*

I couldn't wait to see Issi. There was so much I had to tell her and talk over with her. We had arranged that I would collect her from home so we could go to L'Olivo for lunch.

Her dad opened the front door. 'She's not great today,' he said, wiping away a tear.

I planted a gentle kiss on his cheek. 'Don't worry. We can do this another day.'

'No,' he said, wiping his eyes with a handkerchief. 'Whatever Issi wants, I'll make happen. She's been so looking forward to this.'

'I know.'

'I'll drive you both there so I can help her into the café, and then I'll collect you later.'

How fiercely you protect your children. I felt my heart breaking at witnessing his pain.

Half an hour later Issi's dad pulled up outside L'Olivo and parked on double yellow lines while he helped his daughter inside. Nico rushed to open the door and clucked round her, helping her to sit down.

'God, I hate all this fuss,' she said when we were finally alone. 'You're the only person who's normal with me. Now, tell me everything.'

'Okay. In no particular order – Darren.'

Before I could start, Nico reappeared with three cappuccinos and sat down to join us. He glanced at the scarf covering Issi's wispy hair and gently stroked her cheek with the back of his hand. 'How are you, my friend?'

She glanced at me in a moment's indecision, and then told him the truth about her illness. She was so brave. I wouldn't have had the strength to do that.

'You are a beautiful woman,' was Nico's response. 'I'll make you both a special lunch.' He disappeared into the kitchen, leaving us to resume our chatting.

I smiled at my friend, who was savouring her cappuccino. 'Where were we? Darren. Well, he's still pushing me to make a decision, but I'm not giving in to his pressure. Now he's suggested we go out for a meal – you know, start dating again, but it feels a bit weird, particularly when I'm seeing Rob.'

'Any developments with Rob?'

I smiled involuntarily. 'We just enjoy each other's company.'

'And?'

'No 'and' – he's being the perfect gentleman.' I sipped my cappuccino. 'Actually, there is an 'and' – he had some brilliant news this week.'

'Ooh.' She leaned forward. 'What?' She listened intently as I told her all about his new job. 'That's fantastic,' she said with a smile. 'Tell him well done from me.' She tapped my hand. 'There you go – that's a sign.'

'What do you mean?'

'If he's no longer working at the school, it won't matter if you're dating.'

Nico interrupted our conversation, placing a beautiful salad in front of each of us before reappearing with a basket of warm bread and two glasses of freshly squeezed orange juice. 'On me,' he said, and we smiled gratefully at him.

'So what are you going to do this weekend?' Issi continued.

I couldn't help but grin. 'As the weather's so beautiful Rob's suggested we go to Richmond Park and have a picnic.'

'That sounds so romantic.' She sighed heavily. 'I might suggest that to Jonathan – but in our garden.'

I squeezed her hand. 'That sounds just perfect.'

Issi pushed her salad to one side, nibbling on some bread instead, and I enjoyed watching her, just being with her. 'How are the children coping?' I asked gently.

'So-so. Andrew keeps telling me jokes to make me laugh, Emma wants lots of cuddles and Ben is just Ben.' She smiled at me and I knew from her expression that she wanted to change the subject. 'So what else has been happening?' she asked brightly. 'Has that woman been giving you any more grief in the playground?'

I nearly choked on my salad. 'I forgot to tell you about her,' I said, immediately relaying the story.

Issi's face was full of concern. 'It sounds like she has some terrible issues.'

I nodded. 'I wish she'd accepted my offer of help.'

'Pride, I suspect.' Issi picked at some bread. 'We're so lucky to have good friends who support us,' she added, reaching across the table to squeeze my hand.

I nodded, smiling into the eyes of my best friend, noticing the dullness and the lack of sparkle. 'Are you okay?' I asked. 'Have I tired you out?'

'I'm fine,' she replied. 'Thanks for bringing me out. It's been brilliant and I've eaten more today than I have all week, but I'm going to call Dad now – I could do with a sleep.'

When her dad arrived Nico rushed over to say goodbye and held Issi in a bear-hug. 'Get some rest and come back soon for another special lunch.' He kissed me on both cheeks. '*Ciao*, Becky. Let me know how she's doing,' he whispered.

*

I stretched across the bed, enjoying the strange feeling of being alone. Darren had collected Charlie and Jack on Friday night to take them to his parents' house for the weekend, and I smiled as I thought about spending a whole day with Rob.

I took my time getting ready, and after several changes of clothes I eventually chose a floral skirt and a strappy t-shirt. Rob had told me he was organising the picnic, so I enjoyed the luxury of being able to concentrate on myself without any interruptions.

'You look gorgeous,' he said when he arrived, kissing me on the mouth.

His blue t-shirt was stretched tight across his chest and upper arms, emphasizing his muscles, and then my eyes wandered to his long, khaki shorts, which revealed hairy muscular legs. My pulse rate quickened. Should I suggest cancelling the picnic and just drag him upstairs? Sadly, he was already ushering me out to the car.

As he drove I enjoyed sharing his excitement about his new job. He told me all about his plans for September. 'I'm going to get the parents involved straight away,' he said, laughing. 'We're going to plant the best sensory garden in the country. Somewhere stressed children – or adults,' he added with a rueful smile, 'can find some peace.'

'I know I keep saying this, but I'm so proud of you.'

He glanced over at me, his eyes sparkling, and he pulled my hand to his mouth, kissing it lightly.

I shivered, wishing we'd stayed at home after all.

He told me all about his other plans before shaking his head. 'It's all me, me, me,' he said. 'How's Issi?'

I sighed, not wanting to spoil the mood. 'Okay.'

'Becky?' He took one hand off the steering wheel and linked his fingers through mine.

'Truthfully, I don't know. It's my job to get her better and I just don't think I'm doing it very well.' The words tumbled out in a rush. 'I don't know what else to do.'

'You're a wonderful support to her. Your job isn't to get her better, Becky, it's to be her friend.'

I sniffed and looked away, not wanting to break down and sob on our day out. Rob leaned over and stroked my face before putting some music on. His tuneless singing soon had me laughing again.

We arrived at Richmond Park and strolled across the grass holding hands, watching families and couples setting out their rugs and picnics having carefully chosen their own spot. It was a hot day at the end of May, but we were able to find a shady area under a huge oak tree and Rob spread out our rug.

'Drink?' He opened up his hamper and pulled out a bottle of Bucks Fizz. He passed me a glass, making me laugh as he plopped a strawberry inside.

I clinked my glass against his and tried to peek inside the hamper, but he snapped the lid shut. 'For later,' he told me.

We sat side by side, our bodies touching, and watched some children playing ball in front of us.

'Are you missing Charlie and Jack?' he asked.

'Yes and no. Of course I miss them, but it's lovely to spend time with you.'

He cradled his glass and stared straight ahead. 'Do you

miss being a family – with Darren?'

I linked my arm through his. 'That part of my life has changed. I'm ready to move on.'

He turned and looked at me, his eyes searching mine. 'I don't want to stand in the way of you getting back together as a family. If you think it's important for the boys, I'd rather know now – before I fall too deeply.'

I held his gaze, feeling a sudden rush of love for him, but knowing I had to be honest. 'It's what Darren wants,' I said quietly, looking away.

'And you?'

As the question hung in the air everything became clear to me. 'I can't go backwards,' I said.

I sensed his whole body relax as he exhaled, and he lay on his back, pulling me into him. 'I'm glad,' he whispered.

We lay in the dappled sunshine listening to the laughter around us, our arms wrapped round each other as if we were frightened to let go.

'I nearly got married once.' It was a simple statement.

I froze, remembering the rumours I'd heard about him being jilted. I didn't want him to feel he had to bare his soul, but before I could tell him this he moved away from me, propping himself up on his elbow.

'I want you to know everything about me,' he said. 'I don't want there to be any secrets.'

I reached out and stroked his cheek. 'You don't have to.'

'I know.'

He sat upright and I moved close to him, linking my arm through his.

'I used to live with a girl called Melissa,' he said, staring across the park. 'We'd planned our future out – so I thought. We both wanted lots of children – we had even thought of some names.' He smiled ruefully. 'Funny how things turn out.'

'Rob.' I put my hand in his. 'You don't have to tell me this.'

He turned and kissed me. 'I want to.'

'Okay – if you're sure.'

He took a deep breath. 'In a nutshell – we'd booked the wedding and sent out the invitations, but she came home one day and said she wanted to go off travelling.'

'Oh.' I frowned. 'Couldn't you have gone too?'

He gave a short laugh. 'I got all excited and asked where she fancied going first, but she made it painfully clear that this was her personal voyage of discovery. She loved me, but not enough, was how she put it.'

'I'm sorry.'

'I'm not. If it hadn't had happened, I wouldn't have upped sticks and moved away. And I wouldn't have met you.' He kissed me full on the mouth, our bodies melting into each other. 'I fancied you the first time I saw you,' he said when we surfaced for air. 'It was when you came in to talk about Jack. I was so captivated by you I can't even remember what I said. Was it a load of rubbish?'

'No.' I shook my head and laughed. 'You were very kind. Actually,' I giggled, 'I fancied you when I saw you on my visit to the school.'

He kissed my neck, in a spot that caused ripples of longing through my body. 'I missed my class's nativity play because I spent the whole time staring at you when you weren't looking.'

I laughed and kissed him. 'I'm glad we finally got together.'

Our conversation was interrupted by a ball landing on Rob's legs and he stood up, dribbling it back to the children and having a quick game of football with them.

He laughed breathlessly as he sat back down. 'Lunch?'

I nodded and watched as he laid out fresh bread and patés, mini quiches, a bowl of salad and a selection of cheeses and meats.

'This is brilliant,' I enthused. 'I'm being really spoiled.'

We ate slowly, smiling into each other's eyes, conversation unnecessary. Afterwards we lay back on the rug and fed each other strawberries, laughing hysterically as we both nearly choked.

As we walked back to the car hours later Rob slipped his arm round my shoulders. 'As you're by yourself, would you fancy picking up a takeaway and eating it at mine?'

'That would be lovely.' I smiled back at him. 'But I'm buying.'

We arrived at his small semi-detached house with a bag of Chinese food, and I had a look round while he opened a bottle of wine.

'It's probably a bit minimalist and boring for your taste,' he said as he passed me a glass.

'Not at all. I was just thinking how lovely and peaceful it is. My lounge is filled with toys and games.'

'Funny how we always want what we don't have,' he said, sipping his wine.

'You'd like to live with clutter?'

'I'd love to have children,' he replied simply.

Rob put some music on and we sat down on the sofa to enjoy our meal, talking and laughing. He was part way through a story about his university days when he suddenly stopped and looked straight at me. 'I can't do this anymore, Becky.'

My stomach dropped and tears sprung in my eyes. 'What?'

'I want you so much it's painful,' he continued, grabbing hold of my hands. 'I wake up thinking about you and go to bed thinking about you.'

I swallowed hard. 'I don't understand what the problem is.'

He looked away. 'I can't pretend I'm not falling in love with you. And if you don't feel the same way—'

I cupped his face in my hands and kissed him on the lips. 'I *do* feel the same way.'

He didn't smile back, but continued staring at me. 'Are you sure it's completely over with Darren?'

'I don't love him anymore.' It was a relief to say it out loud.

Rob let out a huge sigh and pulled me into him, kissing me slowly and gently. He slipped his hand under my t-shirt, stroking my breasts through my bra. I wanted this man so much. I pulled my t-shirt and bra off and he pushed me onto my back, exploring my nipples with his tongue.

'Shall we go somewhere more comfortable?' His voice was tight and husky.

I nodded and we ran upstairs, laughing and stripping off. I had never felt this comfortable with a man.

He dived onto his double bed, rolling over and opening his arms out to me. He kissed me deeply and I ran my hands all over his body, the feel of his skin heightening my senses.

'God, I want you.' His voice was raspy.

I wrapped my legs round his back, pulling him into me.

Our first orgasms were quick, fast and furious, but as we began to relax we took more time to explore each other's bodies. His broad back was such a turn-on and I made him roll onto his stomach so I could run my hands up and down it.

'Hey,' he complained, 'I can't see your face. Come here.' He rolled onto his back and pulled me on top of him.

*

I sat up and looked round in confusion.

'Are you okay?'

Rob's sleepy eyes were smiling at me, and I snuggled down next to him. 'I didn't know where I was for a moment. The house is so quiet.' I smiled as I thought about Charlie and Jack. 'Even when the boys are asleep I'm somehow aware of their breathing, and I hear them wriggling around.'

'Wriggling can be arranged,' he said naughtily, sliding under the bed-clothes.

As I lay in his arms afterwards I felt happier than I had in years. I kissed him slowly on the lips. 'I'm really sorry, but the boys will be home just after lunch.'

'That's a shame,' he said, pulling me closer. 'I could lie here all day.'

I looked into his eyes and saw my own contentment reflected back. I smiled at him. 'Is it all right if I have a shower?'

'Only if I can keep you company.'

He dropped me home later, and as he drove away I shut the door and sighed heavily. I had to sort things out with Darren, but it wasn't a conversation I was looking forward to having.

*

I missed my chats with Issi and was desperate to tell her all about my wonderful weekend, especially Saturday evening, but each time I'd phoned she'd been sleeping. I called round on the off-chance, but I was in two minds whether or not to go in because there were already several cars in the drive. I was about to phone Jonathan to check when one of the Macmillan nurses came out of the front door.

'Hello Becky,' she said brightly. 'If you want to see Issi I would go in now. I've just given her some pain killers and she'll be asleep soon.' She held the door open and I walked inside, feeling guilty at disturbing my friend.

'I'll only stay a few minutes,' I told the nurse. 'It's important she gets her rest.'

I poked my head round the kitchen door, where Jonathan was busy making sandwiches. 'Hi there.' I smiled at him. 'The nurse let me in.'

He walked over and gave me a huge hug. He looked tired and thin. 'Good to see you,' he said with such warmth I felt genuinely touched. 'Do you want some lunch?'

I shook my head. 'No thanks. How is she today?'

He sighed. 'Not good. Her dad's upstairs with her, but you can go on up.'

'Are you sure?'

He nodded. 'Could you let him know his sandwich is ready?'

Issi's room was full of flowers and the aroma hit me as I walked in. The last time I had been there she had moaned about her bedroom beginning to smell like a hospital ward, and Jonathan had done his best to disguise this with all her favourite flowers.

Issi looked pale, almost grey, and as she lay there holding her dad's hand I tried to remember when she had stopped looking like my best friend.

I smiled at her dad. 'Your lunch is ready,' I said quietly. 'I'll sit with Issi.'

She turned her head in recognition of my voice and I knew my friend was still there – it was only her body that was letting her down. I sat on the side of the bed and held her hand, stroking it gently.

'How are you feeling, darling?'

Issi murmured something I couldn't catch, so I carried on talking. 'I had the most wonderful day with Rob on Saturday. We just seemed to laugh all day. We went back to his house with a takeaway and well – let's just say it was fantastic.'

Issi was smiling back at me but she didn't respond, so I continued.

'When Darren dropped the boys back he tried again to tell me it would be the right thing for all of us to be together, and I was *going* to tell him it was definitely over, but I lost my nerve. The boys had had such a great weekend with him – it seemed almost cruel.' I sighed heavily. 'He's my head option, and Rob is my heart option.'

I felt Issi's grip tighten on my hand. She was saying something to me, but I couldn't hear what it was. I lowered my head and Issi whispered, 'Go with your heart.'

I kissed her on the cheek and carried on chatting for a while, gently stroking her hand. I wasn't sure if she could hear what I was saying because her eyes had closed and her breathing had become laboured. When I thought she had fallen asleep I kissed her again and whispered, 'See you in a few days.'

As I crept out of the room I noticed the card I had given to her shortly after her scan result. I had somehow been drawn to the angel on the front, and I picked it up now to re-read what I had written.

Take strength from knowing what a beautiful friendship we share – when one of us falls, the other lifts her up. Just remember your angels have spread their wings around you and are holding you tight. Love you always, Becky x.

Chapter Eighteen

What's the time Mr Wolf?
What's the time Mr Wolf?
Nine o'clock to three o'clock...
Time to spread malicious gossip.

I lay in bed staring at the curtains which were blowing gently in the wind. I rolled over, thinking how much I was dreading the day ahead. I pulled the quilt over my head, wishing I could make everything go away.

My mum padded quietly past my room and shortly afterwards the boys popped their heads round the door.

'Can we go down and put the telly on, Mum?' Charlie whispered, seemingly aware of my fragile state.

'We won't make any noise,' Jack added.

My mum was suddenly standing behind them. 'You two go into the kitchen,' she told them, 'and I'll come and make your breakfast in a few minutes.' She placed a mug of coffee by my bed and stroked my hair. 'I'll leave you in peace,' she said. 'You've plenty of time.'

My mum had come into her own since I'd phoned her to say Issi had died. She had dropped everything and arrived the following day, holding me close as I lay in bed, sobbing in my grief. Since then she had taken over the running of the house;

she had made sure the boys were ready for school, taking them and picking them up, and she had cooked and cleaned.

She had told me that Vicente had wanted to come and help look after us, but he had been worried about intruding. Whether it was his influence or not, Mum seemed pleased to be here and she was trying her hardest to bond with me.

'I've spent a lot of time mulling over my faults as a mother,' she'd told me over a bottle of wine the first evening. 'And I want to prove myself as a decent mum, or certainly a good friend, someone you want to spend time with.'

I had cried in response.

'I know I can't make the pain go away for you,' she had continued, 'but I want to help you get through this.'

Mum came back upstairs and disturbed my thoughts. 'You have a soak in the bath while I get the boys organised. Since it's half-term I'll take them to the park later.' She straightened the duvet and plumped up the pillows. 'It's a lovely morning out there.'

'Is it?' I asked. How could it possibly be a lovely day when I was burying my best friend?

'Yes, it is.' Mum spoke firmly as she drew back the curtains, letting the bright sunshine flood into my bedroom. 'Go and get in the bath, and then I'll make you some breakfast.' She held her hand up as I started to protest. 'You'll need something to give you strength.' She kissed me lightly on the forehead, and I appreciated what a supreme effort she was making.

I lay in the bath for what seemed like ages, enjoying the comfort of the warm water and the aroma of the bubble bath. My mind was full and I was finding it difficult to think straight. Darren had a place and Rob had another, but everything was clouded by my over-whelming feelings of grief and loss. I tried to think logically about where my life was leading.

Since Issi's death I hadn't had a proper conversation with anyone, and I was already missing the one person who could have helped me sort out my love-life. I felt racked with guilt. Having told Rob it was all over with Darren, I was still uncertain that what I was doing was the best thing for the boys.

As I tossed these thoughts round and round in my mind I started to shiver. I had been lying there so long the water had gone cold, and there was nothing left to do other than get on with the day.

The morning dragged by. After lunch, with my mum's help, I picked out a suitably subdued outfit to wear. At the last minute I swapped the blouse I had chosen for the red one Issi liked so much.

'After all, it's Issi I'm dressing for,' I said.

'Perfect choice,' Mum agreed.

The doorbell rang and I opened the front door to Darren, looking sombre in his black suit. 'Thanks for coming,' I said quietly. 'There's no way I could have driven today.'

'It's the least I could do,' he replied. 'I want to give you my support.' He looked up and nodded at Mum.

'Darren,' she said curtly, shoving a couple of handkerchiefs into my handbag. She held me close, conveying her feelings without the need for words.

I swallowed hard as I climbed into the car, determined not to cry before I even arrived at the church. Darren and I barely spoke during the short journey, but he reached across several times and squeezed my hand. I found I was almost grateful for this comfort, and I was surprised by how natural it seemed.

We pulled into the church car park and I felt my legs turn to lead. 'I can't do this,' I said, starting to shake.

Darren leaned across and held my hands. 'You'll get through it.' He glanced up and waved. 'Jonathan's there. Go and be with him, and I'll see you after the service.'

Jonathan's face was pale and drawn, his eyes swollen

from crying. We hugged each other for what seemed like an eternity, neither of us wanting to break free.

We had been in constant touch, planning the funeral, and I knew how brave he had been over the past few days for his children's sakes. I felt as if my heart would break.

Issi's dad walked towards us, and as he gave me a kiss he began to tremble in my arms. 'I can't believe I'm burying my daughter,' he stuttered. 'It doesn't seem two minutes since it was her mum's funeral.'

'I know.' I sniffed, tears rolling down my cheeks.

'This is a terrible disease, Becky.' He kept hold of my hand and we followed Jonathan behind Issi's coffin, sitting on the front row with Issi's step-mum.

The service passed in a blur and I was grateful for the handkerchiefs Mum had given me. Jonathan talked lovingly about Issi as a wife and mother, his voice thick with emotion and barely audible at times. When he said he'd lost his best friend and soul mate, I sobbed openly, thinking that I felt the same. The wake passed in the same haze and as I was saying my goodbyes Jonathan passed me a letter.

'Issi gave me this the week before she died.' He took a deep breath and closed his eyes momentarily. 'She knew she didn't have long, and there were things she wanted to say before the drugs took hold, so she wrote it all down.'

I stared at my best friend's writing, tracing it gently with my finger.

'She wrote one for you, one for each of the children and one for me.' He swallowed hard. 'Issi loved you very much, Becky.' He kissed my cheek. 'We'll see you soon.'

I nodded and went over to see Sam, sobbing on her shoulder.

'I just kept thinking about when we were children.' She sniffed loudly. 'All the things we planned to do with our lives. And now…'

'I know. I can't take it all in.' My head hurt and my eyes were stinging. 'I just want to go home now.'

'Do you want a lift with Dave and me?'

'I'm okay, thanks. Darren's waiting for me.'

I sat in the car with him, crying uncontrollably, and he gave me time to compose myself before driving off.

'Do you want to come back to mine?' he asked. 'You don't look ready to face the boys.'

I nodded through my tears. 'That would be great.'

We drove in silence, and when we arrived at Darren's large detached house he showed me into the lounge. I wandered round the well-furnished room, looking at photographs of me and the boys, of the four of us together as a family, laughing and smiling. Suddenly he was standing next to me holding a bottle of wine.

'Merlot.' I smiled. 'Your favourite.'

'I remember you being rather partial to it as well,' he teased.

I sank into the cream leather sofa, and as the smoothness of those first few sips glided down my throat we reminisced about Issi. The second glass slipped down faster than I would normally have drunk, but the alcohol was anaesthetising the pain of my loss.

I was getting drunk by the third glass, but I no longer cared. I picked up a photograph of the four of us. 'Why did you leave me, Darren?' The words shot out of my mouth.

He stared at the carpet without answering me.

'You love the boys and I thought you were happy with our life,' I continued, unable to stop myself. 'So what made you fall for her? What did she have that I didn't?'

Darren still didn't reply and the silence became overwhelming. 'It was never about me not loving you,' he said eventually. His voice was calm and he looked straight into my eyes. 'I always loved you, but it was about me needing to be loved, too.' He looked away. 'Shelley made me feel wanted,' he said. 'You had forgotten about me. The boys took all your time—'

'What?' I exploded. '*Our* children took up my time but I never stopped—'

'I just felt there was nothing left for *me*,' Darren interrupted. 'I needed some affection, but I felt I was simply playing the role of financial provider.'

I stared at him in disbelief. 'How *dare* you accuse me of ignoring your needs?' Months of pent-up anger started to bubble inside me like a dormant volcano. 'Why didn't *you* make more effort to put things right, instead of running to the first tart who flashed her knickers?' Whoosh. The lava started flowing. I was screaming hysterically, tears streaming down my face. 'I was caring for our boys, keeping everything together while you worked away most weeks. Who gave *me* any attention?'

Darren started to cry silently, letting the tears roll down his cheeks unchecked. He moved closer to me. 'I'm so sorry. You're right, and I wish I could turn the clock back.'

We stood staring at each other, contrition in his eyes, anger in mine.

I can't remember who made the first move, but without any conscious thought we were suddenly kissing, fiercely and with an animal passion I had missed so much. We made love on the carpet as if we had never been apart.

Afterwards he held me in his arms. 'I love you,' he whispered.

*

Mum hugged me as I told her what details of the funeral I could remember. 'Jonathan gave me a letter from Issi,' I said, sighing, 'but I can't face opening it.'

'Do you want to do it together?'

'Maybe later.' I shrugged. 'I just need to be by myself at the moment.'

'I understand,' she said, making two strong coffees. 'I met your friend Kate at the park, and the boys are playing back at her house.'

I nodded absentmindedly.

'She said they can sleep over if you like.'

I refocused on what Mum was saying. 'That would be great. I need some time and space. I'll text her.'

I lay in bed that night, unable to sleep. I turned the envelope from Issi over and over in my hands, smelling a faint trace of her. Eventually I opened the letter.

My darling Becky,

I'm so sorry we won't grow old together as we'd planned, but the time we've shared has been so precious to me. I couldn't have asked for a better friend.

I wish I could stay a bit longer to help you through your problems, but just remember how much you've moved on with your life and how strong you've become. I know your sensible side will be telling you to take Darren back, but the best thing for Jack and Charlie is a happy mum and Rob makes you happy. Follow your heart for once – not your head.

You deserve a happy life, Becky and that means being true to yourself.

I love you so much and I can't tell you how much I've valued our friendship. You've been such a special friend – my soul mate.

I'll be watching over you – helping where I can. Love you always,

Issi xxx

I held the letter close. What would my friend have made of the mess I'd got myself into? I pulled the quilt over my head and cried myself to sleep.

*

I got up early to make breakfast for Mum as a thank you. I perched on the end of her bed, enjoying the smile spreading slowly across her face as she saw her surprise. I liked being friends, companions, and I hoped we'd turned the corner in our relationship.

I showed her Issi's letter and explained about Rob.

'What are you going to do?'

'I don't know,' I replied, staring across the room.

We sat in silence, and as she sipped her tea Mum looked at me sadly. 'You always used to tell me how Issi's mum brought you both breakfast in bed when you slept over.'

I nodded, thinking about Issi's mum, with her laughing blue eyes and long blonde hair. She was an Enid Blyton-type mother, who couldn't do enough for her only child – or for me, either.

'I'm sorry I disappointed you, Becky.'

I looked directly at her. There was a sadness in her eyes that I'd never seen before. When we were growing up she hadn't seemed to care whether we ate breakfast or lunch, and the fridge was often empty, but none of that seemed to matter anymore. She was simply my mum.

I suddenly thought about Issi's children and leaned forward, overwhelmed by my feelings of grief for them. 'Who'll make breakfast in bed for Andrew, Emma and Ben?' I whispered.

Mum put her tray down and came and sat next to me, holding me in her arms. 'They'll be fine, Becky,' she said. 'They've got Jonathan and their grandad – and they've got you.'

I looked up and stared at her. 'Apart from Issi's dad, I'm the only one who knows what she was like as a child.' I blew my nose on the tissue Mum handed me. 'I'll write it all down for them,' I said excitedly. 'All the stories of her childhood.'

'Like the one where Mr Sampson next door had to call the fire brigade?'

'Oh, yes.' I started to giggle. 'Issi and I decided to make a campfire in the garden to toast marshmallows, but we didn't know how to make a fire.'

Mum shook her head. 'What was it you used?'

'Rags and newspaper from the shed, I think. But then we got distracted in the kitchen and when we came back out half the garden was alight.'

We laughed together, and then Mum took my hands in hers. 'It's such a shame Issi won't be joining us in Spain.'

'Yes,' I agreed. 'She was looking forward to it.'

'Why don't you ask Rob if he'd like to come with you?'

I stared at her for a while, nausea rippling through me. Would what had happened with Darren yesterday ruin my relationship with Rob? 'It's a lovely idea, Mum. Could I think about it?'

'I don't know what there is to think about,' she said.

*

I wanted my mum's last day in England to be spent doing something fun. She had stayed for over a week, but because I had been so caught up in my grief I hadn't had chance to spend much quality time with her. This was the last time we would see each other before the wedding, so were going shopping for outfits and had asked Sam to come along. The three of us hit the shops and enjoyed trying on different clothes, laughing at each other when we didn't get it right.

'Mum and I are going to have our make-up done,' Sam told

me. 'Do you fancy it as well? They can fit us all in.'

I shook my head. 'I need to go to L'Olivo – I've been putting off telling Nico about Issi.'

Sam hugged me. 'Okay.'

I pushed the café door open tentatively, feeling shaky as I walked inside – memories swamped me immediately. I swallowed hard and was just about to ask for Nico when he came rushing towards me.

'Becky. How is she?'

I let out a strangled sob and my legs buckled underneath me. Nico caught hold of me and gently propelled me into his office, away from the staring diners. He sat down next to me and held me for the next twenty minutes while I sobbed. Guessing what I was unable to tell him, he cried too.

I was finally able to catch my breath. 'She slipped away last week,' I told him.

He nodded, wiping away fresh tears. 'No pain?' he asked quietly, both arms still clamped round me.

'No pain,' I whispered into his chest.

The door opened quietly and I sat upright to wipe my eyes, aware that a man was watching us. Older than Nico, his black hair was flecked with grey and his brown eyes were filled with concern. He knelt down and held Nico in his arms, rocking him gently. 'It's bad news?' he asked in a soft Italian accent.

Nico nodded and the man kissed him gently on the cheek. 'I'm so sorry, *cara*,' he whispered.

I stared in amazement, and when Nico looked up he laughed. 'I thought you knew about me.'

I shook my head, still unable to speak.

'This is my partner, Benito.'

'Partner?'

He nodded and smiled. 'We own this place together.' He looked up at Benito and smiled. 'We've been together for eight years.'

I was staring at them both with my mouth open. 'But…' I stammered. 'All the flirting – we thought you liked us.'

Nico smiled. 'I do like you. I love seeing ladies feel good about themselves and so I love to make them smile, but that's as far as it goes.'

As I shook hands with Benito I suddenly started laughing. 'Oh, how Issi would have enjoyed this one,' I told them.

'She would.' Nico smiled back. He was lost in thought for a moment. 'Becky, we have a private courtyard at the back. I'd like to plant an olive tree in Issi's memory.'

I choked back fresh tears. 'She'd love that.'

'Good. Then I can think of her every time it flowers and bears fruit.'

*

Over lunch I told Mum and Sam what had happened with Darren, needing to share it with someone.

'How does that make you feel about him?' Sam asked.

I shrugged. 'I don't know.' I fiddled with my fork and sighed. 'If it had happened six months ago I would have been delighted.'

'And now?'

My mum tutted. 'Don't forget how he treated you.'

'Mum, let her finish,' Sam said in frustration.

I sipped my drink. 'My work's taking off, the boys are settled—'

'And you've met Rob,' Sam finished for me.

I nodded sadly. 'Do you think he'll still want me after what has happened?'

Mum put her knife and fork down in exasperation. 'Don't tell him.'

'That would make me a hypocrite,' I replied. 'I'd hate myself, and I couldn't start a new relationship with that hanging over me.'

'Well, one step at a time,' Sam said, trying to encourage me. 'Speak to Darren first and get that out of the way.'

'Okay.' I swallowed nervously. 'Should I invite him round?'

Sam thought for a moment. 'When we drop Mum at the airport tomorrow, how about I take the boys home with me and you meet him at a pub for lunch?'

I let out a long slow sigh. 'I wish things were simpler.'

*

'Bye, Mum.'

'Bye, my darlings.' She kissed Sam and me before hugging the boys. 'I'll call you when I'm home.'

I was upset to see my mum leave, knowing that I would miss her more than I had felt possible. We tearfully waved her off through the departures gate, the boys crying too because they had bonded with their grandmother during the week.

Darren was waiting outside the pub and we wandered inside, finding a table in a quiet corner. He bought some drinks and sat down opposite me.

'I've ordered for us,' he said.

'Oh.'

'You do still like salmon?'

'Yes, but that's not necessarily what I would have chosen today.' I shook my head. 'You can't run my life for me.'

He stared back, his jaw clenched in irritation. 'I just thought it would be one less stress for you.'

I sighed. 'I'm perfectly capable of ordering my own meal.'

'Let's not argue.' He smiled and caught hold of my hand. 'It must be hard for you at the moment – I know how much you're hurting.'

He was trying to show me his caring side and I felt a pang

of guilt.

'Becky,' he said after a small silence, 'have you thought about things?'

I fiddled with my glass, and I was glad we were interrupted by the waitress bringing our meals.

'The boys are so pleased you're back,' I started gently, taking a deep breath. 'The thing is – I've just started seeing someone.' I couldn't meet Darren's eyes and I stared at my food until he replied.

'Anyone I know?'

'Rob – the boys' football coach.'

Darren raised his eyebrows and pushed his food round his plate. 'Oh. That's come as a surprise. Is it serious?'

I looked up at him. 'It's too early to say, but that's not the point, Darren.' I lowered my voice. 'He's made me realise I'm not in love with you anymore, and I've finally been able to move on with my life. I'm not bitter, I'm not angry – I'm just ready to move on.'

Darren's eyes filled with tears. 'What about the other afternoon? Didn't that mean anything to you?'

I breathed deeply. 'Of course it did,' I replied. 'Part of me will always love you – but I just don't feel enough for you.'

He pushed his plate away angrily. 'I made a mistake, Becky and I will always regret it.' He sank his head into his hands before looking up at me, tears streaming down his face. 'Are you sure that's how you really feel?'

I nodded, keeping my eyes fixed on the table.

'Then I don't want us to feel uncomfortable with each other,' he stated simply. 'We have so much history and two wonderful boys.'

'Thank you,' I replied. 'I'll make sure Jack and Charlie always know you're the most important man in their lives.'

I wondered briefly if I had done the right thing, but the thought of Rob reassured me. I stared down at my untouched meal, my stomach in knots, desperately hoping he would be able to forgive my indiscretion.

Neither of us had any appetite, and as we left the pub Darren kissed me on the cheek. 'There's still time to change your mind,' he told me. '*Please* reconsider. I haven't signed the divorce papers yet.'

'I'm sorry,' I whispered back. Please don't start being difficult, I thought. I haven't the strength left to cope.

He closed his eyes and nodded. 'I'll see you next weekend when I collect the boys.'

The tears rolled down my face as I drove away. I had said goodbye to my best friend and my husband, all in the space of a week. I hoped things were going to start getting better for me, but I had one more painful conversation to get through.

I pulled up outside Rob's house and while I sat in the car I played the conversation I was about to have in my head.

I walked up the drive slowly and rang the bell.

'Hey.' He smiled, before kissing me on the lips. 'What a lovely surprise.'

I stepped inside, nausea permeating every cell. I wanted to retch; I wanted to run away; I wanted Rob to forgive me.

He stood in front of me, putting both hands on my shoulders. 'Becky?' He frowned. 'You look terrible. What on earth's wrong?'

'I…I just need to tell you something.'

'Oh.' The colour drained from his face. 'Come into the lounge, then.'

Neither of us sat down, the tension almost tangible. Rob took a deep breath. 'You've decided to go back to Darren.'

'No.' I shook my head fiercely. 'He knows it's all over.'

Rob exhaled loudly. 'You frightened me, Becky.' He flopped into an easy chair. 'What's the matter? You can tell me anything.'

I remained standing, tears flowing down my cheeks. Rob

jumped up, starting to walk over to me, but I held my hand up to stop him. It would just make things harder. 'Darren gave me a lift home after Issi's funeral.'

Rob stood in front of me, frowning. 'Yes, I know. You went back to his first. You told me.'

I nodded, wiping my eyes with the backs of my hands. 'We had a screaming row. We both finally talked about why things went wrong.'

'And?'

'And.'

'Becky, this is killing me. What's wrong?'

'We had a lot to drink – an awful lot, and I hadn't eaten anything all day.'

'So?'

'I'm sorry, Rob,' I sobbed. 'One minute we were yelling at each other, and the next we were having sex.'

'What?' He stepped away from me.

'It was nothing – meaningless. I think it was the grief and the emotion…' My voice trailed away. No matter how I dressed it up, it sounded awful.

He turned his back on me, staring out at the garden.

I was rooted to the spot, paralysed by the fear that he wouldn't be able to forgive me. 'Rob? Please say something.'

He didn't turn round when he spoke. 'I think you'd better just go.' His voice was muffled, choked with emotion.

'Rob…Please…Can we talk? I don't want to lose you,' I cried out. 'I just wanted to be honest with you.'

He remained standing with his back to me, his body rigid, and I let myself out.

*

I struggled through the following week. Some days I felt like hiding away and crying, but I had to keep going for the boys' sakes. I worked hard to take my mind off things, but I wasn't happy with a lot of my work, knowing it wasn't my best effort. I finished the leaflet for school and was confident that this piece, at least, was well-written. I took it into the playground to give to Martin, but before I could find him Angela came over to me.

'Hi Becky. Have you seen that Miss Whittaker is back today?'

I could see her preparing for the day ahead through the classroom window. 'That's great news. The boys have missed her.'

'There's been no news on Helen Stevens,' Angela continued. 'She's keeping a low profile.'

I nodded slowly. I hadn't told Angela I'd visited Helen because there'd been enough gossiping going on. 'I keep thinking about those poor children.'

'Me too,' added Kate, who had joined us.

'I don't think we'll see them again. The house is up for sale,' Angela told us. 'I'll catch you later,' she said before wandering off to talk to some other mums.

Mandy and Martin had walked over and they caught the tail-end of the conversation. 'Poor woman,' Martin said.

'I know.' I thrust my hands in my pockets, staring morosely at the ground. 'I keep thinking about something Issi said to me,' I said slowly.

Kate rubbed my arm, and I appreciated her gesture.

'When I told Issi about visiting Helen,' I continued, 'she said we were lucky to have support from good friends.'

Mandy nodded, linking her arm through Martin's. 'You can't put a price on friendship.'

'Helen had her friends,' Kate said, 'but maybe they didn't support her? Maybe she didn't confide in them?'

We all fell silent for a few seconds.

'I wish I'd realised how she was struggling to cope,' I said, 'but I was so caught up in fighting her, I didn't see it.'

'None of us did,' Mandy sympathised. 'She wasn't an easy woman.'

'No.' I sighed heavily. 'Some good has got to come out of this, though. I'm going to write a piece and submit it to as many magazines as I can find.'

Kate frowned at me. 'About what?'

'About women supporting each other.'

'Er, what about men?' Martin interrupted.

'You're right.' I smiled. 'But it is mostly women in the playground.'

'It's a great idea,' Kate said. 'The balancing act we all do is so tough – there have been many days when you and Mandy have picked me up.'

Mandy nodded in agreement and I couldn't help but smile. I had somehow always thought they had given to me – I never imagined they valued what I gave back. Mandy brushed away a tear. 'I'm going to speak to Mrs Jenkins to see if we can all write testimonies for Helen.'

Kate frowned. 'Testimonies? What do you mean?'

'From what Becky said, it sounds like Helen was bringing up the children without much support. I know how hard that is – there have been mornings when I haven't wanted to get out of bed.'

Martin slipped his arm round her shoulders.

'Not now, though.' She grinned at him.

'Great idea,' I told her. 'It might mean the difference between a custodial sentence and her getting the help she needs.'

We all fell silent, lost in our own thoughts, until the bell rang. I suddenly remembered the completed leaflet I had for Martin, and I handed it to him. 'Hope it's okay. I'm pretty pleased with it.'

'Thanks. I'm sure it is,' he said. 'I'll let you know after our next meeting.'

We all saw our children into school and as we walked away Mandy mentioned something about sports day.

'Sports day?' I frowned at her. 'Have I missed another letter?'

'Becky, you are hopeless,' she said. 'It's next Wednesday. We watch the children race and then stay for a picnic, so you'll need to bring a hamper for you and the boys.'

I blushed. 'I probably have the letter, but I'm not functioning properly at the moment. Next Wednesday rings a bell.' I paused for a moment. 'Oh, I know why.'

My friends looked at me expectantly, waiting for me to continue and I blushed again. 'It's my birthday.'

*

I sat at the kitchen table fighting back tears. I was remembering twelve months ago when Issi had turned up on my doorstep with presents and a chocolate cake. As I fingered the necklace she had given me I realised again how acutely I missed her. I didn't want to cry because I knew the boys would be up shortly, and right on cue I heard them thunder across the landing and down the stairs.

'Happy birthday, Mummy!'

I laughed when I saw the assortment of presents they were clutching, desperately trying to not let any fall. They dropped them onto the table, insisting I open them straight away, and the sight of their shining faces banished any gloomy thoughts. Darren must have taken them shopping, and I was touched by his thoughtfulness.

As I started to open the gifts the phone rang and Jack ran to answer it. 'It's Aunty Sam,' he yelled at the top of his voice.

'Hi, Sam.'

'Happy birthday. Have you had anything exciting?'

'I'm just opening the boys' presents—'

'No. I mean from *anyone* exciting?'

'Oh.' I stared at the phone. 'He's still not been in touch.'

'I'm surprised – he must have taken it very badly.'

'Yes.' I sighed. 'If he'd screamed and shouted at me we could have talked it over, but it was the look of hurt on his face when I told him, and the silence that followed, that makes me think he can't forgive me.'

'I'm so sorry. I'll try and give you a good night out tonight to make up for it.'

'Thanks – see you at eight.'

I put the phone down and smiled brightly at the boys. 'You know Daddy is going to babysit tonight?'

'Yes,' they chorused.

'Where are you going?' Charlie asked.

My smile dropped as I thought about how I would like to be spending my birthday. 'I'm going for a meal with Aunty Sam,' I told them cheerily.

'That's nice,' Jack said. 'Can we have some of your chocolates for breakfast?'

*

I arrived at school with my hamper and rug, joining my friends at the side of the running track. I waved to the boys, who were sitting on the opposite side, and as I watched Rob organising the races I fought back the urge to cry at what I had lost.

The adults cheered the children on, waving madly as they ran past, and when it came to the parents' races I smiled at the seriousness of it. I nudged Mandy. 'Look how competitive the dads are. I can't believe they're all limbering up.'

Mandy giggled. 'They obviously don't want to embarrass themselves in front of their offspring.'

'It's the mums' turn next,' Kate joined in. 'They're as bad, look. Anyone fancy it?'

Mandy folded her arms across her chest. 'Not a chance.'

I shook my head, not wanting the embarrassment of being near Rob.

Kate laughed. 'How about the three-legged race, then?'

I really didn't want to, but Mandy thought it would be fun and she dragged me across. Rob tied our legs together and we managed to avoid eye contact with each other.

Mandy frowned. 'I thought you two were good friends?' She grinned wickedly. 'Martin told me—'

'We were,' I said, staring at the ground. 'It's a long sad story.'

'Oh, I'm really sorry,' Mandy panted as we started limping along. 'That's such a shame. How are you feeling?'

'Gutted,' I panted back.

'We'd better win that prize then,' she said. She picked up the pace, overtaking all the other mothers and dragging me along with her.

At the end of the parents' races there was a small awards ceremony with boxes of chocolates being given out by the staff. Mandy and I were called up to receive ours from Rob, and Mandy kissed him on both cheeks and then pushed me forward so he had to do the same to me.

'That must be your birthday kiss.' She kept her eyes trained on Rob.

He raised his eyebrows in surprise. 'It's your birthday?'

I blushed and stared at my feet, nodding dumbly. I have missed you, I thought. Please give me a second chance.

He didn't say anything else, moving on to hand out the next prize, and I walked away.

Once the races were over the parents spread their rugs on the field and the children joined us for a picnic. I sat in a group with Martin, Mandy, Kate and Angela and as we were unpacking our goodies Martin announced that he needed to go back to his car. He returned a few minutes later carrying a bag of presents and a handful of pink and purple helium balloons, which he tied to my hamper.

I shook my head, laughing as I started to thank them, but then the tears poured out and my friends rushed to hug me. I was laughing and crying, hugging my children, and as I opened my presents there was nowhere I would rather have been at that moment.

During the picnic I glanced over at Rob a few times, and each time he was looking over at me. My stomach somersaulted, but he didn't wave or smile and I couldn't read his expression. He was sitting next to Louise, who was chatting away and sharing her picnic with him. Had he turned to her for comfort?

As I was packing our lunch away I became aware of someone standing behind me. I stood up slowly and turned round. Rob was inches away from me, his face expressionless. Neither of us spoke.

Martin walked over to me. 'Er, bye Becky. Enjoy your evening. Come on,' he hissed at Mandy, Angela and Kate, who were hovering.

Once we were alone I took a deep breath. 'I'm so sorry. I didn't mean to hurt you.'

'Shh,' Rob interrupted, putting a finger against my lips. 'It's me who should be saying sorry.'

'Oh.' I frowned at him. 'I don't understand.'

'Because of what happened with Melissa, I immediately assumed the worst – that you didn't want me either.'

'But I explained—'

'I know,' he replied, smiling. 'It sounds ridiculous, but that's what happens when your confidence gets knocked.'

'I'm so sorry,' I repeated.

'I've thought about nothing else for days, and actually it's made me realise how strong my feelings for you are.'

I looked up at him hopefully.

'You're beautiful and clever and...and I just want to be with you.'

Relief flooded through my body, every cell bursting with happiness. 'So can we try again?'

'If you'll have me?' he teased.

'I'd love to,' I replied wickedly.

We walked side by side, oblivious to anyone else around us, and Rob gestured at my balloons. 'I was so jealous when Martin gave those to you,' he said. 'I wanted it to be me.'

I giggled. 'I was jealous of you sitting with Louise – I wondered if you'd got together with her.'

Rob burst out laughing. 'I think she did once have a thing for me – but it was never reciprocated. Actually,' he whispered, 'she's seeing one of the doctors from the hospital.'

'I'm pleased for her.'

'So,' he said, moving as close as he probably thought was decent. 'It's your birthday.'

'Yes, another one,' I replied.

'What are you doing to celebrate?'

'Just out with my sister – nothing special.'

He caught hold of my hand fleetingly, sending shivers down my spine. 'Would your sister mind if you came round to mine instead?'

I giggled. 'I think she'd be delighted.'

*

I stepped out of the shower, humming to myself. I'd had a wonderful day so far and there was more to come. I searched through my drawers for some matching underwear and came across the cream and pink lace bra and knickers Issi had bought me exactly a year ago. They had been an additional present to my necklace – 'For you to wear when you start dating again.' Her voice was as clear in my head as if she'd been standing next to me. 'This year you're going to move on, Becky,' she'd said.

I sat on the bed and held them to my skin, suddenly feeling close to her. 'Thank you,' I said out loud, surprising myself that I didn't cry. I snapped the labels off with a shiver of anticipation. A perfect end to a perfect day.

I took time getting ready, wanting to look my best for Rob, and by the time Darren arrived I was happy with what I'd chosen. I walked downstairs with an air of confidence to find him standing in the hall holding an elegantly wrapped present. He drew his breath in sharply.

'You look beautiful.' He kissed me on the cheek as he handed me the box.

The boys watched as I unwrapped it, and I gasped when I saw the delicate Tiffany bracelet.

'That's pretty,' Charlie said. 'Come on, Jack. Let's go and play Batman.'

The boys ran off and I looked up at Darren. 'Thank you. That's so kind – I never thought I'd own one of these. They cost a fortune.'

'You're welcome.' He didn't take his eyes off me. 'He's a lucky man.'

I turned away but he followed me, pulling me close. 'Don't go out with him tonight,' he whispered as he kissed my neck softly. 'Stay with me – you know we want each other.'

Chapter Nineteen

Rob and Becky,
Sitting in a tree.
K-I-S-S-I-N-G

'No, Darren,' I said, pushing him away. 'Here.' I handed the bracelet back to him. 'If that's what it was for, I don't want it.'

'Sorry.' He put the box on the hall table. 'I just love you so much.'

I opened the front door, turning to face him. 'Don't do this to me. It's not fair.'

As I drove to Rob's my temples thumped. I'd wanted so much to enjoy this evening, but now it was spoiled before it had even begun.

No, I wouldn't let Darren do that to me.

I pulled up outside Rob's house and took a couple of pain killers, breathing deeply to calm down.

I rang the doorbell, pushing away the memories of my last visit, but there was no tension this time. I was enveloped by an aura of tranquillity. He had placed candles all round the house and I laughed as he poured me a glass of wine.

'Happy birthday.' He kissed me gently before taking my hand and leading me upstairs.

I gasped as he pushed his bedroom door open. The whole

room was lit by candles of every size and colour, and I breathed in the heady mixture of the different scents.

We sat on the bed resting against the headboard, Rob with his arm round me as we finished our drinks.

He unbuttoned my blouse, admiring my lace bra before I unclasped it. He kissed me slowly, but then frustration overwhelmed me and I whipped the rest of my clothes off. Laughing, Rob followed suit, and as his skin touched mine I wanted him with a physical ache. I pulled him into me and we made love slowly and passionately.

Afterwards he rolled onto his back, breathing hard, and I snuggled into him. 'Look under the pillow,' he whispered.

I pulled out a small unwrapped box.

'I'm sorry about the lack of originality,' he said as I opened it, 'but by the time I'd finished work the shops were just about closing.'

I held the heart-shaped necklace between my fingers, overwhelmed by his love for me.

*

I had been back to Issi's house several times since she died but the thought of it still filled me with dread. Jonathan had asked me to bring the boys round because he had bought the children a puppy and he thought Charlie and Jack would love to see it.

I pulled into the drive and the boys jumped out of the car, but I sat for a while. I was still finding it difficult to face walking into my friend's house without her being there. I was picturing what she would normally be doing inside as Jonathan walked towards me.

'It's all right,' he said as I stepped out of the car. 'I often sit here and do the same thing. It gets easier.'

He was looking thin and haggard and I hugged him, both

of us holding on to each other.

We linked arms and walked into the house together to be met by five very excited children and one cowering collie puppy.

'This is Alfie,' said Andrew, bending down to stroke him.

Charlie looked at me with what I knew he considered to be his cutest smile. 'Can we have one?'

'He's gorgeous, but no,' I replied resolutely.

I left the children playing and followed Jonathan into the kitchen. Over coffee he explained why he had bought a puppy.

'It's not a substitute for their mum – just a distraction to help ease the pain.'

'I understand,' I said. 'Are things getting any easier for *you*?'

He closed his eyes and breathed deeply. 'I can smell her perfume, I can hear her talking to me and I have so much to tell her, but she's not here.'

'I know,' I said quietly.

'At night I dream she's lying next to me, but in the morning our huge bed is empty on her side. Sometimes it's unbearable, Becky.'

We sat holding hands, both of us crying softly.

'I'm always here for you and the kids,' I said after a while. 'Even if you just want to talk.'

He nodded, wiping his eyes on a handkerchief.

'How about on a practical level? Can I do anything?'

Jonathan shook his head. 'Issi's dad and Maureen are clucking round us – it helps them, too, and I have an au pair starting on Monday.'

'Okay – but let me know.'

The boys wandered into the kitchen.

'I'm starving,' Charlie announced loudly.

'I'm really starving,' Jack added.

'Time to go.' I held my hands up and laughed.

'It's always great to see you,' Jonathan said as he kissed me goodbye. 'It'll get easier – for all of us.'

'We'll see you soon,' I promised, and as I drove away my thoughts were full of Issi and the letter she had written to me. Unconsciously I fingered Rob's necklace. It hadn't cost as much as the Tiffany bracelet, but as Issi had said – follow your heart.

*

I woke up with my stomach churning in nervous excitement. It was the morning of the school fête and Rob was determined that we were going to announce our relationship to the world. I turned onto my side, imagining he was next to me, my senses tingling as I thought back to my birthday evening.

It felt right to make our relationship public knowledge, but I felt guilty. I hadn't told any of my playground friends, although I had a feeling some of them had guessed. Rob and I had enjoyed having our little secret – it had been exciting, and I knew Mandy and Martin would understand this. I was worried about Darren, though. He had said he might come along to the fête for an hour. How would he react to seeing me with another man? At the moment we were barely speaking.

'Are you looking forward to the fête?' I asked Charlie and Jack during breakfast.

They both nodded, too busy concentrating on their cereal to look up.

'Mr Phillips will be there,' I continued. I took a gulp of my tea. 'Mr Phillips and I are friends.'

Charlie put his spoon down and looked at me, waiting for more information.

'We're *special* friends,' I told them both.

Jack paused with his spoon in mid-air. 'Urgh.' He pulled a

face. 'Does he kiss you?'

I was taken aback. 'Sometimes, yes,' I replied. 'Is that all right?'

The boys exchanged bored glances. 'Can I have some more cereal?' Charlie asked.

*

The fête started at eleven, but Rob was collecting for the raffle during the first hour. I met Kate outside school and we walked in together, admiring the school field which had been set out with bouncy castles, a soft play area, a coconut shy and many more stalls and activities. We gave the children a pound coin each and they ran off to spend it as quickly as possible.

As Kate and I followed behind them we spotted Mandy and Martin walking across the other side of the field, hand in hand.

'It's so sweet,' said Kate. 'They make a lovely couple – I'm almost envious.'

'Yes, it's great,' I agreed.

We were interrupted by a familiar voice behind us. 'Raffle tickets, ladies?'

I spun round to find Rob smiling at me. He was being helped by one of the mums, who was tearing off the tickets for him. We couldn't talk, but the smile that passed between us didn't go un-noticed by Kate. She looked me straight in the eyes.

'Yes?' she demanded. 'What's going on?'

I blushed. 'Let's pay for the kids to go on the bouncy castle. It'll give me five minutes to fill you in.'

As the children bounced and screamed, Kate jumped up and down and screamed herself. 'You dark horse. I had no idea, although I did wonder what was going on at the picnic.' She hugged me. 'I'm so pleased for you – he's lovely. Does anyone else know?'

'Not yet, but Rob's planning to make it common knowledge by the end of the fête.'

Later on we met up with Martin and Mandy and the four of us decided to sit on the grass with the children and have lunch. Martin took our orders and headed off for the barbeque while the children ran around, leaving us to chat. After a while Mandy prodded Kate.

'What is wrong with you? You can't keep still. You keep looking round and smiling. Is Robbie Williams drawing the raffle?'

Kate didn't answer. She smirked at me and I followed her gaze. Rob was striding towards us. He walked straight over to our group and sat down next to me. Kate dissolved into a fit of giggles, I blushed and Mandy frowned in confusion. Rob glanced at them both before putting his arm round me and giving me a long, lingering kiss. When we surfaced for air Mandy was sitting with her mouth open, as was Martin, who had returned from the barbeque with a tray full of beef burgers. Rob smiled at them all.

'Shall I get the drinks?' he asked and sauntered off, leaving me with some explaining to do.

I thoroughly enjoyed the afternoon, walking round holding hands with Rob. It felt good and I was relieved Darren didn't show up to take the edge off things. At the end of the fête Rob needed to stay and help cash up, so I took Charlie and Jack home to play.

When Rob arrived he joined us in the garden until it was time for me to take the boys round to Darren's for a sleepover.

As I dropped them off I kissed them goodbye and spoke quietly to Darren. 'My solicitor's just waiting for your signed papers.'

'I haven't had chance,' he snapped back.

'If you could sign them this week, that would be great.' I smiled at him. 'We need to get things sorted.'

Rob had started cooking while I was gone and we ate in the garden, talking and laughing.

Lying in his arms later, when I drifted off to sleep I dreamed I was holding hands in a circle with Rob, Mandy, Martin and Kate, jumping up and down and laughing on a bouncy castle. Just as I was screaming at the top of my voice Darren appeared and pulled out the plug, deflating it.

*

The final week of term seemed to come round quickly, and as I walked to school in the July sunshine I reflected on how much my life had changed during Charlie and Jack's first year of school. My thoughts turned to Helen. Should I have been more understanding of her problems, instead of simply taking her nastiness at face value? I smiled as Issi's voice told me that I'd had no way of knowing what Helen's life was like, and I shouldn't be too hard on myself. I talked to Issi a lot in my head and I always found it a comfort.

I laughed as I walked into the playground and saw Mandy and Martin deep in conversation. It had been quite a year for them, too. Martin looked up and smiled.

'Becky. Just the person. We had a governors' meeting last night and your leaflet was unanimously approved. Everyone loved it.'

I glowed. 'Thanks, I'm really pleased.'

'We're going to start the new parent mentoring scheme in September and we wondered if you'd fancy giving it a go, along with Mandy?'

'Oh, I'd be thrilled. Thanks.'

Kate joined us, slightly out of breath. 'I thought I was going to be late. I stopped off at reception to put some money in Mr

Phillips's collection and there was a queue.'

I laughed. 'He's so embarrassed about it – he hates being in the limelight. Apparently they're having a special assembly for him, although he's not supposed to know.'

As the children burst out of the classroom Angela rushed past us. 'Don't forget about Friday,' she yelled. 'Pub. Twelve o'clock.'

*

We had all drunk far more than was sensible for a lunchtime, and by the time we arrived in the playground I knew a few more of the mums I would be standing with in September.

'Are you going away?' Kate asked as we waited for the children.

'We're going to Spain for two weeks – it's my mum's wedding.'

Kate beamed at me. 'Oh, that's lovely. Just you and the boys?'

I grinned back. 'I finally plucked up the courage to invite Rob – and he said yes.'

She hugged me. 'I'm thrilled for you – you'll have a wonderful time.'

'How about you?'

'We're going down to Devon for ten days, so hopefully we can get together at some point?'

I nodded. 'I'd love to.'

Diana was holding court with her posse and my smile faded when I saw her. 'Some things never change,' I muttered.

'Have you been thinking about Helen?'

'Yes.' I nodded.

'Me too. Those poor children.'

'Let's just hope she gets the help she needs.'

The children rushed out of the door full of chatter about

their last day, clutching bags full of artwork that had been taken down off the display boards. I hugged my friends, promising to call about meeting up in the holidays, and walked home glowing with contentment.

*

I woke up the next morning and stretched, feeling gloriously happy. During the week I had spoken to my accountant, who confirmed that I had earned enough throughout the year to take the summer off without worrying. I intended spending my time with Rob, Jack and Charlie.

'Time to for breakfast,' I told the boys, who were playing in their bedroom. 'Daddy will be here soon.'

'Yippee!' yelled Jack, throwing his Lego up in the air. 'We're going to see Granny and Grandad.'

'Yes, just for a few days, and then we're off to Spain.'

'I can't wait!' Charlie shouted, bouncing on his bed.

Rob and I were going shopping in Maidenhead because I needed everything from suntan lotion to a new bikini. 'It's going to be a long day,' I'd warned him.

'I need lots of clothes, too,' he'd replied.

Darren collected the boys, and while I was waiting for Rob the post arrived. I froze when I saw an envelope from my solicitor. Was Darren playing yet more games in delaying our divorce? I opened it nervously, having to re-read the letter twice to take in what my solicitor was telling me. I grabbed my phone to tell Issi my divorce had come through, but then put it back down again, unable to get used to her not being there.

I was still on a high when Rob arrived. 'My divorce is through!' I beamed, waving the letter at him.

He picked me up and swung me round. 'How do you feel?'

'A little sad, but mostly relieved.' I kissed him on the mouth. 'And I'm looking forward to the future.'

We drove into town, walking round the shops for several hours, holding hands and chatting.

'I'm in need of lunch to revive me,' he said eventually.

'Me too.' I automatically headed for L'Olivo, but when we were standing outside I had reservations. 'I'm not sure why I came here,' I said, turning to face him. 'This is where Issi and I met all the time. It's where we discussed the ins and outs of our lives, made plans, listened to each other, supported each other...' I started trembling and Rob cupped my face with his hands, kissing me gently.

'If it's too painful, we'll come back when you're ready,' he told me. 'But Issi would want you to move on.'

'I know.'

'If it helps you to hear this, then here goes.' He looked into my eyes and took a deep breath. 'I love you.'

I didn't know whether to laugh or cry with happiness, and as we walked through the door I was laughing as I wiped a few tears away. Nico came rushing over to greet me and I made the introductions.

'Benito is here today, going through the books,' he told me. 'Would you like to join us for lunch? We can eat in my private garden and you can see Issi's olive tree.'

As Rob and I relaxed in the courtyard I explained all about Nico and his partner. 'Issi would have found it hilarious.'

'I'm sorry I never got to meet her,' he said. 'I feel we would have got on well.'

'Oh, she already liked you – I talked endlessly about you.'

'Really? I'm flattered.'

I was suddenly overwhelmed by a feeling of sadness. I pressed my index fingers into the corners of my eyes to stop myself from crying. 'I just can't believe she's not here with us.'

Rob took my hand and pressed it to his lips. 'She's here,' he said quietly.

I nodded, swallowing hard. 'There's so much I want to tell her.' I fought back more tears. 'We had such an amazing friendship – the kind that only comes round once in a lifetime, the kind that makes you want to take that person's pain from them when they're so ill—'

'Becky.' Rob grabbed my hands. 'I'm sure Issi felt that way about you, too – and I hope the friendship you're describing comes round twice in your life.'

I stood up and walked over to the olive tree, rubbing one of the leaves between my fingers, missing the physical presence of my friend with an acuteness I didn't think possible.

'She'll always be with you,' Rob said softly, slipping his arm round my waist.

'I know. It's just that it's hard – not seeing her.'

Nico and Benito walked towards us carrying a cold bottle of white wine and four glasses. Nico poured a glass each and as I took mine I glanced across at the olive tree. A small white feather floated slowly downwards, landing on one of the branches, and I knew with certainty that Issi was with me. '*Salute*, my angel,' I told her, raising my glass. Then I turned and clinked my glass against Rob's. 'To the future,' I said happily.

Acknowledgements

My first thank you is to Paul, Chris and Katie for believing in me and for pushing me to publish this book.

My second is to my sister, Gillian Heggs, who is a very talented writer herself. She has taught me virtually everything I know about the technical side of writing, but more importantly, she's the person who tells me not to give up and to believe in my ability as a writer. She has picked me up so many times and has made me keep going. We all need a writing buddy and I'm so lucky to have the best one. 'Thank you' seems so inadequate.

I have so many other people to thank and I hope I've remembered everyone. Here goes: Thank you to Jo Meredith. The original idea for *Playground Politics* was conceived together and this book is my interpretation of it.

Thank you to all the friends who've taken the time to read my work and have given me honest feedback. In particular: Jacky Elkington, Tina Hawley, Debbie MacKenzie and Mel Poskett.

Thanks to Jane Dixon-Smith for the fabulous cover artwork and for holding my hand during the formatting process (www.jdsmith-design.co.uk); to Louise Maskill for her brilliant proofreading (www.lmaskill.wordpress.com) and to Sue Phelps for the amazing author shot (www.suephelpsphotography.co.uk).

Thank you to Cornerstones Literary Consultancy for their brilliant critique, and in particular, Jenn Ashworth for her encouragement and great advice; to the members of my writers' group, who have been a constant source of support, and to my other writing buddy, Harry Dunn (Smile of the Viper published by Caffeine Nights Sept 2012). Our 'office' is the local café, where we meet regularly to discuss writing and life in general.

Judy Bryan lives in Berkshire, England, with her husband and two children. *Playground Politics* is her debut novel.

www.judy-bryan.co.uk
judybryanwriter@aol.co.uk
Twitter: @JudyBryan

15817575R00180

Printed in Great Britain
by Amazon